"Why Should I Believe You?"

Erika asked. "If you can lie to everyone else about us, why should I believe what you say to me?"

"There's no answer to that," Glen said slowly. "You'll just have to trust me . . . trust your own feelings. Could we have shared what we have if it weren't important to us both? Can't you understand? Can't you forgive what you heard?"

She nodded. "I do understand, Glen, and . . . yes, I forgive you. But where are we heading? We're just in a fast lane to nowhere."

She hated the words, but she knew they were true.

NANCY JOHN
is an unashamed romantic, deeply in love with her husband of over thirty years. She lives in Sussex, England, where long walks through the countryside provide the inspiration for the novels that have brought her a worldwide following.

Dear Reader:

Romance readers have been enthusiastic about Silhouette Special Editions for years. And that's not by accident: Special Editions were the first of their kind and continue to feature realistic stories with heightened romantic tension.

The longer stories, sophisticated style, greater sensual detail and variety that made Special Editions popular are the same elements that will make you want to read book after book.

We hope that you enjoy this Special Edition today, and will enjoy many more.

The Editors at Silhouette Books

NANCY JOHN
The Moongate Wish

Silhouette Special Edition

Published by Silhouette Books New York

America's Publisher of Contemporary Romance

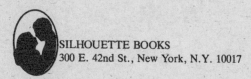
SILHOUETTE BOOKS
300 E. 42nd St., New York, N.Y. 10017

ISBN: 0-373-09238-5

First Silhouette Books printing May, 1985

10 9 8 7 6 5 4 3 2 1

Map by Ray Lundgren

America's Publisher of Contemporary Romance

Printed in the U.S.A.

For John Lowe—

a superb Maitre de Cuisine,
in appreciation of his generous help.

The Moongate
Wish

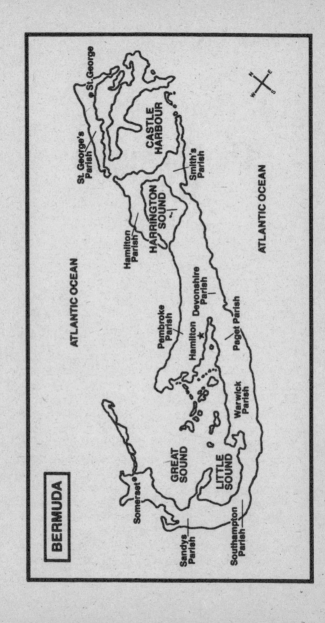

Chapter One

*J*etlag caught up with Erika just as she was starting on the crepes suzette that she'd ordered for dessert. Reluctantly she laid her fork aside, suppressing a yawn. She suddenly felt incredibly tired and a little light-headed, her brain spinning with the kaleidoscopic images of the past twenty-one hours since she had spurred herself from bed. The day before yesterday she had been settled in Yorkshire, managing a relatively quiet residential hotel on the outskirts of Leeds. She'd expected to be there for another three weeks until the owners returned from a trip to visit their married daughter in South Africa. Then her agency had called, begging her to undertake this relief job at the Moongate Hotel in Bermuda, which had been stranded without a manager at the peak of the tourist season due to sudden illness. Since that moment it had been one long mad rush.

The impeccably attired maitre d' was at her elbow. "The crepes suzette not to your liking, Miss Talbot?

Would you care to try another dessert? We have English trifle, Tarte Amandine, and a fine selection of French pastries. Or strawberries? The berries are excellent today."

Erika shook her head. "No, thanks . . . Rigby, isn't it? That was a superb meal. I'm afraid I'm just a bit too tired to have done justice to it."

"Who wouldn't be after all that traveling?" White teeth flashed against his mahogany-dark skin. "Now, how about some coffee in the lounge, and maybe one of our rum liqueurs to round things off?"

"No, I'll skip coffee. I just want to slip through to the kitchen to compliment the chef; then I intend to call it a day."

With a flourish the maitre d' drew back Erika's chair so she could stand up, and she nodded her thanks to him. As she turned to leave the elegant ivory-and-gilt dining room she was careful to acknowledge the few guests who were still at their tables, people she had introduced herself to in the cocktail lounge before dinner: an elderly, stiff-necked English couple, Sir Charles and Lady Willoughby; the Kaplans from Chicago, who were on their honeymoon; and a party from Canada whose names she couldn't be sure of. Prior or Friar was one, she thought. And Greenbaum . . . Or was it Baumfeld? In any case, she couldn't be sure which couple was which. She'd have to study the guest list again in the morning.

Through the swing doors to the kitchen, Erika found the staff beginning to relax after the nerve-taut near-chaos of preparing a superlative dinner for fifty discriminating guests. As they cleared up, the chefs and kitchen hands were able to joke and crease their sweating faces into smiles. Except for one dark-haired youth, scrubbing down a stainless-steel counter, who looked close to tears.

"What's up with him?" she asked the maitre de cuisine, who had come across to greet her. Denver West was a tall, pole-thin man in his mid-thirties. He had wispy red hair, which stuck out from beneath his tall chef's hat, and brilliant green eyes that seemed able to look in ten directions at once.

"Pedro is just oversensitive, Miss Talbot. I bawled him out for letting a batch of egg custard curdle. He's got to learn to take criticism. I run a tight ship here."

"I hope he isn't about to quit," she said. "He looks as if he's in the right mood to."

"I won't let him quit. I'll be nice to him in a minute when he's suffered enough. He's a promising lad."

Erika left it at that. She didn't propose to interfere with Denver's control of his staff. A kitchen that wasn't basically well-managed could never have produced the sort of dinner that had been served tonight. In the few hours that she'd been at the Moongate she'd recognized the hallmarks of a finely run hotel, though it was suffering slightly at the moment from the lack of a manager for the past six days. She would soon rectify that.

"Great dinner, Denver," she said. "That was the best chicken supreme I've ever tasted."

"Thanks, Miss Talbot. We do our best."

"What happened to the venison dish, though?" Denver might as well see that she was on the ball. "The menu featured it as the Chef's Suggestion and a lot of guests asked for it, but it wasn't available."

"That was a real foul-up. Our suppliers in Boston shipped the order on the wrong plane. I've given them a good blasting about it."

Erika nodded. "These things happen. Pity the menu wasn't reprinted, though. That sort of thing leaves a bad impression at a hotel of this quality."

"It sure does," he agreed, conspicuously leaving a lot unsaid.

That meant that the slip-up was the fault of the administrative office. In other words, Lalla Bishop, the administrative assistant who'd been doing her best to keep things afloat since the Moongate's manager had been flown off the island to Boston for emergency surgery. Lalla was a charming, soft-spoken woman of thirty-five or thereabouts, with the lovely milk-chocolate complexion possessed by so many of the Bermudians Erika had noticed on her drive from the airport. While talking to Lalla on her arrival this afternoon, it hadn't taken Erika five minutes to get a strong feeling that she had personal problems on her mind. Man trouble? No doubt she'd find out when she got to know Lalla better.

Erika left by a side exit, stepping gratefully from the heat of the kitchens to the relative coolness of the warm May night. A faint breeze stirred the air, wafting to her the scent of unfamiliar blossoms. She'd not had time yet to look around the hotel's extensive grounds, but she'd noted from the windows that the lawns and colorful flowerbeds were beautifully maintained. Royal palms and other exotic trees and shrubs gave shade from the hot sun, and a pleasant feeling of seclusion. She wanted to explore the gardens as soon as she got the chance, but for now she'd just take a short stroll along the lighted, paved paths to unwind a bit before going up to her room.

The Moongate had been skillfully converted to a hotel from an eighteenth-century mansion. It had originally been built by a sea captain who had made his fortune the tough way and wanted elegance in his retirement. It was magnificently located on the rocky foreshore of Hamilton Harbor. Half a mile across the expanse of dark sea the lights of Hamilton town glittered attractively, rising from water level up a low hillside. Erika could make out the shape of a large cruise liner berthed at the quayside. The air seemed marvelously fresh and unpolluted here on this mid-Atlantic string of islands. Overhead, stars sparkled in the clear night sky ten times more brightly than any stars she'd ever seen in England.

Erika yawned luxuriously, stretching her arms and easing the tension in her neck. She descended a short flight of stone steps and skirted the swimming pool. This afternoon it had been a popular focal point, but it was deserted now. The rippling water was subtly lit from below, cool and inviting. She felt tempted to plunge in and spend a while floating lazily on her back, but it was too much effort to go to her room for a swimsuit.

She wandered on, taking a path that led into darkness. At this distance from the hotel the only sounds were the calls of a few night birds, and a soft chirping sound like crickets. Then she heard the faint strains of a piano. It was a catchy tune, not one that Erika knew, and the player kept stopping and starting again from a few bars back.

Glen Hunter, of course. Lalla had told her that the famous composer-lyricist was staying in a villa here owned by the Moongate and permanently leased to a wealthy American financier.

A few steps on, Erika rounded a hedge of dark foliage with fragrant white flowers and came in sight of a building. Its white-ridged roof had a ghostly gleam in the starglow. Yellow lamplight spilled out from wide French windows that were open to the balmy night sky.

She went closer. Through the wire mesh of the screen door she could see Glen Hunter sitting at a white grand piano, absorbed in his task. She stood for a few moments, fascinated by this cameo of a composer at work. Then, feeling a bit as if she were snooping, she turned to walk away. At that moment she clearly heard Glen Hunter mutter to himself in an irritated voice, "What in hell rhymes with 'mechanics'? 'Panics'? 'Volcanics'?"

Erika retreated, and sat on a low stone wall under the drooping fronds of a small palm tree. Her heartbeat had speeded up. Who'd have thought that she would encounter Glen Hunter again here in Bermuda? Not that he would remember her. Still, it was exciting to know that sooner or later, somewhere around the hotel, she would come face to face with such an attractive, charismatic man.

At this distance she could still hear the piano quite clearly. There was a rapid tapping out of a sequence of notes, again and again, as if their very repetition would supply the composer with the inspiration he needed. Then came a few moments of silence. The screen door was swished open and she heard him walk out onto the veranda. Erika stayed where she was, making no sound, not wanting him to discover her and think that she'd been intruding on his privacy. Probably he wouldn't come her way; most likely he was off to the hotel bar for a nightcap.

She was wrong about that. Glen Hunter came striding across a small patch of grass and stood by the sea wall scarcely five yards from where she sat. Erika could hear him mumbling to himself, obviously running through the lyrics of the song he was working on.

> How long will it last,
> their frantic affair?
> Before they're sated,
> Enervated,
> The itch abated.

How long till they're bored
with the sexual mechanics,
ba-DUM ba-ba-DUM,
ba-ba DUM-DUM ba-DUM-ba,
And look elsewhere,
for a new affair?

What now? she thought. Should she emerge, looking slightly furtive and foolish? Or skulk where she was? Erika dismissed the cowardly option. She was about to stand up when she heard him say, "Give me strength. Why can't I think of a rhyme for 'sexual mechanics'?"

"How about 'passion's galvanics'?" she suggested on the spur of the moment.

"What the deuce?" he exclaimed, swinging around. "Where are you, whoever you are?"

"Right here." Erika pushed aside a low-growing frond and stepped out into the open. Glen Hunter was only a shadowy form in the darkness, as she would be to him. She could just detect the glint of his eyes.

"Do you make a habit of concealing yourself in the undergrowth?" he asked in an amused voice.

"Only on Tuesdays."

He chuckled at that. "Who are you?"

"My name's Erika Talbot."

"You're English, Erika . . . right?"

"As English as strong tea and warm beer."

"You sound as English as a dewy rose. Or the tangle of honeysuckle in a summer hedgerow," he amended.

"Oh! Aren't we poetic."

"You're the poetic one, coming up with a neat rhyme like 'passion's galvanics.' You're staying at the hotel, I take it?"

"No. At least, not in the way you mean."

"Intriguing. You aren't, I hope, just a figment of my weary brain?"

"I'm no hallucination."

"I need proof of that." He reached out and touched her shoulder, his fingers warm and firm through the thin fabric of her silk dress. His hand hovered for a second . . . two, three, four seconds, while for Erika the world seemed to lurch to a halt. When he withdrew his hand she still felt a vibrant awareness of the contact.

"I'm the hotel's temporary manager," she told him, getting a grip on herself. "I just flew in from London this afternoon."

His tone registered surprise. "I heard it mentioned that the temporary manager was arriving today, but I wasn't expecting . . ."

"A woman?" she thrust in challengingly.

"Someone so young. Judging from your voice, that is."

"I'm not so young."

"What's 'not so young'?"

"Didn't your mother ever tell you that it's way out of line for a man to ask a woman her age?"

"Touchy on the subject, eh? Are you Miss Talbot? Or Mrs.?"

"Try Ms."

"One of those," he commented dryly.

"Your chauvinism is laid bare, Mr. Hunter."

"Mr. Hunter. So you know who I am."

"Naturally I checked through the hotel's guest list. I was also told that Mr. Glen Hunter often takes his meals in the dining room. I was half expecting to see you at dinner this evening."

He laughed ruefully. "I'm apt to forget about food when I'm working. I hadn't even noticed that it was dark until just this minute."

"It's well after ten. I was having a breath of air before an early night. If you'd like to come over now, I'll tell the kitchen to rustle up a meal for you."

"It's okay, thanks. I have some bits and pieces in the fridge for when I start to feel hollow. What I want right now is to try out that inspiration of yours. Come on, Ms. Erika Talbot."

He touched her again, this time putting an arm lightly across her shoulders to guide her. Erika felt little curls of excitement skittering along her veins. She swallowed. "No, I'd rather not. It's been a long day for me. By Bermuda time I've been up since just past midnight."

"Matchstick your eyelids for a few more minutes," he urged. "Inspiration has to be followed through while it's still hot. I'll give you some coffee to keep you awake."

Who cared, anyway, about the need for sleep? "Okay," she said. "Just for a few minutes."

Glen's arm remained draped across her shoulders while they crossed the grass to the villa, and lingered there while he slid back the screen door. Once inside, Erika twisted away from him without making a point of it.

Despite its spacious size, the living room was dominated by the white concert grand piano. The decor, in muted shades of beige and brown, provided an elegant setting for it. Windows ran almost the full width of one wall, and Erika guessed that they'd give a fantastic view in daylight. Across from the windows three archways with looped drapes led to other regions of the villa. The ceiling was beamed in a reddish-brown wood that glowed richly in the lamplight, the same wood used for the chairs and table in the dining alcove that she glimpsed through the central arch.

While Erika surveyed the room, Glen Hunter

surveyed her. She was even more attractive than her beautifully modulated voice had suggested. She was tallish and slender, with a shape that would make any man drool. He liked her warm skin tone and the bone structure of her features—classical, except for her short nose. It just stopped her from being a true beauty, but it gave her a puckish look that was reinforced by the vivacity in her golden-gray eyes as she glanced about the room. His gaze rested a moment on her mouth—full and deliciously inviting, just right for kissing. She had wonderful hair, fair and glossy, glinting with amber, and she was wearing it scooped up into a loose chignon with a few escaping tendrils that added to her femininity. His fingers itched to pull out the pins and let its weight fall into his hands in a silken mass. She wasn't a blatantly sexy woman, but there was a thrilling eroticism about the way her dress hugged her breasts and curved in to her slim waist before the silk flared out softly over her hips.

Glen knew already that he wanted to see her naked, that he wanted to make love to her. Strangely, though, he wanted to get to know this woman.

Erika was entirely aware of his scrutiny. She was glad now that she'd taken pains to look well-groomed for her first appearance at dinner at the hotel. Her dress, with its soft cowl neck and graceful flowing sleeves, was very stylish, and its shimmering tones of copper and gold flattered her coloring. Her high-heeled, strappy gilt sandals—far from ideal for strolling outside, as she'd found—gave her a couple of extra inches and helped her to more nearly match his six-feet plus.

"A real golden girl. How lucky can I get!" Glen's tone was warm with admiration. "That was a strange first encounter of ours, Erika . . . a disembodied voice floating to me from out of the darkness."

"Not quite our first encounter."

"No?" His strong, finely planed face, the face she'd remembered so well, was marked by two puzzled frown lines between his eyes. Eyes, it occurred to her now, that were the same brilliant shade of blue as the sparkling ocean surrounding Bermuda. His hair grew lushly, thick and very dark and glossy, with just a few flecks of grey. Right now it was looking a bit tousled from where he'd raked it with irritated fingers when his lyrics wouldn't go right. Determination showed in his mouth. Yet it was a sensuous mouth, too, beautifully carved, its symmetry broken by a small scar on his upper lip. He wasn't so much handsome, Erika decided, as outrageously attractive. The tan acquired from the three weeks she knew he'd already spent in Bermuda showed on his face and neck, on his arms beneath the white, short-sleeve shirt he wore, and on his feet, which were bare apart from thonged leather sandals. No doubt, she thought with a dart of imagination, he was the same bronzed color all over. From what she'd read about Glen Hunter, he enjoyed outdoor activities; she'd seen more than a couple of pictures of him sailing or windsurfing—usually in the company of a radiantly smiling girl friend. Anyway, it was evident from just one glance that he took pains to keep in good shape. She knew he must be around thirty-five, yet he could pass for an athlete still in his twenties.

"Where and when did we meet before?" he demanded. "You'll have to fill me in, I'm afraid."

"You've no cause to remember the occasion. It was four years ago. I was assisting the maitre d' at the Clareford Hotel in Knightsbridge, and there was a mix-up over your table reservation. I had to sort it out for you. But your attention was elsewhere at the time."

"Explain."

"She was a luscious silver-blonde. In between a profusion of 'darlings' and 'sweethearts' you called her Jocelyn."

"Jocelyn? I seem to recall her." The corners of Glen's mouth dented. "She worked for one of the local radio stations."

"And Glen Hunter's interest in her was purely professional? Why didn't I think of that? You were only lining up yet another rave review for your new show which had just opened in London."

He ignored the sarcasm. "How about the coffee I promised you? I keep some permanently on the go. Cream? Sugar?"

"Neither. Straight black."

He disappeared through the left-hand archway, returning in a moment with two green-and-white beakers.

"Sit down and tell me about yourself." He gestured to the deep billowy sofa covered in skin-soft beige hide.

"I doubt that there's much about me to interest a man like you."

Glen gave her a lips-together grin. "What's a man like me like?"

"I meant . . ." She twirled her free hand in small circles, conjuring up an answer. "A show biz celebrity. One of the rich-rich."

"Not so very rich, Erika." He sat beside her on the sofa and drew up a small round table between them.

"If so, it's only because you squander your money on riotous living. The media get a lot of copy from Glen Hunter's activities."

"Do I detect a hint of disapproval? Where would people like you in the luxury-hotel trade be if it weren't for people like me?"

"I was just passing a comment," she said, "not criticizing."

"You were labeling me, Erika. So now you can help me to label you."

"Okay. What do you want to know?"

"Well, for starters, how come you got into hotel management? Your folks in the business?"

"I guess that you could say my mother was, in a small way." Erika chose her words with care. "When she was left on her own she turned our family home at Brighton into a guest house. It seemed to her the only way to make ends meet, but it was a hard struggle, and not much fun. I determined that I'd get into the fancier end of the trade."

"Your father had died?"

"No. They were divorced. My father left her and married a much younger woman. His secretary, would you believe?" Her deep-seated bitterness was showing through, Erika realized. She added lightly, "Oh, well . . . *c'est la vie!*"

"That's marriage."

"Huh?"

"A marriage that works is a miracle, and I don't believe in miracles."

"I guess I don't either."

"Does that mean you've tried it? Or steered clear?"

"I've steered clear."

"Wise lady. You've opted for a career instead. It's quite something to get to be the manager of a luxury place like the Moongate at your 'not so young' age. Even on a temporary basis."

"Temporary jobs are on the agenda of my five-year-plan. I'm gaining experience by taking posts in different types of hotels. When I finally decide to go for a permanent management job, I'll be qualified to tackle anything."

"Even the Ritz?"

"Why not the Ritz?"

Erika Talbot was some lady, Glen thought admiringly. He didn't doubt that she could achieve whatever she decided to shoot for. Yet unlike other ambitious career women he'd encountered—and there'd been more than a few—she still retained a softness and charm that was quintessentially feminine.

"How did you get this job?" he asked.

"Through the staff agency I use. I was doing a stint at a residential hotel in Yorkshire. I'd been there for over four months and the place ran itself; there was no challenge. When the agency called to say that the Moongate's owners were desperate for someone competent to take charge here, I jumped at the chance."

"How long will you be in Bermuda?" he asked.

"Two months. That's to give Bruce Oldfield time to convalesce. I expect you know that he was sent to Boston for major abdominal surgery."

Glen nodded. "How is he? He came through the operation okay, I heard."

"He's doing fine now, Lalla told me. I never met him, of course."

"He seemed a nice guy. I liked him." Glen gave her a slow smile above the rim of his beaker, making her nerve endings tingle. "Still, I admit to finding his stand-in a lot more to my taste. Will you take another job in Bermuda when Bruce Oldfield comes back? This island is like one big forest of hotels."

"It's doubtful, even if I wanted to stay on. Immigration regulations are very tough in Bermuda. Employers have to satisfy the authorities that any vacancy that occurs can't be filled locally."

"So we'll both be here for about the same period

of time. I've been loaned this villa for three months, and nearly a month of that is gone already."

"I guess you're working on a new musical. How's it coming along?"

Glen pulled a face. "It's too soon to say. I'm a cautious guy when it comes to my work. The basics have been hammered out with my producers and the backers, but there's a long way to go yet."

"What's the show going to be called? Or is that still under wraps?"

"We're planning on *Gossip*. As a potential customer, how does that grab you?"

"*Gossip*." Erika tilted her head, considering. "It's neat. It has a real ring to it. A typical Glen Hunter title. What's it about?"

"There isn't really a story line this time. The show's more a pastiche, with various identifiable characters who get brought together on different social occasions. For example, a big society wedding, a race meeting, a royal garden party, where the same people keep turning up and gossiping about each others' affairs and marriages and divorces."

Erika laughed. "You're always the cynic, aren't you?"

"And you're not? Write it on the walls—a hotel manager who isn't a cynic."

"I try to cling to a few illusions." Erika finished her coffee and put the beaker aside on the low table. "It's hard sometimes, I admit. You can't help seeing the flip side of otherwise honest people."

"Guests pocket the silverware even in classy joints like the Moongate?"

"You'd be surprised."

"Try me. I'm not easily surprised."

"Okay, here's a for instance. At a hotel in London I worked in a few years ago, one guest stole a whole crystal chandelier from his suite. And he was a peer of the realm."

Glen's face creased into a grin. "Now that I like. Maybe I can work it into *Gossip* somewhere. Did the guy get away with it?"

"No way. The manager phoned his stately home in Surrey and inquired very politely if by any chance his lordship happened to have packed the chandelier in his bags by mistake. Next day the thing appeared on the hotel doorstep wrapped in brown paper. Incident closed. Well, I'd better be going." She rose to her feet, and Glen noted how the silk dress remolded itself to her figure. He wanted to touch her again, wanted to hold her in his arms and experience the softness of her body against him. The urge to kiss those sensuous lips disturbed him more than a little.

"Hey, what's your rush?" he said. "We're going to run through that number and see how your contribution sounds."

"Oh yes, I'd forgotten." She hadn't really forgotten, but she'd thought that Glen had. She felt a warm little thrill that he was seriously considering her suggestion. "Actually, I'd quite like to have you play the number straight through. Hearing it in stops and starts was tantalizing."

"Will do." He took Erika's hand to lead her over to the piano, and the grip of his strong fingers—light yet very positive—again sent pulses of sensual excitement shooting through her. He was an incredibly attractive man, and she could well believe the media stories of his string of glamorous girl friends. The thought wasn't an appealing one, and she eased her hand away.

"I'll play the melody through," he said. "Then let's see if you can come up with any more bright ideas for the lyrics."

"Oh, I doubt that very much."

"Putting yourself down? That's new from Ms. Erika Talbot."

"I know my limitations."

"I bet you don't have many." The look he gave her was overtly sexual, and Erika gulped under the shock of it. Not that she wasn't used to suggestive looks, but she'd never before felt so susceptible to a man she'd only just met. Glen didn't follow through, but went on, "What's needed in my game is an ear for the pithy phrase. A neat rhyme is valuable; it adds weight and a feeling of intelligence. But that's just one of the characteristics of a good lyric."

He sat down on the piano bench, keeping to one half of it as an invitation to Erika to join him. She remained standing, still bemused by the shock of that look. Glen slipped his hand around her waist and drew her down beside him. She went rigidly tense, all her senses alert, but Glen dropped his hand at once and squared up to the keyboard, gesturing at the stave sheet on the music rest. This sheet was filled with music notation and scribbled words.

"That's what I've got down so far. There are eight bars of intro and then the song begins."

Glen played superbly, she thought, watching his long, sensitive fingers almost lazily stroking out the melody. Heard through from the beginning without interruption, the music delighted her. It was a complicated rhythm with intricate cross threads, but very easy to latch on to. She found herself tapping her foot in time and softly singing the words he'd penciled in. When they reached the line "How long till they're bored with the sexual mechanics?" a matching line sprang into her brain: "The whole Kama Sutra of passion's galvanics". Glen looked astonished, then flashed her a brilliant smile of approval. "That's really terrific!"

"It's a great number," she said when he broke off. "Only . . . do you always have to be quite so brittle and cynical? A more romantic approach once in a while wouldn't do any harm."

Glen refuted that. "My public would think I'd gone soft in the head. Besides, this is my style; I couldn't write any other way. You really do like the song, though?"

"Sure I do; it's fantastic. The sort of number that could be a showstopper, like "Let's Give it a Whirl" in *Circles*."

"You saw that?"

"I've seen every one of your shows."

"Really?" Glen seized the chance to give her a soft kiss on the cheek, one that was over before she could react. "I hadn't guessed that you were such a fan of mine, Erika."

She wanted to touch her cheek with her hand to hold the kiss there. It had been so sweet, so tender. But she wasn't about to let that stop her from deflating Glen's ego a bit. "Put it this way, I'm a fan of musicals as a genre. I cut my teeth on *The Sound of Music*."

"A great show in its time," Glen commented. "Too sentimental for now, of course."

"Oh, I don't know. I remember seeing a revival of *Summer Magic* a couple of years back, and the audience loved it. That was by your father, wasn't it?"

She watched a curious expression flash across Glen's face that she couldn't interpret. Anger? Sadness? Jealousy? "That's right," he said dismissively. "More coffee, Erika?"

"No, thanks. I really have to go. Jet lag is catching up to me with a vengeance."

"I'll walk you back."

"There's no need," Erika told him, but she was glad when he insisted.

They left the villa by the front entrance and walked along the shrub-bordered driveway toward the main hotel building. Glen halted before they reached an area that was brightly lighted by floodlights fixed to the trees.

"I guess I'll see you around, Erika," he said.

"Sure you will."

A short pause. "I'll probably be over for dinner tomorrow evening."

"I'll look out for you."

They stood close, but not quite touching. Erika knew that she ought to say good night and turn to walk away. But she lacked the ability to move, held by his magnetic aura. Was he intending to kiss her? She couldn't be sure. It was what Glen might be expected to try with any woman he found attractive. He wouldn't have gained his reputation for nothing. Yet Glen was hesitating, looking at her with a curious expression, and Erika had the strange feeling that he was fighting against temptation. Why, for goodness' sake?

This was agony. She felt a kind of panic, knowing from the rapid thudding of her heart that she longed for him to kiss her, knowing that the decision was entirely his. Where was her pride? she wondered as the moments stretched and their eyes held in a long, meaningful look.

Getting hold of herself, Erika smiled and started to walk away. In that instant Glen reached out and pulled her to him. All thought of tactical protest was instantly quenched, and she accepted his kiss willingly, eagerly. With a flood of happiness she leaned against the hard warmth of his body and felt his sensitive hands spreading across her back, molding her shape, while his lips feathered softly around her mouth. It was as if she'd been awaiting this embrace for an age, awaiting the feel of this man's arms folding around her and the sweet, sensuous taste of his lips.

Glen broke away with seeming reluctance, held her for a moment longer at arm's length, then let her go. She caught the glimmer of his eyes in the semidarkness, and her nostrils inhaled his subtle male tang that carried overtones of sea-salted, suntanned skin.

"Good night, beautiful Erika," he whispered. "Sweet dreams."

Then he was gone, striding off into the blossom-scented darkness. She took a few token steps toward the hotel entrance, then halted, waiting for her thudding heartbeat to slow, for the high flush of color she felt in her cheeks to cool. It wouldn't do for the manager to walk into the lobby without assurance and poise.

Her pulse continued to skip erratically as she thought about that kiss, savoring every moment of it. Just a kiss, yet it had been a momentous, never-to-be-forgotten experience. You made a fool of yourself, a scolding inner voice intruded. You shouldn't have let Glen see how eager you were. But even so, when at last she felt calm enough to enter the hotel and face people, her heart was singing with joy.

Chapter Two

"*H*ave you ever heard the legend of the moongate?" Erika asked the newly arrived American couple whom she was escorting to their suite. This was a welcoming gesture that guests seemed to appreciate, and one that Erika had always tried to practice if the hotel weren't so large as to make it impracticable. She'd been happy to learn that Bruce Oldfield, the regular manager, had done the same thing.

"The legend of the moongate?" The wife, a slim, auburn-haired woman in her early thirties, raised her delicately arched eyebrows inquiringly. "It sounds intriguing."

Erika paused a moment at the head of a flight of outside steps leading to several guest suites at a level nearer the water, which had been built when the original house was converted into a hotel. Gesturing across the lawn to a stone archway that was shaped to form a complete circle, with a decorative keystone, she said, "The idea of the moongate originally came from China, and was adopted here in Bermuda earlier this century. The legend decrees that honeymooners should walk through the moongate and make a wish, and—"

"That lets us out," the husband cut in with a laugh. "We've been married for eight years."

"And this is the first real vacation we've managed to take together," his wife added feelingly.

"Sounds as if you both lead very busy lives." Erika had already gathered that Harvey and Lois Feldman were a professional couple. He was a corporate lawyer and she an assistant D.A.

"Busy lives! You can say that again. Harv and I meet up to say hi now and then, but that's about all." Lois groaned. "Do we *need* this vacation."

"Well, you'll be able to relax here," Erika assured them. "Our aim is to provide quiet, unobtrusive luxury. And you aren't denied the advantages of the moongate's magic, either. It's a two-pronged legend that goes on, If you aren't honeymooning, make a wish anyhow. Who knows, it might even come true."

"Great! What shall we wish for, Harv?"

He snorted. "You can't believe in that junk, Lois."

"What's the harm in pretending once in a while? Say, Miss Talbot, the taxi driver told us that you have Glen Hunter staying here. Is that right?"

Naturally, the hotel guests were intrigued by the presence of such a celebrity. As manager, part of her job was to protect Glen from unwanted intrusions into his privacy. "He's not really staying at the Moongate," she explained. "Mr. Hunter is occupying a separate villa on the hotel grounds. He's at work on a new show, and he's come here for peace and quiet."

"But we'll see him around, won't we? I sure hope so. I think he's just great, don't you?"

"Yes, I do." Erika was careful to keep her voice level. They had reached the door of the suite, so she was able to close the subject of Glen Hunter. Preceding the Feldmans, she said, "I hope you like your accommodations."

"Oh, this is fabulous," Lois exclaimed, tossing her straw handbag onto a peach-colored sofa.

"Very nice," agreed Harvey.

The sitting room had big windows on two sides that slid back to give access to the private patio. The patio was furnished with a white table and lounge chairs with fringed sunshades. It overlooked the hotel swimming pool, and the harbor beyond.

"Luxury is the word for it." Lois was looking around admiringly.

"I noticed in the brochure that the hotel has a private jetty," her husband said. "That's great. Lois and I want to get in some sailing while we're here. Where's the best place for us to rent a boat, Miss Talbot?"

"I'll let you have the address of a boatyard that we find very helpful," Erika told him. "We can arrange the guarantees for you."

"And we'll need a car, too."

Erika shook her head regretfully. "That's one service we can't offer, Mr. Feldman. There's just no such thing as car rental in Bermuda."

He frowned. "No car rental? How's that?"

"The reason is to avoid congestion on the narrow roads here. Even Bermudians are only allowed one smallish car per household. But there's a first-class bus service and plenty of taxis. Or why not rent motor scooters, as many of our guests do? Then you can get around wherever you want."

"Sounds like a good idea. I haven't ridden a bike since I was a kid, but you never forget how. Okay, Lois?"

"Sure," she said. "It'll be kind of fun."

When Erika returned to the lobby she found Lalla on duty at the reception desk, looking worried. The elevator was malfunctioning, her assistant explained, and the maintenance firm was insisting that they couldn't fix it until the next day. Though the elevator wasn't a vital service at the Moongate, since only the main building had an upper story, it was unthinkable to Erika that *anything* should not be in working order.

"Get those maintenance people on the phone for me, will you, Lalla? I want to speak to the boss himself." A minute later she was through. The man on the line sounded uncooperative.

"We have a dozen jobs waiting to be done ahead of you," he informed her.

"That's your problem. You have a contract with the Moongate to keep our elevator in working order. If you don't get an engineer here at once, I'm tearing the contract up. Is that clear?"

There was silence. Then a grudging, "Well, I guess we could rearrange our schedules. Give me a couple of hours, Miss Talbot. Okay?"

"I'll give you *one* hour. That's sixty minutes. But it had better not be a second more."

Lalla looked at her with admiration as she hung up. "You sure know how to handle people, Miss Talbot."

"It comes with the territory," Erika said lightly. She'd often thought, though, that one of the necessary qualities of a manager was a willingness to take risks and accept the consequences if they didn't pay off. Any failure would weigh heavily against her reputation.

"I'd never have had the nerve to tear him off a strip the way you did."

They were interrupted by a hoarse whisper from the entrance door. "Mum! Mum!"

"Not now, Frankie," Lalla said quickly. "I'm busy."

Erika turned to see a youth whom she'd already noticed working on the hotel grounds. Around fifteen or sixteen, he was well-built and quite good-looking, with the same milk-chocolate complexion as Lalla's. His eyes, soft and brown, held the slightly hazed look of the slow-witted. She gave him a quick, friendly smile.

"Your son?" she asked, turning back to Lalla.

"Yes. I'm sorry, Miss Talbot. I've told Frankie that he mustn't bother me when I'm working."

"It's all right, Lalla. You go ahead and see what he wants." Erika left them, walking through to the manager's private office. A son who was retarded might account for the impression she'd received that Lalla was a woman with problems, but Erika had a hunch that Lalla's present anxiety went deeper than that.

Later in the day, when Erika changed for the cocktail hour, she dressed consciously for Glen. For the guests in general her aim would be to look slick, smart, efficient. For Glen she wanted to look something else. Sexy? Well, why not?

She chose a white jersey dress with a chiffon overtop that had batwing sleeves and was lightly spangled with sequins. She wore her hair down tonight, fastened back by two tortoiseshell combs so that it fell in a bunch of loose waves at her nape. She took even more care than usual with her makeup, especially the eyes, using a subtle tone of pearly-gray on her lids. She touched perfume to her pulse points and took a final check in the long mirror in the center of her range of closets before going downstairs. She didn't bother with the elevator, though it was now working again.

"Hi, Miss Talbot. Come on over and join us," called Harvey Feldman as she entered the cocktail lounge.

"I won't sit down, if you don't mind." She signaled to Amos, the head bartender, to bring her a yellowbird, a popular local cocktail she'd first sampled the previous evening. It was a delicious combination of coconut, rum and pineapple juice on the rocks. "Everything okay I hope, Mr. Feldman?"

"Sure, everything's just fine. Lois might have a complaint, though, if her moongate wish doesn't work out. She rushed off to make one right after we'd gotten unpacked and settled in. She won't tell me what it was, though."

"A wish has to be kept secret," Lois said flatly. "Right, Miss Talbot?"

"That's how I always heard it. I'll keep my fingers crossed for you, Mrs. Feldman."

"I'm looking forward to dinner," Harvey said. "Is the food here as good as the travel agency promised?"

"Even better." Erika glanced around. The lounge was filling up, but there was no sign of Glen yet. "Ah, here are Mr. and Mrs. Kaplan," she went on, spotting the honeymooners from Chicago. "He's in the legal profession, too, so I'm sure you'd like to meet them."

After making the introductions Erika excused herself and started a courtesy round of the other guests. She nursed her drink as an insurance against being pressured into taking too much alcohol—a professional hazard. The elderly English couple, she learned, had taken a ferry to the far tip of the Bermuda islands to visit the Maritime Museum, which had been established in the restored buildings of the old naval dockyard.

"My husband is an ex-naval man," Lady Willoughby explained, "so he was especially interested."

"Glad you enjoyed it," Erika said, smiling. "I must visit there myself, as soon as I can find the time."

"Do that, Miss Talbot," Sir Charles said with an approving grunt. "There's so much British history there."

Erika moved on, glad that she'd penetrated their stiff-necked reserve. Still no sign of Glen. Disappointed, she chatted to other guests, putting on an interested face as they told her how they'd spent their day. She really would have to get around a bit herself, she realized, if she were going to be able to talk about Bermuda intelligently.

This second evening she didn't join the guests for dinner in the dining room. That was something she only intended to do once in a while, mainly to keep a personal check on the standard of food and service. Instead, she had a tray of cold meats and salad brought to her office, where she left the door slightly ajar so she would see Glen when he entered the hotel. He still hadn't made an appearance by the time she'd finished eating.

Rebuking herself for letting him get to her, she went out to the lobby and chatted for a few minutes to the clerk on duty.

"I think I'll take some air," she said finally, and wandered outside.

Once she'd left the lighted pathways it looked

densely dark. Erika waited for her eyes to grow accustomed to the starglow, then made her way slowly in the direction of Glen's villa. Probably he was working at the piano and had lost track of time again. In which case, wouldn't it be a kindness to remind him that it was getting late?

Had she taken the wrong path? she wondered when she couldn't see any sign of the villa's lights. She paused and listened intently. The soft evening air was full of music . . . a breeze rustling the palm trees, the song of night birds and the chirping sound she'd heard last night . . . not crickets, as she'd thought, but tiny tree frogs no bigger than a fingernail. But no piano. Erika walked on with a fast-beating heart, until the villa came into sight. It was in total darkness, its pristine white-ridged roof gleaming with a ghostlike radiance.

Glen wasn't even at home. He'd forgotten—or worse still, dismissed as unimportant—his promise of seeing her this evening. Well, half-promise. I'll *probably* be over for dinner, he'd said, but she hadn't doubted that he would want to see her again soon.

Darn him, she thought angrily. And darn herself for being such a fool. She was a mature woman, way past the age to be thrown because of an offbeat, late-night encounter with an attractive man. From now on, as far as Glen Hunter was concerned, she'd limit herself to ensuring that his needs were properly attended to by the hotel staff.

But out here in the scented darkness the memory of the previous evening was too close, too vivid, too swamping to be shaken off. Glen's kiss, his lips lightly feathering her mouth, had aroused her to an aching awareness of her body and its needs.

She suddenly started shivering as if she were cold.

Turning, she walked back to the hotel entrance, back to her job.

From the upper balcony of an English-style pub on Front Street in Hamilton, Glen moodily contemplated the colorful scene before him. Across the traffic-thronged street, through the interlaced branches of decorative shade trees, the waters of the wide harbor glinted silver-blue. A three-masted sailing ship was tied up at the quayside, a point of interest for the strolling vacationers.

People-watching was an activity that Glen usually enjoyed, but today he couldn't summon up any enthusiasm. He'd taken the public ferry when it called at the Moongate's private jetty this morning with the intention of checking out a couple of queries at Hamilton's reference library. But it had only been an excuse to salve his conscience. The true fact was that he'd found he was too restless to get down to work. And work was what he'd come to Bermuda to do. He'd promised Felix Sylvester, his American producer, that by the end of his three months' stay on the island he'd have *Gossip* in good enough shape to start casting and rehearsals. And Al Friedman, their chief backer, had given Glen use of his rented villa at the Moongate to provide an atmosphere of uninterrupted peace and quiet. So he owed them both.

In the normal way Glen was strong on self-discipline. He liked to play around, and then some, but fun and games had to take a rear seat when he was in the throes of crafting a show. Women and creative work were just oil and water; they didn't mix. No relationship had ever been allowed to threaten Glen's single-minded devotion to his musical career. If a lady grew overly possessive she had to be dropped. That was a risk his girl friends took; it was the name of the game.

During the three and a half weeks since he'd been in Bermuda he'd imposed a rule of celibacy, even though several attractive women had given him the green light. Which wasn't anything unusual. He was pursued by women all the time . . . single, married, and divorced. Glen didn't attribute this simply to his irresistible charm; he was realistic enough to know that the life he led held a lot of glamour. But the reason *why* women chased him was an irrelevancy; the fact was that they did . . . a happy state of affairs that he hoped, and confidently expected, would continue until he was past it.

Erika Talbot was something different, a disconcerting blip on his personal radar screen. Since their meeting two nights ago he had often caught himself fantasizing about her. How great it would be if they could spend days together in this subtropic paradise . . . sailing, swimming, scuba-diving, or just plain lazing on one of the sandy beaches. Erika had a quick mind and a lively sense of humor that appealed to him, and he very much wanted to get to know her better.

It was totally out of the question, of course. They both had jobs to do which needed all their time. *Except,* the thought had persisted, except during the night hours. He'd allowed his mind to flirt around the tantalizing possibility of having Erika in his bed. He'd kept imagining himself undressing her, picturing her naked body. It would be exquisite and perfect in every detail, he felt sure. She was a warm, vibrant woman with a potential for passion; he'd sensed that in those fleeting moments when he'd kissed her. Just a brief kiss, yet he'd known terrible frustration afterward—wanting her, aching for her.

Sexual desire, up until that moment in his life, had been just a lighthearted diversion, a game two people played for their mutual pleasure. Now it had become a torment to him. Nevertheless, he determined, shaking a picture of Erika from his thoughts, he wasn't about to give way to it.

Impatiently, Glen picked up his glass to drain the rest of his beer, then stopped with the glass halfway to his lips. Across the street, walking in the shade of the trees, was a woman wearing a sunflower-yellow dress, the fabric moving beautifully around her hips with each step she took. Her head was half-turned from him as she looked seaward so that he couldn't see her face. But that beautiful amber-glinting hair was Erika's. And that unique body. Even at this distance he felt her magnetism.

Glen sprang to his feet, then stood there, irresolute. Oh damn, he thought angrily, why did she have to show up now, just when he was starting to get his priorities straightened out? What should he do? Ignore her? Just let her go past? In other words, chicken out of a situation he wasn't sure he could handle . . . just as he'd chickened out last night. Too restless to stay home, he'd gone out in search of undemanding company. He'd ended up playing darts at the Ram's Head Inn with some English vacationers who luckily hadn't recognized him.

While he hesitated, Erika turned and paused at the curbside, obviously intending to cross the street. Would she look up and spot him? Glen wondered. But she didn't. Suddenly Glen knew that he couldn't let her walk on; he had to speak to her. When she reached his side of the street, he leaned over the fretted wooden baluster and called down, "Erika!"

She halted and glanced from side to side, puzzled, then turned to look behind her.

"Up here, on the balcony."

She tilted her head and met his eyes. "Glen!" she said in a faint, astonished voice.

"Why not come on up and have a drink? The entrance is straight ahead of you. I'll meet you on the stairs, okay?"

An enchanting smile lit her face. "Okay."

On their way back through the bar, Glen stopped to collect a drink for her—she asked for fresh pineapple juice—and a refill for himself. When they were seated at the table on the balcony, he said, "It was quite a surprise to spot you just now, Erika. You were the last person I expected to see wandering around Hamilton. What brings you into town this morning?"

"I've been taking my driving test. Bruce Oldfield left word that I was free to use his car while I'm doing his job, and luckily Lalla realized ahead of my arrival that I'd need a local license before I could drive in Bermuda, so she organized it. She's really very competent. I'd find the job here a lot more difficult without her to put me wise to the local scene."

Glen nodded. "She's always been pleasant and helpful. I appreciated the trouble she took to get a good piano tuner for me when I first arrived. No one would ever guess the hard knocks life has handed her."

"You mean her son?"

"Frankie is just one of her problems. It's a shame, because he's such a nice lad, and thoughtful. Do you know, he won't use the power mower anywhere near the villa if I'm in and he thinks I might be working. I find that rather touching."

"Good for Frankie. That's the sort of consideration for the guests' comfort that I like to hear about." Erika took another sip of her drink, which was beautifully cool.

"Frankie's as honest as they come, too," Glen said. "The other day I lost my wallet, and he brought it back to me."

"Oh?"

"I hadn't a clue where I'd left it. It contained a wad of cash, too. Three of the bills were hundreds. Before I could report the loss Frankie turned up with it, saying that he'd found it in the grounds by the harbor wall. It must have slipped out when I was sitting reading on one of the seats there. He could easily have pocketed the contents and thrown the wallet away. It could never have been traced to him."

She met Glen's eyes across the table, and laughed. "Let that be a lesson to you not to carry so much cash around."

"Yes, ma'am. Frankie wouldn't take a cent as a reward. In the end I had to go to his mother and persuade her it was only fair that he should have a percentage."

"You said just now that Frankie is only one of Lalla's problems. What else? I guessed that her life isn't a bundle of fun, but I didn't want to start throwing out personal questions the instant I arrived."

"She hasn't much to laugh about, that's for sure. Bruce Oldfield told me about her, just a couple of days before he was taken ill. It seems that when Frankie was only a few months old Lalla lost both her husband and her father in a hurricane that sank their fishing boat out on the reef."

"That's terrible."

"She was left to bring up the boy on her own. Plus take on responsibility for her widowed mother, who was badly crippled with arthritis."

"Is her mother still living?"

"Almost bedridden now, I was told."

Erika let out a breath. "Some people get a load of trouble, don't they? It's a pity Lalla didn't get married again. She's very attractive."

Glen nodded. "But most men would steer clear of taking on a woman who already had a family with so many problems."

"Poor Lalla. It seems so hard."

Watching Erika's face, seeing the look of concern in her golden-gray eyes, it struck Glen with surprise that she was a deeply caring person. As a hotel manager she was capable and determined, the equal of any man. Already, in less than forty-eight hours, she'd made her mark at the Moongate and curbed the slight laxness that had crept in during Bruce Oldfield's absence. Yet Erika had a softer side that was rare these days, certainly rare in a career woman. Was it this gentler aspect of her character that gave her a special sort of loveliness in his estimation? Beautiful women were no novelty to him, but he was accustomed to brittle sophistication that went right through to the core.

He gazed fascinatedly at the pulse that beat under the creamy skin of her throat. He felt an urge to feather kisses against that velvety smoothness, down to the neckline of her dress just above the shadowed valley between her breasts. The beautifully firm, softly rounded shape of those breasts were enticing him to slide in his hands and cup their warm weight in his palms. He could feel his body responding to her.

Closing off the direction of his thoughts, Glen gestured to the two or three small packages Erika had with her. "You've been shopping, I see."

"Just a few things I needed. I left England in such a rush that I didn't have much chance to fit myself up

with warm-weather gear. I'm used to moving somewhere new at short notice, but this is the first time
I've taken a job overseas."

Glen grinned. "When I left London three weeks
ago it was the pits—cold and wet. Had the weather
improved any?"

"Not so you'd notice."

Glen ran his fingers up the cool, polished surface
of his glass, wishing that instead it was the warm,
smooth skin of her forearm. "Who's missing you
back home, Erika?"

"No one, I imagine. Not that much, anyhow."

He lifted one eyebrow. "A very independent
lady."

"That's how I like it."

That was true. She had never been short of male
attention, but she'd always been careful to keep her
relationships from getting too deep. That way she'd
protected herself from the kind of heartbreak and
disillusion her mother had suffered.

Glen was looking at her curiously, and Erika
sensed that he was about to question her on her
private life. To forestall him, she blurted, "You
didn't have dinner at the hotel last night. What
happened?"

He seemed suddenly wary, defensive. "I changed
my plans, that's all." His eyes met hers. "Did you
mind that I didn't come over, Erika?"

She shrugged. "It's your privilege."

"But you were . . . disappointed?"

She denied that a little too fiercely. "Why should I
have been disappointed? I was merely making a
comment."

They both sipped their drinks in an uneasy silence,
while the tension built between them. Glen replaced
his glass on the table and again ran his fingers up and
down the glass's smooth length. She wants me, he

decided, just as I want her. And she's every bit as angry with herself about her feelings as I am with myself. For God's sake, his mind ran on in sudden irritation, why is she holding back? Because Erika *was* holding back, he could sense, despite her warm response to his kiss the other night.

If she were a different sort of woman, he brooded, they could just go to bed together . . . once, twice, a half-dozen times. And then they'd be out of one another's system, and they'd part with no bad feelings. But if Erika *were* that sort of woman, he wouldn't want her as feverishly as he did. Her appeal for him wasn't just a matter of sexual appetite; she reached out and spoke to something deep inside him. Glen shook his head in exasperation, trying to get rid of that last thought. He could do without any complications, especially just now, when he had a deadline to meet. No matter that Erika Talbot was the most attractive woman he'd ever encountered, he just didn't have room for her in his life.

Erika noticed that exasperated shake of the head. Did Glen imagine that she was pursuing him? Maybe he thought that she'd deliberately engineered their first encounter the other evening. And she'd fueled that thought by questioning him about his non-appearance at dinner last night. She wouldn't fall into that trap again. From now on she'd be as pleasantly polite to Glen Hunter as to any other hotel guest. That, and no more.

If he believed she was chasing him, though, why had he called down to her in the street and asked her to join him for a drink? Or had that been just a casual impulse that he was now regretting?

She drank down the rest of her pineapple juice, gathered up her packages and handbag, and rose to her feet. "I have to be getting back to the Moongate."

Glen rose too, leaving his beer unfinished. "By car?"

"Yes, I'm driving back. One of the waiters drove me in, but it's his day off so I told him not to hang around for me."

"That confident you'd pass the test, were you?"

Erika laughed. "I'd have been mad if I hadn't. They drive on the left in Bermuda, just like home."

"Where's the car parked?" Glen asked as they emerged onto the street.

"I found a space a little farther along."

"Can I cadge a ride, Erika? It'll save me waiting for the ferry, or taking a taxi."

"Very well."

"Don't sound so dead keen."

"I'm sorry," she said. "Of course you're welcome to a ride."

The day was really getting hot by now. Erika was glad to keep in the shade of the store arcades as they walked along Front Street. Against the sun-filled blue sky a Union Jack fluttered colorfully. At the intersection a policeman, looking amusingly incongruous in the traditional British bobby's helmet teamed with Bermuda shorts, was directing the traffic from a quaint birdcagelike construction in the middle of the road.

There was a sense of intimacy about being cocooned with Glen in Bruce Oldfield's small car, and she made a hash of pulling out into the stream of traffic. When she reached for the gearshift the back of her hand brushed against Glen's thigh. She hastily apologized.

"Feel free!" he said, not moving his leg. Then, "When will you be getting any time off? Evenings, I mean." Why on earth had he said that? he wondered the instant the words were out.

Erika shrugged. "I fix my own schedule. The

Moongate's owners live in England—they're a family of merchant bankers—so I don't have anyone keeping tabs on me." He could think again if he imagined she was waiting in line to be beckoned. "I shan't be taking much time off for the moment, though."

"Because you're the conscientious type?"

"Is that bad?"

"It can be overdone."

Erika swung the car around the traffic circle and took the road to the Moongate. "Perhaps in your line you can dispense with feelings of responsibility."

"You're kidding."

"So who *do* you feel responsible to?"

"My backers, my producers, everyone else concerned with getting the show staged."

"And your public."

"Them most of all. Without my audiences I'd be nothing." After a moment's silence, he said, "I'm not sure it made sense to come to Bermuda. Maybe I'd work better in a garret in London or New York, without any distractions."

"Distractions? Any that you find here are of your own making."

"Are they?" Erika heard resentment in his tone, and wondered why.

"Anyway," she said, "from what I've read about you in the papers, your life seems to be one long distraction."

"That's just gossip," he said brusquely.

Erika wished she could believe that.

The entrance to the Moongate came up, and she took the branch of the driveway that led past his villa. When she pulled up at the door Glen remained in his seat, watching her. The lines of his face were set in a grim, dark expression. His voice, though, was cajoling.

"How about coming in for a minute? Have a drink or something."

Erika's pulse was suddenly racing, but she shook her head. "No, I've been away from the hotel for long enough. Another time, perhaps."

"You could hear what I've been doing to the lyrics of "How Long Will it Last?" Please, Erika."

She hesitated, debating with herself. It shouldn't be any big deal to go in for a few minutes and listen to his song. But she knew that if she accepted his invitation, she would be acknowledging—to both of them—something she had no wish to acknowledge. She ought to say firmly, Sorry, but I can't spare the time. Instead she said weakly, "Well, it can only be for a minute or two."

In the living room, Glen inquired, "What will you have to drink, Erika?"

"Nothing for me, thanks. That song, have you finished it now?"

"Not really. I've been playing around, trying to get it polished."

"Polished till it's hard and jewel-bright," she said, with a faint smile. "That's the Glen Hunter style, isn't it? So how's it coming along?"

"See for yourself." He crossed to the big white concert grand and sorted out some papers, then laid two or three of them on the piano lid. Erika stood in the curve of the piano, but his scribbled words were blurred as she looked at them. She was too intensely aware of Glen standing right behind her to be able to focus, to be able to *think*. She was only alive to sensations. She could feel his warm breath riffling her hair; then with the back of one finger he gently stroked the skin at her nape. His subtle, sensual, male scent was filling her nostrils, making her head whirl. She stood rigidly tense, pretending to study the music. Glen's other hand came up to rest lightly on her shoulder. An age passed, each second drawn out to an eternity of waiting.

"Have you . . ." She cleared her husky throat and tried again. "Have you altered much?"

"The odd phrase here and there. The melody is still a trifle ragged."

"I . . . I thought the melody was terrific the other night," she said.

"Thank you, Erika."

Glen's hand left her shoulder and skimmed down the length of her arm, bare beyond the tiny cap sleeve of her yellow shantung dress. Her own hand rested on the piano top and Glen laid his over it, splaying his fingers along hers. She could see his hand clearly—the strong, flexible pianist's fingers, the breadth that could span octaves with the greatest of ease. His brown wrist, hazed with tiny hairs, was circled by the gilt band of his wristwatch, and the passing of time shown by its sweeping second hand bore no relevance to this timeless present.

Glen moved very slightly, and the length of his body came into contact with hers. Only a light pressure, but the feel of his flesh kindled fires that flared through her. His lips nuzzled her hair, and he murmured her name with a soft sigh.

From somewhere, Erika summoned up her fragmented will. "Glen, I really must go. . . ." Unwisely, she turned to push past him and escape the seductive snare of his arms. But Glen's arms remained firm, and they were face to face. As he molded himself to her, pinning her against the piano, she felt the surge of his desire. His breathing was rapid, shallow and strained. His hands came up and held her head captive, his thumbs sensuously massaging the tender spots behind her jawbone. His face came closer, closer, until his breath fanned across her cheek. His lips were parted, sweet with promise, and she felt dizzy at the tempting expectation. His kiss would drown her in delight, overwhelm any tiny strand of resistance left in her. . . .

Taking Glen off guard by the suddenness of her movement, she twisted out of his grasp and stumbled a few steps toward the door. For an instant Glen was too puzzled by her abrupt change of mood to move. Then he came after her.

"Erika . . . what's wrong?"

She held up a hand to stop him from touching her. "I have to go. I said I'd only come in for a minute, and look at the time now." In a dramatic gesture she glanced at her wristwatch, and was astonished to see that a full fifteen minutes had vanished.

"Why are you doing this to me?" Glen's voice was harsh and condemning.

"For heaven's sake, I have a hotel to run."

"The Moongate isn't about to grind to a halt because you're not there. Lalla Bishop is very competent . . . remember?"

"It was a mistake to come in with you at all. It was against my better judgment, and . . ."

"So why did you?"

She returned his belligerent gaze, wishing she could just turn and run. "Because you asked me to."

"Yet when I ask you to stay a little bit longer, you refuse."

"I've told you why. I take my job seriously, Glen. There are a lot of things I have to get done today."

"You can't work all the time," he protested. "What about this evening? What will you be doing?"

"There's a barbecue down by the swimming

pool," she said, forcing her mind back to realities. "It's the first since I've been here, so I'll certainly have to show myself at that."

"Oozing hostessy charm." Glen thrust his hands deep into his pockets and studied her. "What time does your working day finish?"

"It never does. I thought I'd made that clear."

"What you made clear was that you fix your own hours."

"I've already taken time off today," she reminded him. "Whether or not I feel free to take any more this evening will depend."

"On what?"

"On whether I'm needed. On whether something goes wrong. This may be a fairly small hotel, but the problems keep coming up just the same."

Glen sighed impatiently. "How about sending me a memo when you have a couple of minutes to spare?"

His face hostile, Glen stood watching her as she got back in the car and drove off toward the hotel garage. She crashed the gears badly, and narrowly missed stripping the crimson blooms from a hibiscus bush.

Chapter Three

During the past ten days Erika had seen Glen on a number of occasions, but always when there were other people around. Whenever he came into the cocktail lounge or dining room he was the focus of attention—especially female attention. Erika noticed how skillfully he handled admirers, switching on instant charm but deftly extricating himself after a rationed few minutes. She'd thought that it would be part of her job to help preserve his privacy, but Glen didn't need any help from her.

One lunchtime, when she was taking a dip in the empty pool, she'd glanced up to the upper terrace and seen Glen standing watching her, his hands on the stone balustrade. Erika had a feeling that he'd been there for several minutes. Shaken, she'd given him a brief wave, and he'd raised a hand in response. Then he'd turned away and disappeared.

It was exactly what she wanted, Erika assured

herself, this guest-manager relationship. She had enough on her plate without the complications that an affair with Glen would bring. This way, when the time came to quit Bermuda, she'd leave heart-whole and with the satisfaction of yet another job competently handled.

This evening, another of the regular barbecues was taking place. The weather was ideal, warm with just a slight breeze. A full moon rode serenely in a darkening indigo sky that was still flushed with orange and crimson in the west. On the far shore of the broad harbor, the lights of Hamilton twinkled with crystal brightness. Harp music floated on the soft air as Erika made her way down the steps to the lower terrace near the pool, where round tables were set out under colorfully striped fringed umbrellas. Here at the Moongate most guests stayed for at least two weeks, so they intermingled and made friendships. Erika could tell from the hum of conversation and bursts of soft laughter that everyone was having a good time. An enticingly savory aroma was wafting from the range of barbecues, where chefs in their tall white hats were deftly dealing with a string of meat orders.

"All okay, Leroy?" she asked, pausing for a word with Denver's deputy, who was busy turning steaks.

"Just fine, Miss Talbot." A grin split his face. "Kinda thirsty work, though."

"Think how great it will be, quenching that thirst with a few nice cold beers, when the pressure's off."

Erika threaded her way between the tables, exchanging pleasantries. One couple, sitting alone over drinks, were looking rather less than happy, and she made her way over to their table by the seawall. They were from Scotland, and had arrived just that afternoon. Erika had taken an instant liking to them. Dr. Montrose was a stocky, sandy-haired man with courteous manners, and his wife, Catrina, was a slender woman with straight dark hair that she wore with a center part and coiled on the crown of her head. They'd told Erika when she'd escorted them to their suite that they had honeymooned at the Moongate nine years previously.

"I hope you've settled in okay," Erika said to them now.

"Yes, thanks, everything is splendid," Douglas assured her in his attractive Scots burr. "The Moongate is even more luxurious than we remembered it."

"That's nice to hear. Most of the suites have been entirely remodeled in the past few years, and the tennis courts are new. Also the sauna and Jacuzzi."

"Yes, I'm longing to try that," Catrina said. "Someone told me, Miss Talbot, that you're only here temporarily. I expect you'll be sorry when the time comes to leave such a lovely place."

"I'm sure I shall. You get used to changes when you do stand-in jobs as I do, but this is definitely the nicest hotel yet."

"Have you worked in many different places?" Douglas asked.

"Quite a few . . . Bristol, London, Brighton, Manchester, and Leeds, you name it."

"You make me seem a real stick-in-the-mud," he said with a chuckle. "Except for holidays, I've never been far from Edinburgh, which is where I did my medical training. After qualifying, I joined a family practice in the small country town where I was born. Now I'm the senior partner in the same practice."

"There must be advantages, I'd think, for a doctor to have strong roots like that. It means he knows his patients through and through."

"That cuts two ways. A small-town doctor has no such thing as a private life."

"You can say that again." There was a note of bitterness in his wife's voice.

Erika was getting the feeling that things weren't going too well between the Montroses. She sensed that they were forcing the conversation with her to avoid being left alone together. The idea of returning to their honeymoon hotel had struck her as intensely romantic, but she began to wonder if they weren't trying to recapture something that was missing in their marriage. She wished them luck. If it could happen anywhere, it ought to happen in an idyllic setting like Bermuda.

Catrina went on impulsively, "Won't you join us for dinner, Miss Talbot?"

"Yes, please do," her husband put in.

Erika hesitated. In the dining room she made it a rule not to join guests; it smacked of favoritism. But out on the terrace the atmosphere was so much more relaxed.

"Well, I'll sit down with you for a while," she agreed, "and perhaps I'll sample something from the barbecue. But I know you'll understand if I'm called away."

"Can I join the party, too?" asked a familiar, heart-stopping voice from behind her left shoulder.

Stunned, shaken, Erika spun around to face Glen. He grinned at her, not quite meeting her eyes, and smoothly introduced himself to the Montroses. "I'm Glen Hunter. It's good to meet you."

Catrina was overwhelmed. "Oh, Mr. Hunter, how nice! Someone mentioned that you were staying here."

"Please, call me Glen."

"This is Dr. and Mrs. Montrose," said Erika,

pulling herself together and signaling Rigby to have two extra places set. "They arrived just this afternoon."

"Douglas and Catrina." They both shook hands with Glen.

Chairs were brought, and Erika and Glen sat down. Seated opposite her, he looked maddeningly at ease. He was wearing a lightweight beige sport jacket that was casual in style yet superbly tailored to fit his tall, loose-limbed frame. With it he wore a striped shirt, open at the throat. Erika had to tug her eyes away from the triangle of bronzed chest that was exposed.

Glen felt anything but at ease. He'd come across to eat at the hotel, as he'd come on a few other evenings, not because he'd wanted a square meal but because he wanted to see Erika again. Away from her he felt starved. But why, he asked himself, had he walked slap into this social trap? With Erika sitting a tormenting three feet away, he had to act out a pantomime before these other people. He was insane. Okay, he had a fixation about Erika Talbot . . . something that was totally different from the way he'd ever felt about any other woman. The intelligent thing would have been to stay cool and ride it through, keep on working and banish her from his mind. Instead, he was sweating out the days and nights, unable to work, unable to think of anything but how it would feel to make love to Erika.

"People are saying that you're here to work on a new show," said Catrina. "That's wonderful. I'm a terrific fan of yours, Glen. I just love your music."

Glen beamed her a smile. "You're too kind, Catrina."

"Oh no. It's just so exciting for me to meet such a

celebrity . . . someone so talented." Catrina was gushing, already under Glen's spell. Her husband was watching her, and Erika noted his tiny frown.

"I just happen to have a knack," Glen said in modest dismissal. "Would you believe that at school my ambition was to become a doctor? But my chemistry teacher told me to forget medicine. And never in a million years would I be able to run a hotel with Erika's charm and efficiency. How about you, Catrina? What do you do?"

"Me . . . oh, nothing at all. I mean, I do the usual sort of charity work that's expected of a doctor's wife in our part of the world. I sit on a few committees and that kind of thing. But apart from that, I'm just a housewife."

"And mother?" he asked.

Catrina's animation vanished. An exchange of glances flashed between the Montroses across the gulf that separated them. So that's the problem, Erika thought. Who was blaming whom? Or did they each blame the other?

"No, we don't have any children." Catrina's voice was carefully controlled. The hand that held her wineglass trembled slightly. She hesitated a moment, then took a large gulp.

"Shall we choose?" Erika suggested brightly to turn the subject, and picked up her menu.

It took a while for them all to decide. When the waiter had taken their orders, Douglas said to Erika and Glen, "Do you play golf? If so, we might make up a foursome. There are some fine golf courses in Bermuda, aren't there?"

"I don't think that's a good idea." His wife vetoed the suggestion before the others could respond. "Douglas is far too good a player for me," she explained apologetically. "I'm just not in his league."

"I'm probably not, either," Glen said cheerfully, "but that's what handicaps are all about, Catrina."

"All the same . . ." Catrina's shrug made it clear that she wasn't going to be coaxed.

Douglas threw his wife a swift glance, looking hurt. Erika spoke up quickly. "I'm afraid you'll have to count me out. I've never held a golf club in my life." Hurriedly switching the subject again, she asked the Montroses, "Have you planned what sight-seeing you'll be doing while you're in Bermuda?"

"Sight-seeing?" Douglas gave her his attention. "Well, as a matter of fact we're taking the glass-bottomed boat cruise out to the coral reef later this evening. I spotted a leaflet about it when we were registering."

"That's a trip I've been meaning to do," Glen put in. "It's supposed to be spectacular—especially at night."

"Why don't you come with us?" Douglas invited. "Both of you, I mean."

"Sounds nice. How about it, Erika?" Glen said it casually, but she could hear the challenge in his voice.

She met his glance head-on. "Sorry, I have work to do."

"Do the work tomorrow."

"Not possible."

His eyes called her a liar. She wrenched her gaze away, only to find Catrina regarding her with a between-us-girls look. It covered a lot of territory . . . knowledge of Glen's reputation with women . . . awareness of the sensual currents between him and Erika . . . a some-people-have-all-the-luck ruefulness.

"There's so much to see and do in Bermuda," Erika rushed on, conscious of a brittle jauntiness in her tone. "I can give you all the details. Some of it will be new, I expect, even though you were here before."

"I wouldn't advise you to take Erika's advice," Glen remarked caustically. "She knows even less than I do about Bermuda."

She shot him a furious glance and was instantly caught again in the spell of his eyes. "That's a slanderous remark to make about a hotel manager," she said, her mouth going dry.

"But true!"

"Is this a private fight?" Catrina queried with a laugh. "Or can anyone join in?"

"Erika's a workaholic," Glen declared. "She spends almost every minute of her time right here on the job. As the manager of a resort hotel she has the perfect excuse to get around and see things. Then she could make recommendations to her guests from personal experience."

The Montroses glanced back at Erika to see how she returned that ball.

"I'll get around to it," she said defensively.

"Make it soon. Why don't we make up a sight-seeing party with Douglas and Catrina one day? Erika," he explained to them, "is like the only boy in the street who owns a football. She has the use of a car."

This time Erika refused to meet his eyes. "I'll think about it," she said.

For the rest of the meal they managed to toss conversation back and forth, and on the surface it was a lighthearted occasion. Erika noted, though, that the Montroses rarely addressed each other directly. She also noted that they drank a shade too much, which seemed to make Douglas more morosely silent and Catrina more brightly talkative. As for herself and Glen, the threads of tension were pulling tighter all the time.

When the Montroses departed for their cruise to the reef, Erika rose from the table too. She didn't trust herself to be alone with Glen. Many of the guests were still sitting over coffee and liqueurs while listening to the harpist. Erika did another tour around, making polite chitchat. All the time she could sense Glen watching her, even though he had now joined another party. It was a great relief when she finally saw him break away and start up the steps.

Ten minutes later, duty done, Erika began to mount the steps on her way back to the main building. She turned a corner and stopped in mid-motion. Glen was there, waiting for her, negligently leaning against a huge marble urn containing geraniums and trailing plants.

"Hi." Straightening, he put an arm around her shoulders and attempted to lead her along a side path.

"No, Glen." She shook herself free.

"I have to talk to you, Erika."

"Well, you've chosen the wrong moment. I'm busy."

He reacted with fierce impatience. "Why do you insist on using your job as a shield against me?"

"That's not true," she said falsely.

"It is true. I want to know why." Glen stood blocking her path, dominating her with his sheer virile personality. His hands came up to hold her by the shoulders. "You aren't going to make me believe that you don't find me physically attractive, Erika."

What could she say? That she found him *too* attractive . . . to such a degree that it scared her silly? She'd never before felt like this about any other man, and she didn't know how to handle it. With Glen, her usual clearheaded way of thinking seemed to have deserted her. With Glen, she felt suddenly reckless, tempted to fling everything else overboard and let herself be swept along on a tidal wave of emotion. She wanted his hands on her naked flesh, his lips warm against hers. She wanted this promise of bliss now, tonight, this instant, and hang the Moongate and her responsibilities.

Those skillful hands and lips of his, she reminded herself chillingly, had caressed a string of other women. Could she settle for being just another of Glen Hunter's casual affairs? How long would it be before he grew bored and dropped her? She was crazy to even consider getting involved with him. But how could she expect to act sensibly when he was holding her, his fingers caressing her shoulders . . . when the tips of her breasts were brushed by the rise and fall of his chest and she could feel his warm breath on her forehead? Don't let him kiss me, she thought despairingly . . . and yet, please, please, please *do* let him kiss me. Yes, no . . . do, don't. She felt stupidly, savagely torn apart.

Glen could feel her trembling uncertainty. What the hell was the matter with Erika? he wondered, irritation needling him. She was a mature, intelligent woman, totally in control of her own destiny . . . except in this one respect. She was showing the sort of eager timidity that any guy stupid enough to fool around with a teenage girl might expect. He ruled out the possibility that Erika was playing a game with him. She was too basically honest for that. So it had to be some kind of hang-up.

He'd asked her straight out the other day if there was someone she'd left behind in England, and she'd told him no. Did she find it difficult to relate to a man . . . any man? The thought filled Glen with gloom. He needed to relate to Erika more than to any other woman he'd ever known. There was a fever for her in his blood. For the first time in his life he was sleeping badly. The quickest way to get a woman off his mind, he knew from experience, was to take her to bed. A short affair, or a slightly longer one, and at the end of it a sense of grateful freedom, when he could get on with his life—and his work— again.

So what should he do? Force the pace with Erika? Override her scruples and charm her into bed? He could do it, he felt certain. But something warned him, a buried sensitivity which he hadn't suspected in himself before, that he'd be making a mistake if he tried to hustle Erika. She was a complex woman, with many facets to her personality, and she couldn't be treated on a superficial level.

Still, she was with him now, alone with him in the soft, cloaking darkness of these fragrant gardens. Be content with that for the moment, Glen counseled himself, and he sought for an unemotional topic of conversation.

"The Montroses are nice people," he said chattily, removing his hands from her shoulders.

Erika had steeled herself to argue with Glen. Surprised by his sudden switch of mood, she unconsciously fell into step beside him. "They're here on a sort of second honeymoon. They came to the Moongate when they were married, nine years ago."

"Trying to recapture the magic?" There was a bite of scorn in his words, and Erika was quick to protest.

"I think it's very romantic."

"Can such tactics ever pay off? Trying to recapture past happiness? Happiness is fleeting, Erika. However hard you try to grasp it, to hold it, to keep it with you, you're going to fail. Inevitably. That's why marriage is such a . . ."

"That's why marriage is . . . what?"

"Forget it," he said. "The Montroses haven't any children. Catrina seemed to mind that."

"I'm sure she minds a lot. I've a hunch that it's at the root of their problem."

"A baby would miraculously put things to rights?" Again there was scorn in Glen's tone, a touch of disgust.

"A baby would probably help a lot, anyhow."

"If they can't have one, for whatever reason, then that's too bad. It's useless, their pining for what they can't have."

"We have to have our dreams," Erika said, surprising herself. "Men, too."

"You could be right."

"I wonder, are men's dreams any different from women's?"

"Maybe not, if Erika Talbot represents the new breed of woman. From what you've told me, you dream of success. Of recognition in your field. Of wealth and all that goes with it, too, no doubt."

A few days ago Erika would have accepted that statement as a compliment. Now it was somehow a hurtful slight. She had discovered new dreams . . . vague, shadowy, unformed dreams that vied with her clear-sighted ambition.

"You must already have achieved most of the dreams you ever had," she said as they changed direction onto another pathway.

"Think so? Just wait, Erika. If you ever do get to manage the Ritz, your next ambition will be to own the place. There's always a new challenge. That's what drives us on."

"And you want the next Glen Hunter show to be the biggest ever smash-hit that breaks every previous box-office record and wins every award there is?"

Glen gave a hollow laugh. "I'll be lucky if *Gossip* even opens, the way things are going. Or not going. I should be working on it right now."

The bitterness in his tone was like a put-down, and Erika felt hurt. "Then I suggest you go and do just that. Don't let me detain you."

"Erika!" He caught her by the shoulder as she spun around to walk away. She waited, the rapid beating of her heart a painful throb. Slowly, Glen turned her to face him and held her by the arms, not pressed close against him but just so that their bodies lightly touched. Each point of contact flared with sensation, and Erika trembled. Glen's hands slid upward, over her shoulders and into the curve of her neck. He trailed his fingertips against her responsive flesh until he had her face cupped between his palms.

"Erika . . ." he said again, this time in a husky whisper.

"Oh, Glen." She leaned against him in a sudden surge of joy, all her hurt, all her doubt dissolving away. Their lips met and instantly melded together with a flare of passion, her tongue flirting with his as they tasted the sweet essence of one another. His hands roved her back, molding her feminine shape, holding her closer against him. Her breasts were flattened against his chest, and she could feel her nipples tautening and tingling. The long, drowning kiss ended at last in a series of tiny, darting nibbles, as if Glen couldn't bring himself to desert her mouth completely. With one fingertip he delicately traced the curving outline of her lips, before starting on an exploration of her face that was incredibly erotic. Her eyelids quivered closed as he touched them softly, gently. Her eyes still closed, gloriously alive to pleasure, Erika felt him outline the arch of each eyebrow, felt him shape her nose and move across the plane of her cheek to stroke the sensitive lobe of her ear.

Then Glen was kissing her again, his lips relentless in their demand, his tongue robbing her mouth of secrets. Now his fingers were interlaced behind her head, tangled into her hair. Erika reached up to grasp his head, to lock him to her, feeling dizzy from the wild thudding of her heart.

The kiss ended, and Glen released a long sigh. "Darling Erika, I'm almost dying with the need to make love to you. Come into the villa."

"No, please . . ." she stammered. "It . . . it isn't what I want."

"No?" His voice was incredulous. "You can't really mean that."

"I do. I'm sorry, Glen, but . . . I'm really not your sort of woman. To me . . . well, we hardly know one another, and it wouldn't feel right."

There was a long choking silence between them. "It seems like we got a few wires crossed somewhere," he said with more than a tinge of resentment. "I thought you were as keen to make love as I am."

"I do find you attractive, Glen. Very attractive. And . . . I'm sorry," she repeated unhappily, "but I don't do this . . . I mean, just go to bed with someone I hardly know. Please don't be mad at me. I know I shouldn't have let you kiss me like that, but . . ."

"I'm not mad," he said in a gentler voice. "Just disappointed." His fingertips caressed her cheek. "So where do we go from here?"

"I think we'd better say good night, Glen."

"There's nothing good about tonight," he responded with a dry laugh. "But I'll walk you back now."

Glen kissed her again before they parted near the hotel entrance, but this time it was just a meeting of lips—almost chaste. And then he turned and strode away.

Back at the villa, Glen poured himself three fingers of whiskey. He carried the glass over to a silver-framed mirror on the wall and stood staring disdainfully at his reflection. He mouthed words half aloud—words of deliberate crudity.

"Well, you didn't score there, buddy. You thought you were the world's greatest stud, and she turned you down flat. In future you'd better go for the easy ones."

It was years since he'd been in a situation like this . . . confident that he was on the brink of a fantastic session in bed, only to have it snatched away from him. Damn Erika!

Yet Glen couldn't find it in him to be really angry with her; he knew that she hadn't willfully rejected him. He had sensed the turmoil in her. She had wanted him, that was for sure, yet she'd been inhibited from letting go and permitting passion to take over.

Maybe tomorrow she would be ready to make love with him. Maybe it would take another week. Or even longer. There wasn't really any hurry; they had plenty of time left. Yet he wasn't used to putting sex on hold. Somehow he had to find a way to throttle back his desire and wait it out.

He went and sat at the piano, letting his hands wander over the keys, playing the phrases of melody that were floating through his mind. But it was hopeless, just sentimental slush. Abandoning the piano, Glen went to the French windows and stared out at the lights of the hotel through the intervening trees. Which was Erika's bedroom? Could he see it from here?

After a restless night Erika awoke, feeling heavy and depressed, to the sound of pouring rain and a gusty wind. She threw back the covers and started her yoga exercises with little enthusiasm. She was showered and dressed before the maid brought her the tea and toast she had first thing each morning.

"Thank you, Millie. What a change in the weather."

"Oh, this'll be cleared away in a couple of hours, Miss Talbot. Then we'll have the sun back. That's Bermuda."

"Glad to hear it."

Discipline and training carried Erika through the morning's routine, her mind still churning with thoughts of the night before. She glanced at the diary, noted the advance bookings, then checked that the tabular ledger was right up to date. The housekeeper came to see her about a delayed order for bed linen, and Erika called the New York suppliers to chase them. While she was doing her rounds—discussing menus with Denver, spot-checking on bedrooms, and planning new floral arrangements with the florist, the sun broke through the clouds. Inevitably it lifted her spirits. By the time she returned to her office she was even humming to herself.

She'd been an idiot, turning Glen down. She was free and uncommitted; what she did with her life was no one's concern but her own. If she came to the end of her time at the Moongate without having made love with Glen, she would call herself all kinds of a fool for having thrown away the chance of a blissful romantic interlude with a very special man. Deep down, despite the stupid way she'd acted, her decision had already been made last night. Today she would give Glen the green light he would be looking for. Today . . .

"Come in," she called, to a tap on her office door. One of the clerks looked in. "Mr. Hunter wants a word with you, Miss Talbot."

Erika couldn't hide the excitement that brought a flush of color to her cheeks. So what? Her relationship with Glen wouldn't be a secret from the hotel staff for long.

"Ask Mr. Hunter to come in, please, Jason," she said, rising to her feet.

A moment later Glen stepped through the door, then shut it behind him. He came no closer. His face was unsmiling, dark and serious. He looked tired, Erika thought, as if he'd had a bad night. A bunch of keys dangled from his little finger.

"What's wrong?" she asked anxiously.

"Nothing's wrong." He stepped forward and dropped the keys on her desk. They made a small, chilling chink. "I'm going to New York, Erika. I'm leaving right now. There's a taxi waiting for me outside."

"New York?" She was appalled. "But why, Glen?"

"I need to."

Tightness seized her by the throat so that she could hardly speak. "But . . . but how long will you be gone?"

Glen didn't meet her eyes. She saw him glance through the window, where the courtyard was steaming after the heavy rain. He said in a quiet, toneless voice, "I don't know when I'll be back, Erika. Or even *if* I will. I've come to say good-bye."

Chapter Four

Glen had been in New York for two days before he decided to visit Felix Sylvester, the man who produced and personally directed his shows on Broadway. Up until now he'd been keeping a low profile at a hotel in the East Sixties, trying to get himself sorted out. A feeling of despair finally drove him to stop by Felix's office, twenty-four floors above Times Square.

"I thought the idea was for you to stay in Bermuda until the show was in good shape," Felix said with a critical frown when his first surprise was over. Though short and balding, with a droopy mustache that gave him a melancholy expression, Felix Sylvester had a king-size personality. Lesser people quailed before him. Glen respected his judgment and valued his friendship.

"Bermuda wasn't working out, Felix."

"How come? Al Friedman's villa should be everything you always claim you need when you're getting down to the nitty-gritty. Quiet, comfort, no distractions. So what's your problem?"

Glen hefted his broad shoulders. "I guess it's just a block. I needed a change of scene to break through it."

"And have you?"

"I'm working on it."

"The question is, are you achieving?"

"Not a lot that's any good," Glen admitted morosely.

"It happens. Don't worry, Glen, you've always been lucky so far. You've hit some bad times, but you'll pull through."

Glen knew, though, that Felix was far more concerned than he pretended. The production schedule for *Gossip* was getting too tight for comfort. No producer expected a show to be complete and perfect in every detail before casting and rehearsals began, but it had to be well on the way.

"Anything in particular you're hung up on?" Felix asked. "What have you written lately?"

Glen was glad to be able to tell Felix of one achievement. "I have a damn good song that can keep reprising through the show. I thought I'd introduce it in the women's powder-room scene. It's a satirical little number called 'How Long Will it Last?' "

"Sounds promising. How about letting me hear it?"

"I don't have the score with me."

Felix shot him a skeptical glance from beneath shaggy eyebrows. "Come on! Since when has that stopped you?"

Felix had a right to ask, damn it! Reluctantly, Glen crossed to the piano. He began to play the song, talking through the lyrics. When he came to Erika's contribution he stumbled a moment, feeling guilty that he wasn't giving her credit with Felix.

"That's really great," Felix said, beaming, as Glen finished. "Nothing wrong there. How many more stanzas does it have?"

"I thought another three."

"You haven't done them yet?"

"Only sketchily."

"Oh, well . . . it's a good punchy melody, and there's a lot of scope. So what else have you done since we talked a couple of weeks back?"

Aside from that one song, Glen's efforts in the two weeks since Erika had intruded into his life had produced little that was anything like in shape. He said with false enthusiasm, "The barroom scene, remember? I have something good coming along for that. A duet for two men. Here's the main theme of it." He played the melody, improvising a little, throwing in the odd bit of lyrics here and there.

Felix wasn't fooled. "And that's about it, eh?"

"There's the title song—"

"Come off it, Glen. You mailed a tape of the title song at the end of the first week you were in Bermuda."

"Yes, well . . . I have a mass of other stuff. Half-formed ideas—a couple of tunes that are nearly there, some neat couplets. It's the way I work, Felix. You know that."

"Sure, I know. It's lucky I also know that you always meet your deadlines, Glen. Otherwise I *would* be worried. Is there anything I can do to help? Where are you staying, by the way?"

Glen named the hotel.

"Hell, that's no use. You need a piano. Let me rent a studio for you somewhere."

"No point. I don't aim to stay here that long."

"Every day counts."

"You think I don't know that?" Glen said irritably. "Don't crowd me, Felix."

"Okay, but I have a question for you. If you don't want to talk about your problem, why have you come by? Not to see my ugly mug, that's for sure."

Glen was tempted to tell Felix about Erika, and his hopelessly ambivalent feelings about her. Felix would sympathize, for he was a deep-eyed romantic. He had three marriages to prove it, and was currently lining up a fourth. But Felix knew damn well that when Glen was in the throes of creative activity, he always foreswore women. If he confessed now to having broken his rule, Felix would probably surmise that this was something serious. It wasn't, though; it couldn't possibly be serious. A woman was a woman. A beautiful woman was a beautiful woman. Okay, so he wanted to go to bed with Erika . . . the mere thought of her made his body throb with wanting. Okay, so he felt keener desire for Erika Talbot than he ever remembered feeling before. If he'd stayed in Bermuda, they would almost certainly be lovers by now.

Would that have been best? Glen agonized. Should he have stayed there and gone through the familiar ritual of an affair? "The whole Kama Sutra of passion's galvanics," in Erika's own witty words. But that wasn't how he wanted it to be with her. Making love with her would be very special. Unique.

If it were just a matter of physical attraction, then an affair would be the answer until she was out of his system. But with Erika there was so much else. For Erika he felt a bewildering confusion of emotions, from which surfaced the knowledge that he wanted to be with her . . . anyhow, anywhere. He enjoyed her company, he liked her style and wit, her spirit, her competence. He loved the look of her, the feel of her. He loved to listen to her soft, beautiful voice, to hear her delightful laugh. Glen gave a shuddering sigh as this complex torrent of thought rushed through his mind once more. He just wanted to be with Erika; he just wanted to be with her. . . .

"Glen, what are you doing for lunch?" Felix had been watching him intently.

"I'll grab a sandwich somewhere, I guess."

"I'm meeting Joni. Why not join us?"

"No, I don't want to intrude."

"Hell, what do you think she and I can get up to in a restaurant?"

Glen was reluctant to join Felix and his current girl friend, who was tipped to become Mrs. Felix Sylvester IV. Not because he didn't like them both, but because he needed to be alone. Contrarily, he'd welcome company as a way to stop him thinking. Brooding.

"Well, thanks, Felix—if you're sure."

"Sure I'm sure." He picked up his phone and told his secretary he was going to lunch. "Let's go, Glen."

They went to a Mexican restaurant a few blocks away. After five or six minutes, Joni joined them. She was big, brashly beautiful, and blond, a look-alike of each one of Felix's ex-wives. When she saw Glen, her large green eyes widened in surprise.

"I thought you were holed up in Bermuda, Glen."

"I was, Joni . . . I am. I mean, I'll probably be going back."

"So this is just a flying visit to little old New York? Missing someone, were you?"

"Glen's going through a bit of an inspirational dry spot at the moment, honey," said Felix. "I've been telling him he'll snap out of it."

"Maybe he needs some help. There'll be no shortage of volunteers in New York City."

"Cut it out, honey. You know that's not Glen's style when he's doing a show."

They ordered lunch, and it came very quickly. Glen found that he had no appetite for the hot, spicy food. In a rare moment, he envied his producer. The relationship with Joni, who owned a beauty salon in the West Fifties, was to Felix beautifully romantic and simple. How long will it last? Glen wryly wondered. A couple of years, perhaps. Felix wasn't into long-term fidelity. But at the breakup they'd part still friends, without recriminations. Felix had the amazing knack of remaining on good terms with each one of his ex-wives and their mutual offspring. Maybe, Glen mused, it was the best way of handling liaisons in this imperfect world. But imperfect was the word. It wasn't a way of life that appealed to Glen. What was, though? He suddenly felt a sense of dissatisfaction with his past, with all those fast-living years. He'd worked hard, damned hard, and it had paid off. He'd known success, wealth, and acclaim. But there was a hollow quality now about these achievements. For the first time in his life Glen felt a yearning for something more. But what? If only he knew.

Glen glanced surreptitiously at his watch, and was vexed to see that Joni's shrewd eyes had noted the action. Allowing for the hour's time difference, it was just about the same time of day that he'd spotted Erika in Hamilton and called to her to come up and join him on the pub balcony. He recalled how he'd wished, as they drove back to the Moongate, that they could take off for a whole day to some deserted beach. Better still, that they could spend a week, a month, cruising around in a rented launch. Just the two of them alone. Even that day Glen hadn't fully read the danger signals. That had only come later, during the tormented nights that followed. He had finally quit Bermuda to put a safe distance between himself and Erika, so that he could begin to concentrate on work. What a laugh! His creative block was now total. Glen knew that he wasn't going to be able to get anything done in New York. Was the answer to take himself off even farther away from Erika? To hole up in South America, China, Australia . . . wherever? In God's name, what had happened to him? He was riddled through with doubts and uncertainties, unable to make a clear decision.

He glanced at his watch again, openly this time. "Hell, is it that late already? Felix, Joni, you'll have to excuse me. Got to rush. Nice lunch."

"What's your hurry?" asked Felix.

"Tell him to mind his own business, Glen," Joni advised. "You mustn't keep the lady waiting."

Glen gave her a vague smile as he rose to his feet. "I'll call you, Felix . . . soon. That's a promise. See you."

Outside in the street he strode off briskly. The snarled-up traffic of New York throbbed in his ears, and the hot city air choked him. He spotted a phone booth before he'd started looking, and felt in his pocket for a dime. When he'd found the number and dialed, he said abruptly, "Flights to Bermuda. Soonest available. What do you have?"

"Hi, nice lady! I need a jumbo-size favor." The voice on the phone was male, American, and wheedling.

"What favor?" Erika inquired warily.

"Can you handle a banquet tomorrow night, honey?"

Behind the wheedling tone she detected a note close to panic. "What did you have in mind? How many people?"

"Fifty-three. Mostly men. We had a shindig all

nicely organized in Bermuda for the last night of our computer sales convention, and then there's this foul-up with the hotel. Make alternative arrangements, Harry, the president tells me. Just like that. Wouldn't you know something terrible would happen to me?"

"Where would your party be coming from?" Erika asked to give herself a few seconds of thinking time.

"Washington. Touchdown in Bermuda seven P.M. your time. If you've got a heart, sweetie, say yes."

"When do you need to know?"

"Now. Five seconds ago. Please say yes. Please!"

Erika weighed the pros and cons. Twenty-four hours was hellishly short notice, but banquets were a profitable sideline for a hotel.

"You can stop praying, Harry," she said crisply. "You've got yourself a deal. Now, about the menu . . ."

"I leave it to you, honey. We want the very best."

"Right." Erika reached into a side drawer of the desk and pulled out a file. Flipping it open, she said, "Our terms will be—"

"Forget terms," he said. "I love ya, baby."

Erika talked to him for five minutes longer, checking credentials and getting a clear understanding about terms. Maybe Harry Seidel could afford to be casual, but she knew from experience that a pre-event ready agreement could well be a post-event wrangle about the bill. When she put down the phone, she sat back in her swivel chair and flexed her shoulders. The easy part was done . . . saying yes into the phone. Now for the hard parts. First, Denver. Without the chef's enthusiastic cooperation, the whole project would be a fiasco. Any banquet provided by the Moongate had to be a memorable meal, one that would get talked about in convention circles and further enhance the hotel's high reputation.

She pushed aside the diary which she'd been glancing through before the interruption and headed for the kitchens. Preparations for lunch would be reaching a climax, so it wasn't the ideal time to choose. But this couldn't wait.

"Denver," she said brightly from behind his shoulder, "I've just accepted a banquet booking for tomorrow evening. A party of fifty-three, from Washington."

The maitre de cuisine was running a critical eye over a row of prepared salads, rather like a top-sergeant inspecting his men. At Erika's words he froze, then slowly swung on his heel to meet her eyes.

"Feel up to handling all that cooking on your own?" he inquired sardonically.

"Denver, don't be negative. Treat it as a challenge."

He inclined his head in appreciation of her tactic. "That's what I'm to say to my crew, is it? Treat it as a challenge, boys and girls."

"You don't need me to tell you how to handle your staff," she said demurely.

"Neat! I'm not fooled for a second, Erika, but I like your style. Okay, so what are the details?"

"Mostly men—computer executives. They want the very best, the man said."

"What else, at the Moongate? If it's mostly men, we'd better make it steak. . . . Entrecote, with sauce béarnaise and a selection of vegetables. For the fish, I'll wait to see what's best of the local catch in the morning . . . serve it pan-fried, with bananas and almonds. Chilled soup to start with . . . avocado would go down nicely, and a mixed salad.

Desserts from the trolley, and a cheeseboard. Sound good?"

"Sounds wonderful. I knew I could depend on you, Denver."

He grimaced. "Well, you would say that, wouldn't you?"

Thank heaven, Erika thought as she walked away, for a maitre de cuisine who was not only in the first rank, but totally unflappable. Operating a hotel in Bermuda, she'd discovered, had special problems and hazards. With so little produce grown on the island, most of the meat, vegetables, and fruit had to be flown in from the United States. This meant being at the mercy of plane schedules and weather hold-ups.

After Denver, she talked to the maitre d'. They went together to the large room kept for private functions to plan out the seating and discuss the additional waiters he'd need. Also wines. Then Erika had to lay on transport from the airport, and a motor launch to ferry the party over to Hamilton for a last fling before flying back to Washington. And there was an extra flower order to place.

She snatched a quick lunch, finished checking through the diary, then turned to the bank reconciliation statement which had arrived in the morning's mail. There was a discrepancy she couldn't make sense of. In the end she called Lalla, who was in the linen room doing an inventory check with the house-keeper.

"I'll be through here in five minutes," Lalla told her. "Will that be okay?"

"Sure. Whenever."

The instant Erika relaxed and eased off the pressure, thoughts of Glen swept back remorselessly. Once again she tried the philosophical line. What had she really lost, after all? She'd known from the start that she would be getting into something that could lead nowhere. Just as well, then, that their romance had turned out to be a non-event.

But all the intellectualizing in the world couldn't drive out the image of Glen's face, that fascinating face with those compelling, brilliantly blue eyes, and determined, sensuous mouth. The memory of his mouth on hers brought an aching throb low in her abdomen; the memory of his hands caressing her started a shiver in her limbs. Erika sat in her chair and gazed wistfully into space. . . .

A tap at the door brought her back with a start.

"Oh, come in and sit down a moment, Lalla. I'm having a problem tallying the cashbook with the bank statement. There seems to be a shortfall of over eight hundred dollars. Probably I'm just over-looking something." Glancing up inquiringly from the bank's computer printout, she was astonished to see that Lalla had gone rigid. Her hands gripped the chairback as if she needed something to cling to.

Oh no, Erika thought wretchedly, not Lalla! Any hotel manager had to keep a constant watch for petty dishonesty. If left unchecked, it would have a disas-trous effect on staff discipline. But she'd sensed when she first arrived that the Moongate was re-markably free of this sort of malaise. On the other hand, Bruce Oldfield's sudden illness had thrust Lalla into a position of exceptional responsibility and trust. It looked as if she'd fallen prey to temptation.

"You'd better tell me about it, Lalla," she said in a quietly insistent voice.

Lalla sank down into the chair, and her fine-boned face took on a tragic cast. "Will I be fired, Miss Talbot?"

"I can't say until you've explained."

"I'd have paid it all back, every last cent. That's the truth." Seeing Erika's impatient frown, Lalla went on hurriedly, "It was like this . . . my Frankie got into trouble, and . . . and I was desperate."

"Frankie? What sort of trouble?"

Lalla made a helpless gesture as if her throat was too choked to form the necessary words. Then she stumbled on. "He likes to hang around with other boys . . . be one of the gang, so to speak. Even though they tease him a lot, it seems better to let him go with them than make him stay home on his own. One day, about three weeks back, some of the older boys had been twitting him because he couldn't ride a motorbike, and Frankie wanted to show them. So he borrowed one of the boys' bikes without his knowing and took it out on the road. He crashed into a wall and the bike was badly smashed up, though Frankie escaped with hardly a scratch, thank heaven. But the boy who owned the bike said that Frankie had to pay for the damage or he'd go to the police, which would put Frankie in bad trouble for riding without a license. And he's underage, too. I was at my wit's end, Miss Talbot. I had a tiny bit put by, but nothing like that sort of money."

"So you helped yourself to some hotel cash?"

"Not to keep, I swear it." She looked at Erika imploringly. "If Mr. Oldfield had been here I'd have asked him for an advance against my salary, but he'd already been taken ill by then. There was no one I could turn to, and . . . and there seemed no harm in my borrowing the money temporarily. I worked out that I could save seventy dollars a month out of what Frankie and I earn between us," she finished.

Erika let her stern expression relax a little. "I do understand, Lalla. It must be terribly hard to have lost one's husband and be left alone to bring up a

small son. Especially when he has a handicap like
Frankie does. And I gather that you have an invalid
mother, too."

Lalla nodded, her eyes filling with tears. "I know
it's no excuse, Miss Talbot, but I really was desperate."

Erika pondered. She could decide to treat the
money as a loan, if she chose, but was it ever wise to
compound an offense? Given the same circumstances, she asked herself, what would she have
done in Lalla's shoes?

Compassion won. "Listen, Lalla, this business is
not to go beyond the two of us. We'll work something out. As long as the money is repaid eventually,
no one else need ever know."

"Oh, Miss Talbot, you're so good. I don't know
how to thank you."

"I don't want your thanks," Erika said uncomfort-
ably. It had been easy to pronounce a few reassuring
words from her lofty position. "Just make sure that
you don't let me down, Lalla."

Later that afternoon Erika took five minutes for a
stroll on the hotel grounds. The sun was blazing hot,
and she kept to the shade beneath the trees. Bare-
chested above his denims, Frankie was hoeing a
flowerbed containing tall spires of yellow and pink
snapdragons. The boy worked hard, and he was
always polite to the guests. It was such a pity that he
was somewhat lacking in mental capacity, an inno-
cent in the adult world. Lalla had brought him up to
be strictly honest, as witness his return of Glen's
wallet. Yet to save her son, Lalla had herself acted
dishonestly. Erika felt a pang of sadness as Frankie
looked up and acknowledged her shyly with one of
his slow, sweet smiles.

"Taking a break, Erika?"

She swung around to see Catrina Montrose, clad

in a yellow suntop and a black and white wrapa-
round skirt. She carried a paperback novel with her
sunglasses wedged into it as a bookmark.

"Hi, Catrina. Are you coming or going?"

"Just having a walk. I've been reading on the
terrace since lunch, but I got a bit restless."

"Where's Douglas this afternoon?"

"Playing golf with Harvey Feldman."

"And Mrs. Feldman . . . Lois?"

"She's gone on a shopping spree in Hamilton. It's
her last chance before they go home tomorrow."
Catrina's glance was questioning. "I heard that Glen
Hunter has gone to New York. Will he be coming
back?"

Erika kept her voice carefully neutral. "He didn't
say. He can come and go just as he likes, of course.
The villa is leased permanently to one of Glen's
American backers, who isn't using it this summer."

"Nice for some! Were you sorry that Glen took
off, Erika?"

"Why should I be sorry?"

She received a direct, challenging look from Catrina. "He's terribly attractive, isn't he? I felt quite
envious of you the other evening when Glen joined
us for dinner."

"You have an overactive imagination, Catrina."

"Oh, come off it. Glen fancied you; that was very
clear. Still, you were probably wise not to let him get
to you. That guy's supposed to have notched up
quite a score. I wonder how many of his girl friends
went through a bad time when he dropped them?"

Erika felt a shaft of pain, but managed to sound
detached. "I'm sure they only had themselves to
blame."

Catrina had slipped the sunglasses out of the book
and shaken them open; she was nibbling one of the
sidepieces. "You could be right. All the same, he's a

really gorgeous hunk. What I really envy you for, Erika, is having an interesting career. It must be great to know that you're independent and can make what you want of your life."

Erika sensed that Catrina was working around to confiding in her. Much as she liked Catrina Montrose, she wasn't sure she had the emotional energy right now to get involved in another woman's problems. Still . . .

"How about a cup of tea?" she suggested.

"Yes, I'd like that, Erika, if you can spare the time."

They descended to the lower terrace, and Erika chose a table a little away from the others, shaded by an oleander bush that was bright with rosy-pink flowers. The scent was heavenly. A young white-jacketed waiter slid up instantly. Erika ordered a pot of tea and cucumber sandwiches. English-style afternoon tea was one of the many small touches that added distinction to the Moongate.

"It's nice to relax for a few moments," Erika said as she settled back in the white-slatted, blue-cushioned chair.

"I can imagine. You can't get much time to yourself in your job. Me, I have far too much time on my hands."

"Isn't that something you could alter?"

"Not in the only way I really want." Catrina gave a long, sad sigh. "You must have noticed that things aren't too good between Douglas and me."

Erika didn't deny it. "It's a terrible pity. You're both such nice people. I thought the idea of coming to the Moongate for a sort of second honeymoon was very romantic. Isn't it working out?"

The waiter arrived and set out the delicate bone-china cups and saucers, the silver teapot, and a platter of wafer-thin sandwiches. "Will that be all for now, Miss Talbot?"

"Yes, thanks, Ossie. We'll let you know if we want any cakes."

After Erika had poured the tea, Catrina took one sip from her cup, then put it down and slipped on her sunglasses. Erika knew it was more to hide her eyes than for protection. In a voice that sounded pent-up with emotion, Catrina said, "It was a mistake for us to come here. Douglas suggested it, and I suppose it was a last attempt to make a fresh start. I should have known that it would never work out."

"Isn't a marriage that's lasted for nine years worth trying to preserve?"

"Why? To go through a few more miserable years together? This vacation may have served a purpose after all, if it makes us see that we're all washed up. At home, Douglas and I have no real contact at all. We don't even fight. We're just carefully polite as we drag on from day to day, caught up in the family doctor's routine."

"Is there someone else involved, Catrina? Another woman? Or maybe you're interested in another man?"

"Oh no, nothing like that. At least, not as far as I'm concerned." Catrina frowned, considering. "I don't *think* Douglas is playing around."

"Then I don't suppose he is." Erika couldn't altogether hide her impatience. "You can't seriously want to end your marriage, Catrina. Douglas is such a nice man, intelligent and thoughtful. And he's good-looking, too. A lot of women would envy you."

"They wouldn't know what I know about him."

"Oh? I can't believe that it's anything so very terrible. Not Douglas."

There was a long pause while Catrina carefully bit into a cucumber sandwich. "Erika, do you want to have children?" she asked at length.

"I've never really thought about it." That wasn't quite true. She'd never *let* herself think about it. "Maybe I'd like to, one day."

"It's only natural, isn't it? Most women long to have a child to hold in their arms, a child to love. I had a child, Erika."

"Had?" She said it quietly, invitingly.

"It took me ages to get pregnant. Alistair was a darling little boy. He was so cute, so bright and clever. He walked at ten months, think of that, and he was really talking by the time he was two. Oh, he was a wonderful child, and I had such hopes and plans for him. We were so close." The fevered brightness in Catrina's eyes dimmed, and she nervously pulled at a thread in her cotton skirt. "I lost him just before his fourth birthday, and it was Douglas's fault. He let Alistair die."

"Douglas let your son die?" Erika echoed in a stunned tone. "Surely that can't be right, Catrina."

"He's a doctor. He's been trained to spot the early signs of illness, but he didn't."

"Doctors aren't infallible. If Douglas overlooked . . ."

"He saw so little of Alistair; that's the point. He was always too wrapped up in other things."

"How do you mean?"

"He was scarcely home except in the evenings, when Alistair was in bed. On the rare times he did take a few hours off from his medical practice, he played golf. He said he needed the exercise." Catrina's voice grew more bitter by the moment. "When it came to his patients, Douglas couldn't do enough for them. But when it came to his family—his one and only child—all his medical expertise was no use at all, because he didn't see enough of Alistair to know that something was badly wrong."

"But Douglas wouldn't have been his own son's pediatrician, surely," said Erika, frowning thoughtfully.

"He should have noticed the early signs, though. By the time I decided that something must be the matter with Alistair and asked Douglas what he thought, it was already too late. Douglas fixed an appointment with a consultant for that same day. It turned out to be a brain tumor. They told us that the operation was very risky, but it was the only hope." Catrina paused, then added in a choked voice, "Alistair died on the operating table."

Erika felt moved by compassion. The loss of a much-loved child in such circumstances would have been a terrible blow. But the charge that Catrina was making against her husband was too outrageous and shocking to be dealt with by words of conventional sympathy. After a few moments, she asked, "What did Douglas have to say about it?"

"What could he say? Facts are facts."

"You mean he accepted the blame?"

"Oh, at the time he tried to explain how it was . . . made excuses for himself. But he knows where the fault lies. Now, we don't discuss it anymore. What's the point? No amount of talking will bring Alistair back."

"Maybe you *should* talk, Catrina. However you look at your son's death, it was Douglas's loss, too. Your attitude, holding him to blame, must have made his suffering ten times worse."

"He brought it all on himself," Catrina said with quiet emphasis.

Erika was tempted to really let fly, but she bit back the words. "What made you decide to come to Bermuda again?"

Catrina was linking and unlinking her fingers, unable to keep her hands still. "I knew it was crazy, but Douglas kept on and on about coming. He seemed to imagine that we could go back and start afresh. Stupid of him."

"The way it looks to me, Catrina, you're the stupid one. You're willfully throwing away your marriage when it could be good again. Okay, so you've suffered a tragedy. I'm not trying to minimize that. But so have lots of other people, and they survive. They pick up the pieces and carry on, as Douglas is trying to do. You should meet him halfway."

"You just don't understand," Catrina said in a reproachful voice. "I should never have told you."

"I agree. You should be talking to your husband, Catrina, not to me. Why don't you try to get pregnant again? Having a baby to love and share with Douglas would help you get things into perspective."

It was almost as if Catrina had been waiting for that suggestion to deliver her trump card. "I *was* pregnant again . . . four and a half months pregnant. But when I lost Alistair the shock caused a miscarriage. I was ill for weeks."

"I'm sorry," Erika said sincerely. "Are you saying that you can't have any more children now?"

"I could, I expect, but I won't. I just won't take the risk of losing another baby. Besides . . ."

After a pause, Erika prompted, "What were you about to say?"

"It's academic, anyhow. Douglas and I . . . well, we don't sleep together anymore."

"And he accepts that?"

"He has to, doesn't he?"

"He hasn't given up on your marriage, though. He must still love you, Catrina. Why not let this vacation turn out the way he hoped it would? Make it a real second honeymoon."

"I . . . I just can't. I was a fool to agree to come to Bermuda. We'd be better to split up than just let things drag on." Catrina gave a little snort of self-disgust. "What a moaner I must sound, pouring all this out on you." She forced a laugh. "Now you know why I envy you so much, Erika. You've really got it made."

"Have I?" Erika's own laugh masked the bleakness she'd felt since Glen's sudden departure. "I'll tell you this, Catrina . . . much as I love my job, if I was married, my marriage would always come first."

"Since you rate marriage so highly, Erika, how come you've never taken the plunge? You must have had lots of chances."

"Cowardice, I guess."

"Cowardice? That doesn't sound like you."

Erika picked up the sandwich on her plate, then put it down again. "My parents got divorced, rather messily, when I was ten. I saw the damage it can cause . . . the lasting scars." She had never talked to anyone about her childhood before; the memories were too painful. Suddenly, she felt a need to spill it out. "I know I'm not unique. But it was the way it happened, I guess, the bitterness and misery it brought in its wake. I was an only child, and I was very close to my parents. You could say that I was spoiled rotten. Anyway, I was very happy. It just never occurred to me that the good life could suddenly crash in ruins."

"What happened?"

"My father was having an affair with his secretary and got her pregnant. He just walked out on my mother and me. Somehow it made things worse that I knew the woman. I'd even liked her, because she'd been nice to me on the couple of occasions when my father took me to his office. . . . After I found out, I hated them both."

"Your mother took it badly?" Catrina queried.

"It really broke her up. I hardly ever heard her laugh again. She never got over the way he'd treated her, and she died of cancer while I was at college. Maybe she would have died anyway, but I can't escape the feeling that it was because of what had happened."

"Are you reconciled now with your father?" Catrina asked. "Is he still alive?"

"He's still alive. I used to see him as a child, but the visits were always a total disaster. He sent me presents for my birthday and Christmas, but when I grew older I wrote and told him not to anymore. He and Phyllis had a daughter, who must be around eighteen now. But I've never met her. The only time I've seen my father in years was at my mother's funeral. He asked me if we could bury the hatchet, but it was too late for that."

She and Catrina parted then, with a lot said, but much still unsaid. It was strange, Erika thought, that she felt such a bond of closeness with Catrina, which seemed to be reciprocated. Even so, she had surprised herself by talking so freely, but she had felt the need of a sympathetic ear. This feeling of emotional insecurity, of uncertainty, was something quite new in Erika's adult life. She was suddenly forced to question her basic concepts, her philosophy of life, the thrust of her ambition. All this since meeting Glen. And losing him . . .

"About your banquet this evening," said the woman from the staff agency. "I'm afraid we have a problem, Miss Talbot."

"Oh? In what way?" Erika wedged the phone

between her ear and shoulder while she reached for the special functions file.

"You're going to be two waiters short. Unfortunately, silver-service waiting staff is hard to come by at this time of year."

Erika exploded with fury. "Now you tell me! Not a word about problems when I called you yesterday. Just promises."

"We did our best for you," the woman objected peevishly. "It's just one of those things. I'm sorry."

"I should think you are sorry. And you're going to be even sorrier. That really *is* a promise. The Moongate won't forget this in a hurry." Erika banged down the phone, then had to waste precious time calling around before she finally managed to engage the two extra waiters she needed.

No sooner had she sighed with relief than a tap at her door heralded the maitre de cuisine. One look at his face was enough to make her groan.

"I don't really want to hear what you're going to tell me, Denver."

"The motor on the main freezer has burned out. We have a couple of tons of assorted food that will be turning rotten in this heat."

"That's just terrific! Isn't life a riot? So we now have to find a temporary home for our perishables—and pronto. Any suggestions?"

Denver named a couple of nearby hotels. "We've done favors for both of them in the past, so you can tell them that we're collecting."

Erika reached for the phone, flipping through the desktop directory with her other hand. "No hitches on the banquet front, I hope?"

"Now that's something you *don't* need to worry about, Erika. Delectable dishes will appear through the service doors like magic tonight, and never mind the mayhem and near-murder it took to produce them." He turned to the door. "You don't know how easy you have it up on the bridge, compared to us in the engine room."

"Want to change places?"

"You kidding?"

She winked at him. "So get back to the engine room, Denver, and leave the real headaches to me."

Chapter Five

Harry Seidel, the organizer of the banquet, looked like his voice had sounded on the phone: harassed, expecting disaster to pounce on him from around every corner. He was middle-aged, a thin, wiry man with gold-rimmed spectacles and a bristly mustache. As he and Erika moved among the boisterous throng of computer experts who'd just piled out of the bus from the airport and were having drinks on the upper terrace, he gripped her elbow the way a drowning man would grasp a life preserver.

"I hate to break it to you, sweetheart," he said into her ear, "but somehow or other there are four more of us than I told you."

Darn him, Erika thought. She said brightly, "No problem." Signaling a drinks waiter, she told him to inform Denver and Rigby of the revised number. But Harry still wore his haggard face. Living on the brink of disaster, she reflected with inward amusement, was how people like Harry Seidel got their highs.

"Look at them," he grumbled. "The way they're drinking, I'll have some drunks on my hands before the evening's over. I hope to God the president gets the names right when he starts thanking everyone in his speech. I gave him a list, but that's no guarantee."

"You should have my job," Erika said with a laugh.

"Bad, is it? There's not going to be a problem with the food, I hope."

"Don't worry, everything's going to be fine." But even while she jollied Harry along, soothed him, tried to inject confidence, Erika felt a strange premonition of something about to happen. She tried to eliminate the thought, but it wouldn't go away. Maybe the Harry Seidel brand of foreboding was contagious. Oddly, though, she felt excited, not apprehensive.

Presently she and Harry started rounding up the drinkers and herding them through to the private room where the banquet was to be served. Suddenly she froze in her tracks. Glen Hunter was standing in the archway that led to the lobby. Erika's initial reaction was disbelief. She had to be hallucinating. Glen was in New York. Glen was never coming back to Bermuda. Not while she was there.

"What's up, honey?" asked Harry. "Something wrong?"

"No . . . no, it's okay. You go ahead and I'll join you in a minute."

"Don't go far," he said. "I need you."

Glen had remained standing where he was, watching her intently. His blue eyes carried a message, but Erika couldn't interpret it. Quelling the weakness in her legs, she walked over to join him. She pitched her voice for the benefit of any staff and guests within earshot.

"Mr. Hunter! We weren't expecting you back so soon . . . if at all."

"I just arrived." In a softer tone, he added, "I have to talk to you, Erika."

She made a helpless gesture. "I'm terribly busy at the moment. We have this banquet party from Washington, and . . ."

"I need the keys to the villa. I gave them to you when I left, you remember."

"Oh, yes. I have them in my office."

It was the excuse they needed for a few moments alone—but a few moments wasn't enough. There was too much to be said, too much to be explained. She led the way into her office, but left the door wide open.

Glen closed it. "I've missed you," he said. "Have you missed me?"

"Yes." Her throat was tight, her voice husky.

"You look wonderful, Erika. We have a lot of catching up to do." He stepped forward with his hands outstretched, but she hastily moved behind the desk, out of reach.

"I can't stop to chat with you now, Glen. I'm up to my ears."

Anger flared in his eyes. "Isn't that just great. You've missed me, but now that I'm back I don't rate a couple of minutes of your time. What do I have to do . . . make an appointment?"

"You've picked one hell of a moment to turn up," she retorted. She had to stop him from getting close; she had to stop him from touching her. With Glen back, so near, it was going to be hard to get through the evening. If he took her in his arms and kissed her, it would become impossible. She pulled open a drawer of her desk and fumbled inside for the keys to the villa. The bunch fell from her hands with a clink, and she slid it toward Glen. "Here, take the keys and go. I'll talk to you some other time."

"Tomorrow? Or next week? Whenever you happen to have a free slot in your crowded schedule?"

"Don't be like that, Glen. I have a hotel to run, and this evening I happen to be extra busy. It's not fair of you to turn up like this and expect me to drop everything."

He picked up the keys. "I'll go . . . on one condition."

"What's that?"

"Come over to the villa just as soon as you're finished here. Is it a deal?"

"No, it isn't."

"Then I stay right here."

"Please, Glen. You can't do that to me."

"No? Give me your promise and I'll leave. It's up to you."

She felt hounded, unbearably pressured. Yet she would have gone to see Glen later, whether or not he'd asked her to. How could she survive the night without knowing the reason behind his sudden reappearance?

"I'll come over for a little while later on," she said huskily.

Glen gave a brief nod, but he still didn't move. Erika felt her heartbeat accelerate under the intensity of his gaze, and her palms grew damp. The atmosphere in her small office seemed charged with emotion and breathlessly hot.

"Please go now," she whispered.

"Okay," he said at length. "But I'll be waiting for you."

As she returned to the banquet, Erika felt totally unnerved. Fortunately, her careful pre-planning paid off and there was scarcely a single hitch as course after course was smoothly served. At the end of the meal there were calls for the chef to show himself. A reluctant Denver hastily changed into fresh whites and made an appearance to a hail of congratulations.

As Erika saw the party off on the launch she had rented to take them across the harbor to Hamilton's nightspots before they were bused back to the airport, Harry said with astonishment, "It's all gone just great so far. I only hope we catch the plane, that's all."

Erika had to laugh. Harry was a tonic. "Or the launch might sink."

He paled visibly. "Don't even say it, honey. Good-bye, and thanks a million for everything. We'll be back next year, barring accidents. That's a promise."

"We'll look forward to it," Erika said mechanically. Where would she be next year? she wondered with a wistful sigh. Not in Bermuda, that was for sure. Whatever the weeks ahead might hold for her and Glen, this brief summer would be just an episode in her life. If she wanted to avoid getting badly hurt, this was the moment to call a halt. Yet she knew that no number of logical arguments would prevent her from making the short trip across to the villa. It was kismet.

Eleven-thirty. Activity at the hotel had wound down to almost zero, and the night man was on duty at the desk. Erika left her room stealthily by the door to her small private balcony. From there a flight of steps led down into the gardens. No one was around to notice her as she slipped silently along the pathways to the villa, dappled moonlight her guide when she left the proximity of the hotel.

She saw lights first, warm and beckoning. Then she heard the soft lilt of the piano. It was a number Erika recognized, the hit song from *Overtures*, Glen's last show but one. When she reached the steps she paused a moment to listen, watching him through the screen door. The light from a floor lamp threw his face into silhouette, accentuating his strong profile: the carved ridge of his brow, and his firm, straight nose; the determined, sensuous lips and thrusting chin. Erika's pulse began to race. A thousand butterflies danced in her stomach.

Glen must have heard her. Or sensed that she was there. He stopped playing midphrase and rose from the piano to cross the room. The screen door swished back. He held out a hand to her.

"So you finally made it. I was two minutes from coming to fetch you."

"I said I'd come." Her voice was thin and breathy with nerves. Evading Glen's outstretched hand, she walked past him into the room.

Glen closed the screen door, then pulled the cord to draw the beige linen curtains. He came forward to take Erika into his arms, but she checked him with an upheld hand. It cost her an effort, but she didn't intend to be used by Glen. First she had to know where she stood with him.

"I think you have some explaining to do, Glen."

"About why I've come back?"

"That, and why you went away, too."

He ran long fingers through his hair in a distracted gesture. "I needed to do some thinking, Erika."

"Go on."

Glen turned away from her. He went back to the

piano and stood looking down at the keyboard. "I came to Bermuda to put in some hard work on *Gossip*. It wasn't getting done . . . not anything useful. That was why I left."

"And now you've returned. Does that mean you've broken through your block?"

"I'm not sure yet. Going away did nothing to solve my problem. I was worse off than ever."

"Get to the point." Erika spoke sharply, but hope was soaring through her, and her breathing was shallow and fast. She willed Glen to offer an explanation that she could accept. The one explanation that she yearned to hear.

Glen touched one of the ivory keys. Its single note shivered out, pure and wistful. "When I'm supposed to be in a creative phase, a woman like you is bad for me."

"A woman like me?" Disappointment swamped her, almost drowned her. Somehow she rallied and asked coolly, "What precise category do I fit into, Glen?"

"You're a damned attractive woman, that's what you are."

"Oh, isn't that terrific! I'm lumped in with all the other women you've found attractive. One of . . . how many thousands, would you say?"

"You're one of the loveliest women I've ever met."

"That narrows things down a bit. Am I meant to be flattered, Glen?"

He left the piano to take a step in her direction, but the bright glitter of Erika's eyes stopped him.

"What do you want me to say?" he asked in a low voice.

"Try the truth, if that won't strain you too much."

"The truth? I'm not sure I know what the truth is,

Erika. I don't begin to understand my feelings where you're concerned. All I know is that I can't keep away from you. I've never felt this way about any woman before. I've never before let a woman interfere with my work. From the first moment you arrived here, I was thrown. I couldn't concentrate. I couldn't get you off my mind. Everything I turned out was slush. I couldn't stop thinking about you, wanting you. In the end I decided that I'd better quit Bermuda and hope that I'd find inspiration again if I put some distance between us. New York was just a place to go. But I soon found that I wasn't going to be able to work there either. I felt even worse away from you, not seeing you. My only hope of ever getting this show finished was to stop fighting and come back to you. But whether . . ."

"So this is an experiment? Thanks a bunch. You want to have me on hand, available. Then you can do a balancing act between your need for a woman and your need to be free of distraction while you complete your great opus. You can forget that, Glen. Go find yourself some other woman. There's no shortage in Bermuda."

"I've tried to explain how I feel. You're the woman I want right now. No one else. Please, Erika, don't be so difficult."

"Difficult? You have some nerve. You took off a few days ago without a word of explanation. Now you've come back expecting me to fall into your arms."

Glen ran restless fingers through his dark hair again. "Okay, so I was wrong to walk out on you the way I did. What do I have to do, grovel?"

"You don't like saying you're sorry, do you?"

"Who does? Okay, so I was a jerk. But now— can't we forget all that and start again?"

"Forget it? Just like that?"

"You've already admitted that you're attracted to me," he protested.

"Correction. I *was* attracted to you. You can very easily go off people."

"Then why are you here now?" he challenged. "Why did you come tonight?"

"You blackmailed me into it, remember?" she threw back. "Besides, I was interested to know what your story would be. I admit that I was puzzled— hurt, too—when you took off for New York so suddenly. If there was some reasonable explanation, then I wanted to hear it."

"You've had my explanation."

"I said *reasonable.*"

Glen's mouth tautened. His eyes held an angry, bewildered expression. "I don't know what else I can say."

"You're right, Glen; there's nothing left to say."

She had turned and taken a step toward the door, but Glen moved faster. He caught her wrist and whirled her around to face him again. "Erika, please listen to me."

"No, not anymore."

She tried to pull away, but her determination was weakening. Glen was so close, so underminingly close. She could feel his breath warm on her face, smell the unique scent of his body. A wave of heat washed over her. Even when his grip loosened she stood spellbound, unable to move away.

"Stay . . . give me a chance." His voice was a husky caress.

Erika tried to cling to her anger and resentment. Why should she meekly accept the way he'd treated her? But outweighing that, why should she punish herself for no valid reason? He was Glen Hunter, she rationalized, *the* Glen Hunter. She'd known the kind of man he was right from the start. After his fashion, he was being totally honest with her. He wanted her . . . here and now he wanted *her*. He pretended to no more than that simple need.

"Through my stupidity we've wasted too much time already," Glen said. "Let's not waste any more."

Erika still hung back. "How do I know you won't just take off again any time the whim grabs you?"

A grim smile flitted across his angular features. "No fear of that. Here I am, and here I stay now. I just have to hope that I can find some way to turn out a show."

Erika felt a flurry of anxiety. He was putting too much responsibility onto her shoulders. "You'll *have* to find a way, Glen."

"Then help me."

"How? Just because I came up with a snappy line out of the blue, that doesn't mean I could ever do it again."

"I meant help me by just being here."

"Being available, that's what you really mean."

"I'm asking you to be honest with me about your feelings," Glen said in a low, pleading voice. "And honest with yourself. We're two mature people, Erika—or we're supposed to be. So why don't we accept our need for each other?"

"But you can't expect me to just . . ."

"Yes, darling, I do expect." He smiled bewitchingly. "I have the most wonderful expectations where you're concerned."

He held her head between his hands and drew her toward him. Erika raised her face to receive his kiss. Her last drowning thought was that this was her own decision. Glen's breath seared her cheek as his mouth descended, lips parted, to take hers in a greedy search for sensation. Her arms went around his waist to pull him even closer. She felt a swift thrill as the hard strength of his body met hers. There was no gentleness in the lengthy, drugging kiss. They were both gripped by a passion that threatened to overwhelm them too quickly, too violently.

Glen broke the kiss at last. He said with a shaky laugh, "I'd better slow down. I don't want you thinking that I'm one of those wham, bang, thank you ma'am types, darling."

"You'd better not be." Her own laugh was as shaky as his.

Glen took a long, shuddering breath as his hands began to caress her, shaping her soft curves, tracing endless silken patterns on the bare skin of her shoulders. "In New York, I don't think you were out of my mind for a single second. I had to get back here to you, come what may."

Come what may. Cold, threatening words. But the nuzzling of his lips in her hair, the brush of his fingertips skimming the length of her arms, dispeled any feeling but the sheer joy of being with him.

"Did you really miss me, Erika?"

"And then some. But I had a job to get on with. I'm not my own boss as you are, free to come and go as you please."

"Free?" Glen laughed ruefully. "You had me arrested and brought back in chains. It's nothing less than slavery."

Erika wished she had the power to keep him chained to her till the end of time. But that was like crying for the moon. She'd have to settle for a flashing meteorite . . . bright while it lasted, over all too soon.

"If you're my slave," she said, "I'm going to see that you get down to some hard work on *Gossip*."

"Tell that to Felix Sylvester. He'd be relieved."

"Felix Sylvester?"

"My American producer. I talked to him while I was in New York. Felix is a worried man."

"Why?"

"Because I admitted to him that I'm having problems with *Gossip*. He gave me one of his standard morale-boosting pep talks."

"Was it something he said that made you decide to come back?" Erika asked, a little chill touching her spine.

"No way. In fact, Felix imagined that I was still in the Big Apple till I called him just now to say that I was here. He's relieved, I think, but kind of puzzled. He's scared that I won't meet the deadline. The show's due to go into rehearsal in mid-September."

"So soon?" she said, dismayed. "No wonder you've been uptight."

"I vote we forget about my work for now. Is it a deal?"

"It's a deal."

Glen touched his lips to her cheeks, her brow, in tiny whispering kisses, and Erika responded with a blossoming of need. But there wasn't the same explosion of passion as before. This time there was a wonderful sense of closeness, of togetherness.

Glen led her to sit on the long, billowy-cushioned sofa. One by one he pulled the combs and pins from her hair, tossing them aside onto a glass-topped table. As her hair tumbled down he nuzzled the soft waves.

"You smell of flowers," he said. "Heavenly, fragrant flowers like these in Bermuda."

"And you smell of man."

"*Man?* That's not the brand of after-shave I use."

"After-shave is just a part of it. Your scent is made up of . . . oh, I don't know. Fresh air, sunburn on skin, the tang of sweat and soap, and . . . and man. That's you, Glen."

He picked up a strand of her hair and twirled it testingly in his fingers. "It's like pure silk, soft and fine yet springy."

"I love the strong, wiry feel of *your* hair," she said, taking a handful and giving it a tug.

"Ouch!" He let his hand trail downward around the curve of her cheek and jaw, on until he touched the pointed tip of her breast through the thin fabric of her turquoise dress. "Now let's make some more interesting comparisons between us."

Erika gasped at the electric sensation that his delicate touch provoked, but she didn't move away. It was beyond her strength to bring such tingling delight to a halt. Soon Glen slipped his hand under the scooped neckline of her dress and pushed her bra aside to seek the warm fullness of her breast.

"You have such a soft, smooth, perfectly formed body," he whispered appreciatively.

"I have no complaints about yours."

"Want to know what I think?" he asked.

"Yes . . . no. Well, what?"

"I think the time has come for us to come clean."

"Come clean?"

"I want to see all of you, down to the very last dimple and the tiniest mole." He pressed his lips to hers in a soft, lingering kiss. "Do you have any moles in intimate places, Erika?"

"I don't think so."

"I'll be able to tell you soon, won't I?"

"You're very confident."

"I feel very confident. You can report on the exact shape of my birthmark."

"What makes you think I'm that interested? Where is it, anyway?"

"You'll have to look."

His hand cupping her breast, the thumb teasing the nipple, was liquefying all sensation for her. It was as if their bantering existed on a lower plane than this joyous bliss. Dimly, she was aware of his other hand at her back. She felt her dress grow loose about her as the zipper slithered down. Glen drew her to her feet, and the dress fell with a hiss of silk around her ankles. Her bra was off an instant later, and then her satin panties. Erika felt a wave of shyness and raised her arms to cover her breasts. But Glen gently pulled them aside, and his gaze was so reverent that all embarrassment was swept away.

"You're so beautiful," he said huskily. "Even more beautiful than I've been imagining." He trained his sensitive musician's fingertips across her responsive skin, circling her breasts and moving downward to the curve of her waist, sliding around to clench the soft roundness of her buttocks. "Oh, Erika, I'm crazy for you."

Glen perched on the arm of the sofa to allow him to pay leisurely homage to her breasts, holding each in turn with both hands and letting his tongue caress the dark aureole. He smiled in satisfaction as he watched the even harder peaking of her nipples. Then he dropped his head to tongue her abdomen and probe teasingly into the cavity of her navel.

Trembling with joy, Erika urged him to his feet. She had a need to see him naked too. Her fingers shook as she fumbled with the buttons of his shirt, then tugged it from the restraining waistband of his cotton slacks until she could push the garment from his shoulders. His torso was magnificent, as she'd known it would be, firm and taut. His tanned skin was beautifully supple under her searching palms as she fondled his chest, riding over the contours of bone and muscle. Glen gasped softly and reached out to drag her against him. But Erika resisted, her fingers now at the clip of his slacks, freeing it and tugging down the zipper with timid, eager impatience. In a moment his clothes were off, joining hers in the pile on the floor.

For a long moment they were both still, just looking—and delighting in what they saw. To Erika the night seemed clamorous with the noise of her thudding heartbeat, and she gazed on his tall, naked figure as if through a swirling mist. All doubts and uncertainties, all reservations, had fled away. There was only glorious certainty. . . .

Glen moved; she moved—not in response, but of her own volition. They came together with a sigh . . . a sigh that quickly became a groan of tormented pleasure from Glen as she provocatively arched her body to him, and he ground his hips against her softness. He bent to press his lips to hers, mouth to open mouth, his tongue slipping in to trace the smooth perfection of her teeth, to taste her sweetness, then withdrawing, enticing her to do likewise. Their tongues met and curled together, flirting, teasing, writhing together in mounting passion.

"I want you, Erika. . . . How I want you." Glen drew back to look at her questioningly. She saw the glow of desire in his eyes, and its sparks flickered through her body, starting fires everywhere.

"Yes," she whispered. "Oh, yes . . . yes."

With his lips Glen blazed an erotic pathway across her face, her throat, down to the soft swell of her breasts, teasing and tugging each peaked nipple in turn until Erika was moaning with rapture. Both hands cradling his head, she pulled him closer, her fingers raking into the crispness of his hair.

"Yes," she whispered again, hardly realizing it. "Yes, Glen, yes."

In a swift, smooth movement Glen lifted her in his arms and laid her down on the sofa. He stretched out beside her, skin to skin, while his hands restlessly shaped her body, kneading the soft, springy flesh. Erica was floating, adrift in sensation, beyond the point of conscious thought. She was scarcely aware of their surroundings. It was just Glen and herself climbing toward the beckoning ecstasy until it was suddenly upon them in a great breaking wave.

Afterward, they lay in one another's arms, their breathing heavy, their skin moist with sweat. Now that their passion was spent, little shivering echoes remained as a reminder of the splendor they had known together.

"Darling Erika," said Glen softly. "I knew how perfect it would be with you."

Erika closed her eyes. There was a sting of pain for her in those words. She had proved to be a good lover, Glen was saying, in comparison with the other women he had slept with. She was one among many . . . a long line of bedmates stretching back into his past and reaching forward into his future. She thrust the chilling thought away, and in doing so gave a little whimper.

"What's the matter?" Glen inquired tenderly. "Is something wrong, darling?"

"No," she said. "I was just . . ."

"Just?"

"Nothing. Nothing at all."

Was she regretting it now? he wondered. There was no reason he could see why she should. But in so many ways Erika was different from every other woman he'd known; perhaps she viewed sex differently, too. Still, she'd been as ready to make love tonight as he had been, and there was no doubt that it had been wonderful for both of them. So why had he sensed that slight withdrawal just now?

He studied her face. Her lids were softly closed, shielding her eyes from him, and Glen felt oddly shut out. He was filled with a strange yearning he didn't understand. There was an emptiness in him that their lovemaking, magnificent as it had been, still hadn't satisfied—and Glen realized that the mere repetition of lovemaking with Erika would never be able to satisfy it. He rebuked himself impatiently. Hadn't he achieved his aim? An obstacle in the path between him and his ability to create should have been removed. Instead, it loomed larger than ever. He felt despondent, scared. What had happened to his father must *not* be allowed to happen to him.

Erika roused. Opening her eyes, she found Glen looking at her intently. For how long? she wondered. What was he thinking?

"I'd better get going," she said with a wavering smile.

"It's early yet."

"Early morning, you mean. Come on, let me get up."

Glen sighed a protest and rolled himself away. Then, wanting to recover their earlier lightheartedness, he joked, "Hey, I never did discover if you have any moles."

Erika stood up, scooped her clothes from the floor, and headed briskly for the bathroom. "You'll have to take a rain check on that," she called over her shoulder.

A rain check, Glen thought as he pulled on his trousers. Yes, there would be a next time, and a next and a next. He was into this thing with Erika now, and he didn't want out. How great the prospect would be if only there wasn't this heavy gloom weighing him down.

Tonight he didn't want to be parted from her a moment before he had to. When Erika returned from the bathroom, he said, "I'll walk you back."

"You won't, Glen. I don't suppose there's anybody about at this time of night, but if there should be, I wouldn't want to be seen with you." Noting his frown, she added, "Can't you understand that? It's best for us both."

"I guess so."

There was an odd restraint between them now, after the wild abandon of their lovemaking. Rather awkwardly, Glen laid his hands on her shoulders and lowered his head to kiss her on the lips.

"You're wonderful, Erika," he said in a hushed voice. "Everything a woman should be. Plus, plus, and plus again."

"I think you're wonderful, too." There was a lump in her throat as she turned away. Glen parted the curtains for her and slid back the screen door.

"Take care!" he murmured as she stepped out into the moonlight.

Thankfully, there was no one to see her as she slipped like a pale ghost through the night-scented gardens. The stone circle of the moongate cast an elongated shadow on the grass. On an impulse, Erika switched direction to go and stand within the enchanted circle. What should she wish for? Happiness with Glen . . . just for a few short weeks? That was the very most she could dare hope for. Anything more than that was just a beautiful, impossible dream.

Erika shook herself and walked on. The moongate legend was a charming piece of nonsense, a game for happy lovers to play. She'd be better advised to accept the world as it really was. For her and Glen, there was definitely no long-term future.

All the same, the beautiful dream lingered in her thoughts as she wended her way back to the steps that led up to the balcony of her room.

Chapter Six

"You look marvelous, Erika." Glen's eyes were warm with appreciation as she emerged from her office after checking through the morning mail and dictating a couple of letters to Lalla.

"Thank you." She was glad that her purchase of a sunsuit had been so successful. It was a pale apple green, trimmed with white, and it fitted her perfectly. There was a matching bolero jacket which she was carrying, and she wore a white bandeau to hold back her hair.

They stood chatting in the lobby while waiting for the Montroses to join them for an outing to St. George. It was an arrangement that had been made in the cocktail lounge the previous evening.

"If they don't turn up in the next couple of minutes," Glen said with a glance at his watch, "why don't we skip off on our own? It isn't such a good idea teaming up with them."

"I thought you liked Douglas and Catrina. Especially Douglas."

"Liking is one thing. Having them along when you and I could be alone together is something else."

"It was your idea in the first place to make up a foursome and go sight-seeing," Erika pointed out. "Or had you forgotten?"

"That was days ago. At the time it seemed the only way to get you to come out with me."

Erika laughed. "So now you're stuck with it. That'll teach you not to make impulsive suggestions."

For the first time since her arrival, Erika was allowing herself a real slice of time away from the job. Things at the Moongate were running so smoothly now that she felt entitled to leave it for a few hours.

"Next time," Glen said, "just the two of us. Right?"

"If that's the way you want it."

"Don't you?"

"Maybe."

"Just maybe?"

She smiled enigmatically. "Anyway, please be nice to Douglas and Catrina."

"Aren't I always nice?"

"No, you can be very un-nice at times."

"You're talking about some other guy, not me. I'm the one who . . ." He bent his head and whispered in her ear. "Remember?"

"Behave!" she said, stepping away and fixing him with a severe look.

Glen, she had discovered, could be alarmingly changeable in his moods. When they were alone together in the evenings he was usually cheerful and lighthearted. He was a skillful, tender lover, and she knew that she made him as happy as he made her. Yet sometimes, especially if she chanced to run across him during the day, he seemed very gloomy. She knew that he was concerned because his work wasn't going well, which bothered her a lot. She had to hope that his present mood would survive the day with the Montroses.

"Here they come," she said warningly. "Hi, you two. All set?"

"Sorry to have kept you waiting," Catrina said. "My sandal strap broke, and Douglas had to fix it for me."

With Erika at the wheel they took a route through the narrow leafy lanes that were colorful with the bright blossom of oleander and crape myrtle. At every bend there were breathtaking new views of the sparkling ocean. Overhead, the sun shone down from a cloudless blue sky. It was perfect weather, in a perfect vacation setting. Like Erika, Catrina was wearing a sundress, and the men were both in shorts. Erika determined that she would enjoy her day out.

Reaching St. George, they left the car in the square and strolled across a wide bridge to visit the small island, where there was a full-size replica of an old-time sailing ship, the *Deliverance*.

Erika, with Glen's cracks in mind, had studied her guidebook about Bermuda so that she knew more about the *Deliverance* than any of the others.

"It was built as an escape ship by the first people ever to live on Bermuda, after they'd been shipwrecked on the reef."

"They were English, I suppose?" Douglas queried.

"Yes. It was in 1609, and they were on their way to the new colony of Virginia when they were struck by a hurricane. There were a hundred and fifty people aboard, including women and children, but miraculously they all survived. When they managed to get ashore they found this cluster of uninhabited islands that abounded with food—fish, wild pigs, and fruit. Over the next few months they built a new ship from the wreckage of the one that had brought them from England, and then most of them sailed on to Jamestown. But they'd staked a claim to this territory for England. That, in a nutshell, is the early history of Bermuda."

They were standing on the high poop deck of the vessel, and Glen laid an arm across Erika's shoulders. "There's more to her than just a pretty face, isn't there?"

"You needn't sound so amazed." Erika wasn't trying to conceal her relationship with Glen, but neither did she want to flaunt something that was very special and private between the two of them. So she moved away from him as she continued, "Did you know that Shakespeare's *The Tempest* was based on that episode? He wrote it the following year, so I read."

"What about you, Glen?" asked Catrina. "How do you get the ideas for your shows?"

"I keep my eyes open. Listen. Observe what's going on around me."

Douglas chuckled. "Are you planning something on an attractive woman who comes to Bermuda to take on the running of a luxury hotel?"

"It's a thought."

This possibility hadn't occurred to Erika before. Maybe Glen always regarded his girl friends as raw material. She didn't like the thought one bit. "Let's go belowdecks," she said.

While following the Montroses down the steep companionway, Erika noticed Douglas grip Catrina's arm to assist her. Catrina quietly but firmly pulled away, evidently not wanting him to touch her. It was so sad, Erika mused. They were two people divided by tragedy. Yet they were locked together by that same tragedy, too, because it was theirs and only theirs. She didn't believe that Catrina had ever seriously considered leaving Douglas. But unless they could somehow find a way to bridge the gulf between them, they were condemned to live their lives side by side on terms of distant politeness.

Her solemn thoughts were instantly dispeled as Glen slipped an arm around her waist and drew her hard against his side, bringing back a flood of memories of the times they had lain in one another's arms. Each of the three nights since his return from New York she had crossed the dark garden to the villa. Each time their lovemaking had been more wonderful than before. It was only when she left him in the early hours that a feeling of despondency caught up with her. She didn't know how she'd be able to cope when the time came for them to go their separate ways.

Belowdecks, the four of them marveled at the ship's cramped, spartan conditions. How people in olden times had suffered to seek a new life for themselves in the New World, Erika reflected. As happened so often, she suddenly felt the weight of Glen's gaze resting on her. She turned and fleetingly caught his expression before he changed it into a smile. His face had been sombre, marred by a frown. It was as if one part of him disliked her, she thought with a shiver. He was a man at war with himself. She clung to the memories of their tender passion . . . passion which had blazed briefly just a few short hours ago. But the chill feeling had taken hold of her.

"I'm going up on deck again," she said.

They left the *Deliverance* and wandered back across the bridge to King's Square to look at the ducking stool and stocks, the harsh punishments meted out to miscreants in Bermuda's early days. Now they were a favored background for pictures. Glen unslung his camera and handed it to Douglas.

"Take a couple of snaps of Erika and me, will you?"

"Oh!" Douglas handled the camera gingerly. "I'm a bit of a duffer with these things. I'm still at the aim-and-press-the-button level."

"That's all you have to do with this one. The film advances automatically."

Glen positioned Erika and stood beside her, his arm around her shoulders. She felt suddenly nervous, uncertain that she wanted the pictures taken. In one way, it solidified their relationship, and she hoped that Glen would give her a copy. Not that she'd need a picture to remember him. At the same time she felt uneasy at the thought that he wanted a picture of her to add to his album, along with all his other girl friends.

The instant the two shots were taken, she moved away from Glen. "Give me your camera, Douglas," she said, "and I'll take some of you and Catrina. Stand over there by the ducking stool. Closer. Douglas, put your arm around Catrina. Right, that's fine. Now hold it and say cheese."

They did a tour of the Carriage Museum, with its interesting exhibits of elegant phaetons and barouches and broughams and other forms of horse-drawn transport that had been used on Bermuda's narrow roads until the first automobiles were permitted in 1946. Then they decided it was time for lunch, and looked for a nice restaurant.

They found one close to the water's edge, with

tables set out in the open air, shaded by a trellis of climbing foliage. The food fell well short of the Moongate's standard, but it was still very good. Erika always enjoyed a meal more when she had no kind of responsibility for it. She felt particularly happy to be sitting next to Glen, with his thigh touching hers. Several times he unobtrusively ran a hand over her bare knee, sending sparks of excitement shooting through her.

"I'm going to look around those gorgeous boutiques we passed just now," said Catrina after they'd finished eating. "Coming, Erika?"

"Okay."

The men went to get up, but Catrina waved them down. "You stay here and have some more coffee. You'd only spoil our fun. We won't be too long."

Erika purchased a suntop and a pair of espadrilles; Catrina found some gifts to take home with her, made from the fragrantly scented Bermuda cedarwood. Walking back to rejoin the men, they passed a vacant bench in the shade of a royal ponciana tree.

"Let's sit here for a minute and cool off," Catrina said. "This weather is glorious, but it does sap the energy."

"I like the heat," said Erika.

"Lucky you." Catrina's glance was speculative as they sat down. "So you and Glen did get together, after all."

"Oh, it's nothing serious."

"Meaning?"

"Just that. Can you imagine Glen Hunter being serious about a woman?"

"But you'd like him to be serious about you."

"I didn't say that."

"Funny, I thought you just did. You look to me, Erika, like a woman who's fallen headlong."

"Do I?" Erika turned her head so that Catrina wouldn't see the color flooding to her cheeks.

"I'm right, aren't I?" Catrina persisted.

"So you're right. What of it?"

"A woman in love can't help dreaming. In this case impossible dreams, I'm afraid."

Erika swung back to face her. "I'm not naive enough to imagine that Glen is in love with me. Or that he ever will be. So . . . end of story."

"Not quite the end, yet. There's no reason why it shouldn't last as long as you're both in Bermuda."

"Maybe." Why did she feel this strange dichotomy in her emotions? One half of her wanted to slap Catrina down hard; the other half wanted to spill out her heart to her.

"If the thought of parting depresses you," Catrina said philosophically, "remember that Glen would be a disaster as a husband. He'd never settle down, and you'd never be able to trust him."

"I know that; you don't have to spell it out."

"All the same," Catrina went on, "Glen does seem very keen. It's surprising. . . ."

"Thanks a bunch!"

"I didn't mean it like that, Erika. What I meant was, for a man who's famous for his many affairs, it's surprising that he should seem so caring about his current girl friend. He's really fond of you, Erika; I can tell from the way he looks at you. So I wonder if . . ."

"Forget it," Erika said, and stood up.

They arrived back at the Moongate at the cocktail hour.

"I'm dying for a drink," said Catrina as they got out of the car. "Let's have one before we go and get changed, Douglas." She glanced at Erika and Glen. "Will you join us?"

"I'm easy," said Glen, and looked at Erika.

She shook her head. "It's okay for you all, but not for me. It would never do for the manager to appear looking too casual. I'll slip into something more suitable; then I'll join you."

"We'll have a drink waiting for you," said Catrina. "A yellowbird?"

"Yes, fine. I won't be long."

Erika looked in at her office on the way upstairs, having asked Lalla to leave her a note about anything important that had happened during the day. She was glad to see that there had been nothing to cause any problems. She checked that the expected arrivals had turned up safely. She'd make a point of introducing herself to them during the evening.

Up in her room Erika stripped and showered, then put on a favorite dress that she hadn't yet worn here at the Moongate. She was dressing, as always now, to please Glen. As she stepped into the softly floating skirt, then arranged and tied the velvet cords of the loose overblouse at hip level, she thought with a thrill of expectation that Glen was the one who'd be taking off this dress later, as a prelude to their making love once more. Erika could hardly wait for the time to pass; she was drawn to him as irresistibly as a moth to a flame. She shrank from the sudden thought that eventually the moth brings about its own destruction.

Downstairs, she entered the cocktail lounge and smiled around at the guests, on the alert for new faces. Two she immediately spotted were at the table occupied by Glen and the Montroses. The man was rather short and balding, with a droopy mustache; the woman, some years younger, was stridently good-looking, with long blond hair falling to her waist and heavily made-up eyes. She wore a black jumpsuit in a shiny fabric, and a mass of bangles and chains. Erika couldn't place the couple. They didn't look like she'd imagined any of today's arrivals.

As Erika walked over to the table, Glen rose to his feet. "Erika, I'd like you to meet Felix Sylvester and Joni DeWitt. Felix is my producer in New York. This is Erika Talbot, who's the manager here."

Erika said good evening and shook hands with them both.

"Your drink's waiting for you, Erika," said Catrina. "We timed it just right. Amos only just brought it over with our second round, so it's nice and cold."

"Thanks a lot." As Erika slipped into the chair between Catrina and Glen, she was wondering about the sudden arrival of Felix Sylvester. Glen had given her no hint that his producer was coming to Bermuda.

"Were you hoping to stay at the Moongate?" she asked Felix. "We do have one or two suites free, although I'm afraid they're not the ones with the best views."

"Felix and Joni will be staying with me at the villa," Glen told her.

"I see." Erika had to check herself from adding, For how long? Her spirits took a dive. While these two were at the villa it meant an end to her nightly trysts with Glen. She looked at him, catching his eye, but his expression was impassive. Then she became aware of Felix's gaze. She glanced at him and forced a smile. "I expect you'll want to take some of your meals in the hotel, Mr. Sylvester?"

"If it's no problem, Miss Talbot."

"None at all. Just let us know beforehand if you can." Then she asked, because she *had* to find out, "How long are you planning to stay?"

"Who knows?" His well-manicured hands gestured uncertainly. "As long as it takes, I guess."

"Felix has come to discuss the new show with Glen," said Catrina. "Isn't it exciting? If I get the chance to visit London when *Gossip* is on, I'll certainly go see it. I'll feel that I had a hand in it, having been here while it was being created."

Glen's laugh was rueful. "I'm glad somebody is having fun. For the people involved, Catrina, it's hard work and worry that go into creating a show. Right, Felix?"

"Hard work and worry is putting it mildly. How I've survived nearly fifty years without a heart attack I'll never know."

"How do you actually set about it?" Catrina asked Glen. "Do you compose the music first, and then the lyrics? Or the other way around?"

Glen lifted his shoulders. "Sometimes one way, sometimes the other. More often a bit of both."

"I read somewhere about composers who've had a sudden inspiration and written a whole number in a matter of minutes. Can it really happen like that?"

"It *can*, but it rarely does. Gershwin composed 'Swanee' in fifteen minutes flat. Sondheim's 'Send in the Clowns' was written in just one evening."

"Glen did it too, once," said Felix. "In *Switchback* we had to drop a number that wasn't working in rehearsal. Glen sat himself down at a piano backstage and came up with 'Love Gets Around.' He did the whole thing, words and music, in less than an hour. These creative types sometimes produce their best work when they're under pressure."

"'Love Gets Around.'" Catrina raised her eyebrows. "That's a fabulous number. I love it."

"Thanks. I wish I could do the same thing again."

"Don't we all?" said Felix. "Hey, I'm getting hungry. When does dinner start around here?"

Erika glanced at her watch. "In just over thirty minutes."

"Good. We'd better go get changed, I guess. We left our bags on the stoop at the villa. Okay, sweetie?" he added to Joni.

"I could do with a shower." She paused. "Will you be joining us for dinner, Miss Talbot?"

"Afraid not. I have some catching up to do on work."

"I gather," Joni said, reaching down with a jangle of bracelets for her handbag, "that you spent the day showing Glen and Douglas and Catrina some of the local sights?"

"Not really. We were all exploring together. I'm not very knowledgeable about the local scene, I'm afraid."

"Oh yes, of course. Catrina was telling me that you're just the temporary manager. How long do you expect to be staying?"

"A few weeks more. Then it'll be back to Britain."

"You'll be here for about as long as Glen, then?"

"Just about."

Joni stood up, towering inches above Felix in her high-heeled sandals. "Better make the most of your time in Bermuda."

Erika met her glance head-on. "I fully intend to."

The party broke up, the others all going off to get changed. Erika strolled around among her guests for a few more minutes, exchanging the usual pleasantries, then headed for her office. That had been a silly, defiant message she'd given Joni. It must have sounded as if she were chasing Glen. She shrugged.

Did it matter? Her relationship with Glen was their business, and only theirs.

No doubt Glen felt the same. He might, though, have given her a secret little message of reassurance. It would only have taken a regretful smile, or a slight raising of the eyebrows, to convey that they'd make new plans to meet while Felix and Joni were around. Instead, during the whole time they'd been chatting in the cocktail lounge, Glen had scarcely looked her way.

While dinner was being served, Erika stayed in her office. After the lavish lunch they'd had in St. George she was happy to have just a small chicken salad for dinner, with no dessert. She spent the time checking through an estimate Lalla had prepared for a small international conference of oceanographers due to be held in Bermuda during the coming October. With the peak of the vacation trade over, it would be useful business for the Moongate. Already Erika was having to involve herself in events that would take place after she'd returned home. It seemed to bring the end of her affair with Glen that much nearer. Which was supposing, she reminded herself with a shaft of pain, that Glen wanted it to last even *that* long.

Miguel, the wine waiter, appeared in the open doorway. "Sorry to bother you, Miss Talbot, but it's about Mr. Ephron."

"Oh no! Is he acting up again?" Walter Ephron and his wife had only been staying at the Moongate for two days, and already he had become a number-one menace. A brash, loud-mouthed man, he was a demolition contractor from the Midwest. He'd made his money fast, Erika guessed, and now he wanted to let everyone know that he was loaded. This took the form of complaining about anything and everything in an effort to prove that he was accustomed to even better than the Moongate's luxury.

"Is this the best suite you have?" he'd demanded critically when she'd shown the couple to their rooms on arrival.

Erika had summed him up instantly. "All our suites are furnished to the same high standard, Mr. Ephron," she'd told him with a pasted-on smile. "I do happen to have a couple of others free that I could show you. If you'd prefer one facing the gardens rather than the harbor, the rate would of course be slightly lower."

That had got him, the hint that money mattered. "I guess we'll take this, then," he grunted, and Erika thought she detected his wife's quiet sigh of relief.

At dinner yesterday evening Mr. Ephron had made a fuss about the lobster he'd been served, maintaining that it was off. It had been replaced at once with a fillet of sole. But Denver, when he'd heard, had needed to be restrained from charging through the swing doors to the dining room and letting fly at the man. Tonight, judging from the bottle Miguel carried, it was the wine that Walter Ephron was making a fuss about.

"He says it's corked, Miss Talbot, but it definitely isn't. He's insisting on another bottle."

"So serve him another bottle," she said wearily.

Miguel looked shocked. "But this is the '78 Cabernet Sauvignon, Miss Talbot. It's forty-two dollars."

"You know the rule, Miguel—the customer is always right."

"But . . ."

"I have another rule for people like Mr. Ephron . . . the awkward customer always pays. Make sure that *both* bottles go down on his account."

A joyous smile spread across Miguel's olive-skinned face. "Now *that* I like."

She chuckled. "You'll like the Cabernet Sauvignon, too, when you get to drink it later on tonight."

Erika had been expecting, hoping, that Glen would look in to see her before returning to the villa after dinner. She had decided that if he asked her to join them there for a drink later on, she would accept.

He hadn't come, though, and it was getting quite late. A quick visit to the dining room, and then the cocktail lounge, showed her that Glen and the other two had left the hotel. Perhaps he would call to invite her over to the villa.

By ten-thirty activity in the hotel had wound down. A few people sat reading or chatting in the lounge; a few of the more determined drinkers still propped up the bar. A splash from outside told Erika that a late swimmer was using the pool.

She grew increasingly tense and irritable while waiting to hear from Glen. Maybe the best thing was to call it a day, go upstairs to bed and read herself to sleep. But that seemed feeble, cowardly. It could be, she supposed, that Glen imagined she might be embarrassed by an open acknowledgment to Felix and Joni that they were involved. She smiled to herself. There was no need for him to be so protective.

She picked up the phone to call the villa. But what was she going to say? I've been waiting all evening for you to ask me over? No way. She'd pay him a visit, instead, as if it were the most natural thing in the world.

Armed with determination, Erika left the hotel by the front entrance. Clouds had blown up since sunset, and the night was very dark. After she had left the lighted areas near the hotel, she felt lost for a moment. Then the lights of the villa showed up through the trees. As usual, the French windows were open, with the drapes undrawn. Through the screen door Erika could make out three figures in the room. When she drew near enough to hear voices, she realized that the two men were arguing.

She halted. This wasn't the ideal moment for her to walk in on them. Maybe it was foolish to have come over tonight. Glen and his producer would have a great deal to discuss. Felix's arrival in Bermuda possibly meant there was some change of plan in the production schedule of *Gossip*. Possibly there was a problem over financing. She knew it happened in the theater world that a backer would drop out so that a projected show would suddenly be starved for cash. Thinking about it, all kinds of reasons occurred to her why Felix might need to talk to Glen.

No, she decided, this was definitely the wrong moment for her to show up. She turned away to return to the hotel, but was arrested by hearing her name spoken. It was Glen's voice.

"What do you mean, what's with me and Erika Talbot?"

"Are you denying it?" asked Felix.

"I want to know what damned business it is of yours."

"Relax. I'm not criticizing your taste. She's a good-looking lady, and she has loads of style. Good luck to you, just so long as you get the show finished on schedule. You've got me guessing, though, Glen. Before, you've always stayed away from women when you're working on a new show. So do you wonder that I'm curious now?"

"Leave my private life out of this, Felix."

"Glen Hunter doesn't have any private life; you

know that. What you do is always red meat for the gossip columnists. If you do have something going with this woman and it's helping you, I'm not complaining. There's no publicity in having you holed up like a hermit. We can let the story break that there's a fascinating new lady in Glen Hunter's life—a classy English rose this time. The press would give it the full treatment."

"Lay off it, Felix." Glen's tone was dangerous.

"Why should I? The publicity would be worth a million to *Gossip*."

"You're way off beam," said Glen. "Erika Talbot is the manager of this hotel; that's all. The Montroses and I spent the day out with her because she has the use of a car and could offer us transport. I see Erika around; I have a drink with her sometimes out of common courtesy. But that's the beginning and end of our relationship."

"Joni says she can read the signs," Felix persisted, "and I'd back her judgment in that area."

"You'd lose your money, then. Joni has it wrong this time."

"Have I, Glen?" It was the first time Joni had entered the conversation.

"Damn right you have, if you seriously imagine that I'm having an affair with Erika Talbot."

"I was watching her, and that doesn't fit with what I saw in her face."

"Then Erika must be imagining things too. As I said, I see her around. I quite like her. That's all. End of discussion."

Felix made some comeback, but Erika didn't hear what it was. Already she was stumbling away across the grass, heedless of in what direction. She just needed to put some distance between herself and Glen. She felt furiously angry, and she wanted to weep.

Chapter Seven

"Erika, darling," said Glen on the phone. "I've missed you. When can you come over?"

Erika had taken the call in her office, so she didn't need to hide her feelings. "I can't," she said fiercely.

"It doesn't have to be right this minute. Whenever you can make it. Felix and Joni have gone to catch the ferry to Somerset Village, so they'll be out most of the day. They'll be back for dinner, though, so we won't have a chance to get together after that."

"How delicately you term things, Glen."

"Hey, don't get huffy with me. I didn't know that Felix would turn up yesterday and mess everything up."

Erika thrust aside her anger, and inquired, "Why did he come, Glen?"

"To talk about the show. Time's getting on, and he wanted to check on my progress."

"I thought you discussed the show with him while

you were in New York. That was less than a week ago."

"I guess Felix wanted a bit of reassurance about how things were going."

"And you were able to reassure him?" she asked coolly.

"We're planning to run through what I've done after dinner this evening. Look, Erika, how about you slipping over when lunch is finished? Things at the hotel are usually quieter then."

"No, I can't do that."

"Too busy?"

"Definitely."

"Don't you *want* to see me?"

"Since you ask, no, I don't."

She heard his quick hiss of breath. "I'm just as miffed about Felix being here as you are. So don't hold it against me."

"I'm not—not that."

"What, then?"

"You wouldn't understand. The Glen Hunters of this world see things differently from ordinary people."

He swore under his breath. "What's the matter with you? You lost me way back. If you won't come over here, I'll come over there. We have to get this straightened out."

"Don't bother," she said. "I can't see you."

"You mean you won't."

"That's it, Glen; I won't. Now, if you don't mind, I have a million things to do."

"Hiding behind your job again, Erika?"

Furious, she felt like slamming down the phone. Controlling the impulse, she said icily, "If that's what you want to think, think it. Good-bye, Glen."

She was trembling, and her head was spinning. Hot tears pricked behind her eyelids. So she'd made a fool of herself—these things happened. But why did she feel such a sense of grief? What had she lost other than a few weeks of an affair that couldn't last long anyway?

Erika counseled herself that this was the best way: a quick, decisive break before she was in too deep. She felt angry, *furious* with Glen. That was good, encourage it! That should ease her heartache. Did Glen Hunter really imagine that he could repudiate her like that and get away with it? Flatly deny that she had any importance in his life to Felix and his girl friend, then expect to carry on with their affair just as before? Thank heaven she had her job at the Moongate to keep her busy. Thank heaven she had exciting career possibilities to dream about and work for. She'd been right all along in her outlook. Whatever role she might allow men to play in her life, it would never be a vital one. She couldn't imagine ever finding a man whom she would want to marry.

Except Glen.

The afternoon hush was shattered by a shouting voice in the lobby. That sort of thing couldn't be permitted at a hotel like the Moongate. Erika rose quickly from her desk and went outside.

Walter Ephron, looking apoplectic, was towering over Lalla and raging at her. He swung around on Erika. "I want something done about this, do you hear?"

"If you'd kindly lower your voice and tell me what's bothering you, Mr. Ephron, I might be able to help."

He blustered on in the same ranting tone. "It's that damned half-witted boy you have here in the gardens. He hangs around grinning all the time. It's an insult to the guests. You offer precious little in the way of comfort as it is, without forcing that idiot down our throats."

Erika saw tears in Lalla's eyes, and she laid a sympathetic hand on her shoulder. To Walter Ephron she said curtly, "Come into my office, if you please."

He stalked in after her, swaggering, seeming to imagine that he'd scored a victory. Erika closed the door behind them. She did not invite him to sit down.

"Perhaps you didn't realize, Mr. Ephron, that the woman you were bawling out is the mother of that boy. It's upset her terribly, having her son called such things."

"I'm sure it's not the first time. The boy's a mental case. He should be put away, not allowed to mix with decent people."

"That's an outrageous thing to suggest. I'll have you know that Frankie Bishop is a valued member of the staff here. He's a hard worker, and our head gardener is very pleased with him. Frankie is invari- ably pleasant and courteous to the hotel's guests, and he has a sweet nature. I have never heard anyone else, his co-workers included, say a critical or unkind word about him. It took you to do that, Mr. Ephron."

"It's about time someone spoke up, then. Most people are too damned soft. They don't like to draw attention to themselves, so they put up with any amount of slipshod treatment and rudeness."

"Rudeness? I'd say you'd cornered the market on that." Erika steadied her voice. "Mr. Ephron, I'd like you to listen very carefully to what I'm about to tell you. The Moongate has a fine reputation, which it richly deserves. It's a superbly run hotel. I can claim that without immodesty because it's not my achievement—I'm only here as manager in a temporary capacity. A large proportion of the guests are regulars, people who return here again and again, which is a testimony to the high standards they always find here. Yet you, Mr. Ephron, have done nothing but grumble and make complaints from the first moment you entered the door. If you find the Moongate so uncongenial, I suggest that you move out at once and go to a hotel that's more to your taste."

"Now look here," he blustered, "you can't do this. I know my rights."

"And I know mine, Mr. Ephron. I have a right to expect my clients to observe the normal rules of decent human conduct. I'm willing to put up with the occasional unjustified complaint as part of the job. People have high expectations when they come on vacation, and sometimes they're hypercritical. But you've gone way over your permitted ration of unreasonable behavior. I shall be thankful to see the back of you."

"Suppose I refuse to leave?" he roared. "You can't make me go."

"Why should you wish to remain here, Mr. Ephron, if the Moongate's standards are so far below what you'd hoped for? There are plenty of other hotels if you want to stay on in Bermuda."

Walter Ephron stood glaring at her while he sought around for his next line of attack. Then, "I'll take this up with the authorities. There must be some kind of controlling body here."

"There is," Erika confirmed. "Would you like me to give you the address?" She felt a streak of envy that the wretched man could vent his rage on her, when she was obliged to keep her temper in check. She would love to tell him just what she thought of him in specific detail. Reaching into a drawer of her desk for a booklet, she said, "Here's a list of hotels in Bermuda, according to classification. I suggest you start calling around."

"To hell with that. I'm leaving for home on the first plane."

"Fortunately there's an excellent schedule of flights. You shouldn't have any difficulty. I'll have your bill prepared at once."

With a muttered curse, Walter Ephron turned and strutted out of her office. Erika followed, anxious in case he tried to have another go at Lalla, or Frankie himself. But he headed for the elevator, presumably making for his suite. Erika pitied his wife.

"Where's Lalla?" she asked the clerk at the reception desk. "Has she gone out to see Frankie?"

"That's right, Miss Talbot. What a nasty scene that was. Mr. Ephron sounded as if he wanted to explode."

Erika nodded. "He and his wife will be leaving shortly. Have their bill ready for them. But let me see it first, to make sure that he's been charged for everything."

"Will do." The girl frowned. "It was really horrible of him to turn on poor Frankie like that."

"How much do you know about it, Trixie?"

"Well, we all heard. We couldn't help it, the way Mr. Ephron was shouting and screaming."

"You don't know what sparked it off, I suppose?"

"Well, yes I do, actually. Amos was on his way back from taking drinks to someone in the Jacuzzi, so he saw it all. He's just been telling me. Mr. Ephron was playing croquet with his wife, and they got into an argument. He was walking backward, waving his mallet at her, when he tripped over one of the hoops. Apparently it was a really funny sight because he was staggering around all over the place, trying to recover his balance, before he ended up by collapsing into a rose bush. Frankie was right there, doing some pruning, and immediately went to help Mr. Ephron get untangled. But Mr. Ephron shook Frankie off and swore at him before stomping into the lobby."

Erika regretted now that she hadn't asked the man to leave sooner—she'd had enough provocation. "Well, Trixie, we must console ourselves that Mr. Walter Ephron is a one-off. We aren't likely to meet anyone else as nasty as he for a long time."

Erika was just returning to her office when she saw Glen walk into the hotel. He came straight over to her.

"Erika, I want to talk to you."

If Trixie hadn't been sitting at the desk she'd have refused him. But she knew Glen wouldn't go away without making a scene. "I hope this won't take long. I'm rather busy."

Glen didn't speak as he followed her into the office. Once inside, he closed the door and stood with his back to it.

"What I want to know, Erika, is why I'm getting the freeze treatment from you."

"We've already had this conversation on the phone."

"And I got no answers. I want some now."

Defensively, Erika adopted a puzzled attitude. "What is all this? You seem to be making heavy weather about something that's not that important, Glen."

"Our relationship not important? I can't believe you really mean that, Erika. What's bugging you?"

"I don't owe you any explanations," she said frostily.

"No? I thought you and I had something special. We *do* have something special."

"Like all your other affairs are special? I guess that every single one is the greatest ever while it lasts."

Glen's eyes narrowed. "What's this—jealousy? You knew about my life-style before we started out, Erika. I didn't try to hide anything from you."

"As if you could! The Glen Hunter life-style has been very thoroughly documented. Prize stud of Broadway and Shaftesbury Avenue."

"Greatly exaggerated. Anyway, nothing in the past makes any difference to the way I feel about you."

"Which is . . . how?"

"You know the answer to that, Erika. I don't have to spell it out."

She met his gaze directly, steeling herself against its sensual impact. "I'll tell you how I feel about you, Glen. I'm attracted to you, I won't deny it, but we were getting too intense. We were getting in too deep, and I can't afford the time for a serious involvement right now any more than you can. So I think this is the moment to ring down the curtain."

Her words seemed to have taken Glen's breath away. Then he said, in a grating voice, "My God, you're as hard as nails, Erika. I thought you were different. I thought you had a softer side, but I was wrong. I've never been so completely wrong about a woman in my life. Still, I guess I owe you a vote of thanks for putting me wise before I made an all-time idiot of myself."

He was about to open the door when Lalla burst in. She stopped short at the sight of Glen. "Oh, I'm sorry, Miss Talbot; I thought you'd be alone."

Lalla's stricken face told Erika that something was badly wrong. She set aside the whole problem of Glen and became brisk. "What's the matter, Lalla? Is it . . . Frankie?"

"I can't find him. He's disappeared. I've searched everywhere, all over the hotel grounds. No one has seen him. That awful man must have scared him half to death. He's never walked out on his job before, not ever."

"What's this about?" asked Glen.

"Frankie was yelled at by that horrible Walter Ephron." Erika filled him in rapidly, their personal hostility forgotten for the moment. "Now Lalla can't find him. Do you think Frankie might have gone home, Lalla?"

"No, he's not there. I called my mother, and she hasn't seen him." Lalla put her hands to her head. "I'm so worried. I just don't know what to do."

"I'll go look for him," said Glen. "Poor kid, he's probably hiding someplace. And when I've found him, I'll deal with that bastard Ephron."

"I've already dealt with him," said Erika. "He's leaving the Moongate this afternoon."

"He won't be missed." Glen touched Lalla's shoulder in a compassionate gesture. "Don't worry; we'll find Frankie. I know he's been badly upset, but he's young. He'll soon forget about it."

While Glen went off to search in the gardens, Erika organized a thorough search of the hotel itself, calling on all the staff members who could be spared. She had people look in every possible place where a confused, unhappy Frankie might have hidden himself, right down to the small dugout that housed the pool's filtration plant, and the stifling hot roof of the main building. Glen checked back a couple of times to see if Frankie had turned up, having had no luck himself.

The afternoon wore on with no news, and Lalla's desperation grew. Erika had sent her home to be quite certain that Frankie wasn't there, perhaps hiding in some place her invalid mother wasn't aware of. She'd also told Lalla to check with any friends of Frankie that he might have run to. But all these suggestions had led to a dead end.

"I just can't imagine what can have happened to him," Lalla wailed for the hundredth time. She was only a hair's-breadth from breaking down.

"I wonder if we ought to contact the police," Erika said to Glen quietly, out of Lalla's hearing.

Glen's lips tightened as he considered. "I'd say best not, not yet. It would terrify the life out of the boy if he were approached by uniformed men. He'd imagine that he'd committed some terrible crime."

"I expect you're right." Did Glen know about the incident of the motorbike? she wondered. Or was it just shrewdness on his part that he could guess how someone like Frankie would react to the police?

Erika was just hanging around, waiting. She didn't know when she had felt so useless. Glen hung around with her, and she felt grateful to have him there. He was the only person to whom she could let her concern show. She had sent Lalla off to wait in her private office. It seemed the kindest thing to do in view of the other woman's distress. Erika had suggested to her that she should sit quietly and think of other possible places where Frankie might be, and also phone her friends again.

Guests kept coming and going through the lobby, stopping to chat with Erika for a few minutes as they usually did when they saw her. She took the chance to ask, without betraying the depth of her anxiety, whether they happened to have seen Frankie. But no one had. Several people had heard about or witnessed the row with Walter Ephron, and they were sympathetic, also glad to hear that the Ephrons had left the hotel. Erika kept regretting that she hadn't told them to leave before this, but throwing guests out wasn't something that a manager did lightly. It fell into the "last resort" category.

During the afternoon the weather changed, and a strong wind sprang up. The trees outside the front entrance were being tossed around, and Erika could hear the wind whistling under the eaves of the old mansion. By the cocktail hour it had grown quite dark, with heavy clouds piling up in the western sky.

At a little after seven Felix and Joni walked into the hotel, and exclaimed at seeing Glen waiting around in the lobby.

"So here you are," said Felix, not looking too pleased. "We've been back for ages. We changed and then hung around waiting for you, but it's getting toward dinner, so we thought we'd better come over on our own."

"Sorry. You two went right out of my mind."

They glanced, puzzled, from him to Erika, and Felix asked, "Something wrong?"

"A young chap on the garden staff has gone missing after an unpleasant incident with one of the guests," Glen explained.

"You mean he beat it?"

"It's more a case of going somewhere to lick his wounds, I guess. The way it looks, some extremely nasty things were said to him."

"Gee, that's too bad. Nothing we can do, I suppose?"

"No, you and Joni go on through, Felix. I'll join you in the dining room later, when I can."

A few minutes later, Douglas and Catrina came walking through from the cocktail lounge. "We've been waiting for you," said Catrina reproachfully, "so we've come to dig you out, Erika. It's our last evening, remember? You promised to have a farewell drink with us."

"I'm terribly sorry, but you'll have to excuse me."
Erika explained the situation briefly. "You do understand that I can't come with this hanging over us."

"When did the lad go missing?" asked Douglas.

"This afternoon. Around three o'clock."

"Three? It must have been just around then that
Catrina and I saw him."

"Where?" asked Erika and Glen together.

"Down on the hotel jetty. We were waiting for the
ferry to take a last trip into Hamilton."

"Oh yes, I remember," said Catrina. "He went off
in one of the boats."

"A boat?"

"It was a little blue-and-white dinghy with one of
those . . . oh, what do you call them, Douglas?"

"An outboard motor."

"Blue and white? That must be the one the
Lichtmans have rented," said Erika. "You mean
Frankie started the motor himself?"

Douglas nodded. "He seemed to know what he
was doing. I thought nothing of it at the time."

"Don't forget," Glen put in, "that he's used to
using the power mower for the grass here. So he'd
know about engines."

"And he can ride a motorbike, too," said Erika
with a frown. This news certainly altered the picture.

"So, Frankie's taken off in a boat," Glen said
thoughtfully. "But where in the hell has he gone?
There are a thousand places he might have gone
ashore around the coastline. Or on any of the
smaller islands. Have you any ideas, Erika?"

She shook her head and didn't voice the additional
possibility that Frankie might not have tried to land
but kept on going until he ran out of fuel. In that
case, he would now be drifting on the open ocean.
With night coming on, it was too frightening a
thought.

"How about asking his mother if she has any fresh ideas now?"

"Yes, Glen, I'd better." Erika dreaded the prospect, guessing that Lalla would become even more agitated.

"Lalla," she began gently, entering her office, "I want you to keep calm. That's the best way you can help Frankie. Now, there's no real news yet, but we have a new line to explore. This afternoon Dr. and Mrs. Montrose saw Frankie get into a boat that was tied up at the jetty and start off in it."

"A boat?" Lalla gasped in astonishment.

"So does that give you any clue to where he might have gone?"

Lalla shook her head, but her eyes had grown alarmed. "No, he couldn't have . . ."

"What are you thinking, Lalla?"

"I'm sure Frankie couldn't have . . ."

"Tell me, Lalla. However unlikely it seems."

"Well, Miss Talbot, there's a little island that Frankie is very fond of."

"An island?"

"The first time he went there it was years ago, on a children's picnic organized by our church. Frankie had a wonderful day, and he kept on talking about the island. So one time, for his birthday treat, I paid someone to take us there in his boat. You should have seen Frankie's excitement. He just loved it, exploring every inch of the place and pretending that it was *his* island. That he was the king. So after that I made it a regular thing each year on his birthday. It was worth every cent."

"So it's possible, you think, that Frankie might have headed for this island if he was very upset? He'd have felt comforted there? Safe?"

Lalla nodded. "Yes, he'd feel safe there. But I'd never have thought he'd be able to find his way there on his own. Oh, Miss Talbot," she gasped, and the sudden distress in her eyes made Erika realize that all the other possibilities had crowded into her mind.

"Where is this island?" Erika demanded crisply.

"It's in the Great Sound. It's very small, just a grassy mound with a few trees, and there are lots like it."

"Could you point it out on a map?"

"Yes, I think so."

Erika remembered seeing some navigational charts in Bruce Oldfield's desk. She fished around and found one of the Great Sound.

"Come with me, Lalla. I want Mr. Hunter to know about this." It was only after she'd spoken that Erika realized she was instinctively turning to Glen for support.

Three heads turned at once as she and Lalla emerged into the lobby. Erika explained about the island that Frankie loved so much.

"I'd say that's where he's gone, then," Glen said. "Is that a chart you have there?"

"Yes." Erika unrolled it and spread it across the reception desk. "Now, Lalla, can you show us?"

Lalla studied the chart for a few moments, then pointed a finger. "There. You go past Hinson Island, and between Darrell and Marshall islands. It's that tiny one there, I think. Yes, that's right. I remember it has a tongue-shaped piece sticking out. That's where we landed."

"Okay," Glen said, giving Lalla a confident smile. "If that's where Frankie's gone, I'll find him."

"You?" Erika exclaimed. "Shouldn't we call in someone official? I believe there's a police marine division."

Glen shook his head. "*We* might all feel certain that it's where Frankie has gone, but it would take time to convince the authorities. It's quicker to handle this ourselves. Now, what about a boat I can use?"

"The McKuens have a rented motor launch. And they're in the hotel . . . I saw them go up to their suite a half hour ago. We could ask them."

"No," Glen said. "I think this is a case of take first and ask afterward. Don't worry; I'll square things for you."

"But you'll need keys."

"There're ways. Let's go look at this launch."

"I'll come with you, Glen," said Douglas.

"Thanks. I could use some help. Do you know anything about navigating?"

Douglas gave him a brief grin. "Enough. I've sailed the Scottish lochs in all weather."

"So come on."

The two men started for the nearest exit, the others following. Erika ducked into her office to fetch a flashlight.

Catrina said, "Douglas . . ."

"Yes, dearest?"

Her brow was puckered with anxiety. "Take care."

"Don't fret. We will." He paused fractionally, looking into his wife's face. Then he turned away.

They were halfway to the jetty when the rain began. A few huge drops, carried by the wind, soon turned into a heavy downpour.

"This is going to be a big help," said Glen morosely.

"Can you still go?" Erika asked. Already, in only a few yards, her silk blouse was soaked through.

"Why not? Once we're wet, we won't get any wetter."

"But you will be able to find your way?"

"Sure. I have eyes that see in the dark. So does Douglas. Right?"

"Right." The message was to stop fussing and let them get on with it.

The launch was rocking at its moorings in choppy water. The lights of Hamilton showed only vaguely, and out across the water in the direction Glen and Douglas would be heading there was only blackness. Erika shivered. She would rather go with them than be forced to wait on the shore, imagining all kinds of things. She suddenly knew that she still loved Glen, despite what she had overheard last night. If anything were to happen to him, she would be devastated.

The two men jumped aboard, and a few moments later the engine sprang to throaty life. Erika handed Douglas the flashlight. There was also, she was relieved to see, a swivel-mounted spotlight fitted in the prow.

"Cast off," Glen shouted to Douglas, and revved up.

Erika, guarding her fear, called cheerfully as the launch surged away from the jetty, "Free drinks all round when you get back."

Chapter Eight

*B*ack in the hotel, Erika took Catrina and Lalla upstairs to wait in her own room. From there they had a good view of the jetty. They dried off, and Erika lent the other two sweaters. Rain continued to lash the windows, and the high wind buffeted the trees. It would be very rough out on the open water, Erika thought anxiously.

"My husband is a first-class yachtsman, Lalla," said Catrina suddenly, "and I'm sure Mr. Hunter is too. You couldn't have two better men searching for Frankie."

Lalla jerked upright on the blue-striped chaise longue. She gave a wan, appreciative smile. "They are both very brave men, too, setting out on a night like this."

"They'll be fine." Erika spoke with a confidence she didn't feel.

They fell silent. Then Catrina said in a strained

voice, "It's at times like this when you realize . . ." She trailed off, but it was enough. Erika understood.

Around them, the hotel continued to function in its usual smooth fashion. Dinner would be in full swing, Erika thought. Before coming upstairs she had instructed the staff to say nothing about the rescue operation that was under way. Better that the guests were unaware of the drama, especially the McKuens, who might react badly to the appropriation of their rented launch.

Erika saw from her watch that an hour had passed since Glen and Douglas had set out. Time ticked away relentlessly. She said nothing to the other two, but surely the men should have returned by now, if nothing had gone amiss? She picked up the phone and ordered coffee and sandwiches to be sent up.

The arrival of the refreshments, the bustle of pouring the coffee and passing the cups, carried them through a bit of time. Munching on an unwanted turkey sandwich for appearances' sake, Erika surreptitiously watched the sweep of her watch's second hand. Minute by minute her anxiety intensified. At what stage, she wondered fearfully, should a general alarm be raised? Had it been an act of reckless folly for Glen and Douglas to set out across the dark water in this weather? Had she been wrong to permit it? She suspected, though, that she couldn't have stopped Glen once he'd decided what must be done. For an easygoing playboy type, he could be very stubborn.

Horrifying images were forming in her mind, sending throbs of panic pulsing through her. How could such a small craft survive the battering of storm-whipped water? It would be swamped, overturned. Erika saw two figures struggling in the water, and gripped her cooling cup of coffee with tense fingers. She closed her eyes, but the fearful images wouldn't go away.

And then . . . a pale light shone out across the water, flickered, and was gone. All three women were instantly alert, eyes strained. There it was again, quite definitely, and nearer. Erika dragged open the door to her balcony and they ran down the outside steps, careless of the rain that soaked them in seconds. As they reached the jetty the spotlight of the launch streamed out, and the engine chugged. It came alongside and scraped; then a figure jumped ashore with a mooring rope.

"We found him," Glen shouted. "He's hurt, but he's okay."

"Frankie!" Lalla would have flung herself into the cockpit, but Erika and Catrina held her back. Glen leaped down again and threw a second rope, which Erika secured. Then Douglas appeared from the cabin, bearing in his arms a limp figure wrapped in blankets and protected by a yellow oilskin. The two men carried Frankie to the side, and as Glen once more jumped to the jetty, Erika and Catrina lent a hand with the injured boy.

"Careful," Douglas instructed. "Mind his head. He's all right," he said to Lalla, "but we must get him to the hospital. He needs stitches, for a start."

"Oh, my poor darling!"

"Can he be taken by car?" asked Erika. "Or should I call an ambulance?"

"Better get an ambulance."

Erika ran off to the nearest phone and made arrangements. The ambulance would be just a few minutes, she was told. She returned to find the others carrying Frankie up the steps. They entered the hotel by a rear entrance, and took him through to the staff lounge.

The ambulance arrived and Frankie was safely stowed inside; then Douglas went with him and Lalla, indifferent to his own sopping wet state.

Erika had sensed that Glen preferred not to say too much in front of Lalla. Now she said, "Well, tell us what happened."

"We were right in our thinking," Glen said. "Frankie *had* headed for that island. But he only just made it. The way it looked to us, Frankie hit a submerged rock as he tried to beach the dinghy, and its keel was ripped open. He must have hit his head on something. He'd bled profusely. But somehow he managed to drag himself onto the beach, and he must have been lying there for hours, either unconscious or semiconscious."

"What a blessing you found him when you did," said Erika.

"The sound of our engine probably roused him, and that's how we spotted him. Douglas and I were shouting and flashing the spotlight around when we saw this shape lumber up and start to run . . . away from us. I guess Frankie got the idea we were the police come to arrest him for stealing the dinghy or something. We beached the launch and followed him, but he'd crossed the island before we reached him. It's very small. I shouted again, telling him who we were, and that there was no need to be afraid, but he obviously didn't understand. He started wading into the water, and then the current caught him and swept him away."

"How did you manage to get him out?" Erika asked in a shaken voice.

"It was Douglas, more than me. I rate myself a strong swimmer, but he left me behind. And the way he handled Frankie! The lad's as strong as an ox, and he was panicking. But Douglas coped."

"He won a gold medal for lifesaving when he was

at university," Catrina said, and there was a ring of pride in her voice.

"Just as well. Anyway, between us we hauled Frankie ashore again. Douglas had to try to do several things at once. I fetched the launch and brought it around to give him some extra light. The gash on Frankie's forehead had opened again, and his lungs were full of water. Plus, Douglas thought he was concussed. He did a marvelous job. Thank heaven he insisted on going with me. I couldn't have managed on my own. He's quite some guy, that husband of yours, Catrina."

Quite suddenly Catrina was weeping, tears streaming down her face. Erika had a feeling that a good cry might do her good. "Come along," she said briskly. "Get to your room and into some dry clothes."

Glen said, "I'd better get back to the villa and get changed myself."

"No, don't go. It . . . it's much too wet," Erika said. "You can have a hot shower here in my bathroom. I'll find you something dry to put on."

Starting to object, Glen looked at her and gave in with a quick grin. "As long as it's not a waiter's monkey suit."

"I'll find something of Douglas's for you," Catrina offered, pulling herself together.

After showing Glen to her room, Erika went to the Montroses' suite. Catrina had already sorted out a pair of jeans and a sweatshirt for Glen, plus some sneakers.

"The jeans will be a bit short on him," she said with a giggle, "but what they lack in length they make up for around the waist."

Catrina was joking, Erika realized, to cover her feelings. Feelings, perhaps, that she was only beginning to appreciate.

"It's certainly been an eventful last night for you, Catrina."

"Yes. A night to remember."

Erika brought her back to practicalities. "What do you want to do about food? Will you come to the dining room, or shall I have a tray sent up?"

Catrina pondered. "Right now I couldn't eat a thing. I'll wait until Douglas gets back, and then we'll call room service."

"Whatever suits you." Erika moved to the door. "Good night, then. I'll see you in the morning. Take care."

"And you."

Erika walked back to her room, calling as she opened the door, "Are you decent?"

"More or less."

A bath towel was cinched around Glen's waist, and his torso gleamed golden-brown in the lamp-light.

"Here," she said, holding Douglas's clothes out to him. "They should be a passable fit."

"Thanks." A pause, then, "Erika . . ."

"I thought it was wonderful what you and Douglas did tonight," she said hastily. "I know that Lalla will be eternally grateful. I . . . I'd better go and tell the McKuens that their rented launch is back safe and sound. They're sure to have heard about it by now." She laughed wryly. "It's just as well that the Lichtmans have been out all day and won't be back till way past midnight. I can explain to them tomorrow about the dinghy. I suppose it's a complete write-off?"

Glen nodded briefly. "Erika, don't go."

"I must. Get dressed, Glen; then come down-stairs. I guess you'll be hungry; you missed dinner."

"What I want is for you to stay right here. We have things to talk about."

"We've already done all the talking that's necessary. You decided that you'd made a sizable error of judgment about my character—remember? Let's just leave it there."

Glen met her eyes with a strange, long look. "Out there in the boat, Erika, I was thinking about the two of us. . . ."

"You had time to spare for thinking about us?"

"Believe it." His voice was deep, serious. "There were a few really nasty moments when I wasn't sure that we'd come through. And do you know what was uppermost in my mind? Regret about you and me. What we've shared . . . it was too good for you to lightly throw it aside."

"Lightly?" she protested.

"That's how it looks to me. How else can I see it, if you won't explain why you've suddenly gone cold toward me?"

"Put it down to a blinding flash of insight."

He shook his head. "No, I want a better answer than that."

"It's the only one you're getting." She opened the door. "See you downstairs."

Glen came to her swiftly, making her flinch in anticipation of his touch. But he didn't touch her. He merely closed the door again. "Get this into your brain, Erika. It's not finished between us yet. Felix and Joni will be gone tomorrow. I'll expect you over at the villa in the evening to get things sorted out."

"You'll be unlucky."

His eyes flared. "I have the right, damn you."

"You haven't any rights where I'm concerned, Glen, except the rights of any other guest of the Moongate." Very deliberately, she opened the door again and stepped outside. As she walked away, she heard Glen call after her, "We'll see about that, Erika."

Glen didn't show up for the meal she'd promised him, so he must have gone straight back to the villa. She didn't see Douglas either. She first knew he was back from the hospital when she heard that the Montroses had supper from room service.

Later, Erika called Lalla's home to see if she was there. She'd just arrived, and said in reply to Erika's inquiry, "They're keeping Frankie in the hospital for a couple of days in case he's slightly concussed. But otherwise they say he'll be fine."

"That's great. You'll want to go and see him tomorrow, Lalla. Take whatever time off you need."

"Thanks, Miss Talbot, you're real good to me. Thanks . . . for everything. I can't begin to tell you . . ."

"Not at all. If you want the truth, Lalla, I feel partly to blame for what happened to poor Frankie. I tolerated that Ephron man's appalling rudeness for too long. I should have foreseen that he might cause real trouble."

Next morning, Douglas and Catrina came to settle their account and say good-bye. A single glance told Erika that there had been a reconciliation between them. Douglas had a sleekly contented look; Catrina was radiant. She met Erika's eyes and smiled a smile that said it all.

"Back to the Scottish mists for us," Douglas chuckled as he pocketed his wallet. "Maybe it's good for our souls' sake that we can't afford this kind of perfect climate and pampered luxury all the time. Eh, Catrina darling?"

"But we'll be coming back to the Moongate again one of these days. Douglas and I are agreed on that. It's a very special place for us."

"Don't leave it nine years next time," said Erika. "Did you make a moongate wish while you were here?"

"We did," Catrina said. "This morning."

"I hope it comes true for you; I sincerely mean that. Douglas, in all the drama last night I didn't get a chance to thank you properly for what you did, saving Frankie like that. It was marvelous."

"Don't mention it. I was very glad to be able to help. Very glad." His eyes flickered to Catrina, and Erika noted the other woman's quick, reassuring nod.

"I called the hospital this morning," Erika said, "and apparently Frankie is doing fine."

"Good. We've arranged our airport taxi early so we can drop in to see him for ten minutes en route. By the way, what's happening about the dinghy that got smashed up?"

Erika pulled a wry face. "I still have to break the news to the Lichtmans. They haven't appeared yet after their late night, but I guess they soon will."

She walked with the Montroses to the front entrance to wave them off in their taxi. She felt really sorry to see them leave, and promised Catrina to keep in touch, also to visit them in Scotland if she ever came their way.

An hour later, still trying to shrug off her sense of anticlimax, Erika found the Lichtmans by the pool. Luckily, though, she didn't have to face a difficult explanation about the wrecked dinghy.

"Glen Hunter has already told us what happened," Hank Lichtman said in his soft southern voice, seeming entirely unbothered. "He said that we shouldn't worry; there'd be no problem."

"No problem?"

"He said that he was going to take care of things with the boatyard people."

"I see."

"In fact," his wife put in, "Glen said that he'd bring a replacement dinghy over for us later on."

"Oh, good," Erika said, swallowing her astonishment.

Glen, she reflected as she walked back to her office a few minutes later, had acted fast to avoid what could have been a nasty situation. With the dinghy a write-off, the boatyard would have made a claim against their insurers, and the insurers would have brought a charge against the person who had taken—stolen—the boat: Frankie. Glen's intervention could only mean that he intended to bear the cost out of his own pocket. She wondered if Lalla knew . . . if Glen would want her to know. She had a feeling that he wouldn't. Glen Hunter was a strange mixture . . . a playboy who indulged in frivolous affairs with women, yet a caring person, too. She doubted that she'd ever understand him fully. Instantly the bleak thought followed that she wasn't going to be given the chance to.

"Why the hell can't you take an hour off to visit one of your staff in the hospital, Erika?" Glen sounded impatient. It was midafternoon, and he'd found her in the lounge, where she was picking up a few loose petals that had fallen from one of the large floral arrangements.

"It's not that." She avoided Glen's challenging glance. "I plan to go and see Frankie later on, but . . ."

"You won't go with *me*, is that what you mean?" When she didn't answer at once, Glen went on, "That boy must be feeling wretched. Douglas and I pulled him off that island and got him to the hospital, but it hasn't canceled out what it was that caused him to take off in the dinghy like that. I reckon that it's up to us to try and counteract whatever it was that Ephron said to him. Don't you?"

"I . . . I guess you're right."

"So come on. Get the car out."

"I really can't get away right now, Glen. Honestly. I'm expecting an important call from Boston.
Look, meet me in the lobby in a half hour. Right?"

"Okay," he said, and strode briskly away.

They were sitting in Bruce Oldfield's car, ready to
go, when another car swung into the driveway and
pulled up in their path. Denver jumped out. He was
carrying a stereo radio recorder.

"Glad I caught you," he said. "The staff took up a
collection for Frankie. When I heard you were
visiting him this afternoon, I nipped down to the
store to get this for him. Give it to the poor kid with
this card we've all signed, will you?"

Erika took the radio through the window. "Oh,
Denver, you are a sweetie."

"Aren't I just?" He winked at Glen. "Sweetie
isn't what she calls me when I spoil the dinner."

"Wasn't that a kind thought?" she said to Glen as
she drove off. "People are really nice."

"But not me?" When she made no comment, he
went on, "Felix and Joni have gone now. They left
directly after lunch."

Erika chose to ignore the implication behind this
statement, and asked, "Was Felix satisfied with your
progress on *Gossip?*"

"Producers are never satisfied."

"But I mean . . ."

Glen swung in his seat to face her. "Why ask? You
don't care."

Her hand shook as she reached for the gearshift at
a bend in the road. "Yes, I do care. I want your new
show to be a huge success—even bigger than your
others were."

"You could have fooled me."

"What have I said or done," Erika said bitterly,
"to give you a different impression?"

"It's the way you're acting. Switching abruptly from hot to cold."

"That's purely on a personal level," she said. "Nothing to do with your work."

"You imagine that my work isn't on a personal level? Creating a musical show is a bit more than just sitting down at a piano and waiting for inspiration. I have to live and breathe what I'm creating if it's to have a hope of succeeding. My shows aren't just a part of me; they *are* me. My emotional state when I'm working affects the end product."

This time, luckily, she didn't need to find a reply, because they had reached the hospital.

They found Frankie sitting at a window and gazing moodily in the direction of the Botanical Gardens. A large bandage covered the wound on his forehead.

"Hi, Frankie!" Glen greeted him. "How's tricks?"

He looked pleased to see them, but his soft brown eyes were wary. They took seats beside him, and Erika at once handed over the chocolates and fruit they'd brought for him, and presented him with the radio/recorder.

"This is from all the staff at the Moongate, Frankie, with their best wishes. See, there's a get-well card."

"Gee," he said, "that's great." Frankie read the message on the card, mouthing the words in the way of a slow reader. He sat hugging the radio as something very precious. "Mum told me what you did, Mr. Hunter . . . you and Dr. Montrose. Only you shouldn't have bothered. I'm just a nuisance to everybody."

"That's just not true," Erika said fervently. "A great many people are very fond of you, Frankie. Do you think the staff at the Moongate would have sent you that radio if they didn't think a lot of you? And what about your mother and your grandma? They love you very dearly. They'd be heartbroken if anything happened to you."

Frankie looked a bit shamefaced, but he still wasn't convinced. "I smashed up someone's motorbike," he confessed, "and it cost Mum a lot of money to get it mended. And now there's the boat I took."

"That's all been taken care of, Frankie," said Glen. Cheerfully lying, he went on, "It wasn't as badly damaged as you seem to think. So you can forget about the boat. Nobody's going to come chasing your mother about that."

Frankie seemed very relieved, accepting Glen's word without question. "Dr. Montrose and Mrs. Montrose came to see me this morning. They said they were on their way to the airport. Dr. Montrose told me that I'll be fine, except that I'll have a scar." He touched the bandage on his forehead.

Glen grinned and put a finger to the scar on his own upper lip. "See this? All the best people have scars, Frankie. They're a useful reminder not to do the same stupid thing again."

"Stupid?" He looked at Glen in sheer astonishment. "Did you do something stupid, Mr. Hunter?"

"You bet I did. It was when I was a kid, much younger than you are now. I picked a fight with a boy who was heavier than me." Glen smiled reminiscently. "Still, I managed to leave my mark on him."

Frankie didn't smile. "I felt like I wanted to hit that Mr. Ephron," he confided solemnly. "I was trying to help him get up, but he pushed me away. He swore at me and called me names."

"Well, I'm certainly very glad you didn't hit him, Frankie," said Erika. "You'll be happy to know that

Mr. Ephron and his wife have left the hotel now. He wasn't a nice man; nobody liked him. So you must just forget the nasty things he said to you."

"But it wasn't my fault he fell into that rosebush, Miss Talbot. I hadn't done anything, honest I hadn't."

"We all know that, Frankie. It was entirely his *own* fault, and that's why he got so angry. Men like Mr. Ephron can't bear to look foolish, you see. You just happened to be the nearest person, so he vented his fury on you. It could have been anyone."

Frankie had believed Glen's falsehood about the damage to the dinghy, but he wasn't deceived by this attempt on her part to reassure him. "The boys I know call me names like that too."

"You call them names right back," Glen advised. "They only do it to tease you. It's just the way boys are."

Erika and Glen stayed a while longer, skirting around the subject, till Frankie became more cheerful. By the time they stood up to leave, he had worked out how to listen to his radio through the earpiece. Erika gave him a little hug.

"Come back to work just as soon as you're well, Frankie. The Moongate's gardens will suffer without you there to take care of them."

Back in the car, Erika said, "I heard about the wrecked dinghy . . . what you did. The Lichtmans told me. You're very generous, Glen."

"If you truly think that, Erika, it's a reputation I've bought on the cheap."

"You didn't do it to impress me."

"How do you know I didn't?"

"I just do."

They sat in silence for a few tense moments. Erika knew that Glen was watching her face and she could feel her nerves stretch almost to the breaking point.

As they came to a traffic circle, Glen said suddenly, "Don't let's go straight back to the hotel. Let's just drive."

Hands trembling on the wheel, Erika drove around the circle and took the road for the Moongate. "I have to get back."

He didn't argue. "Erika, please come over to the villa later on."

"I've already told you, no."

"Change your mind," he urged. "Whatever you say, we do need to talk."

"No, Glen."

"Because you're afraid?"

"Why should I be afraid?"

"Then come. Coffee and conversation, that's all. I promise."

"Some things are best left unsaid, Glen."

"Not between us, they aren't. This has to be brought out into the open, whatever it is."

Her hands gripped the wheel tightly. Maybe Glen was right. What use was clinging to her pain, hugging it within herself? Maybe it would be best to throw it at Glen's head and clear the air. Then he'd stop pestering her.

"Okay," she said in a clipped voice. "You win. I'll come, when I'm able to get away. I don't know exactly what time."

Out of the corner of her eye she saw Glen move his hand, as if to touch her thigh. For a moment it hovered; then he withdrew it.

"I'll be waiting for you," he said.

Chapter Nine

The delayed arrival of a plane from Toronto kept Erika on duty longer than she'd expected. She fixed with Denver to serve a late supper for the four arriving guests in place of the dinner they'd have been expecting, and she made sure she was in the lobby to greet them.

It was a family party, a middle-aged couple plus their daughter and son-in-law. But the parents both looked so young they might almost have been all of the same generation.

"Are we glad to get here!" the mother exclaimed, slipping off the chiffon scarf from around her blond curls. "I hope we haven't missed anything special by being so late."

"Not this evening, as it happens, Mrs. Praeger. When you're ready, there'll be some supper waiting for you in the dining room. Tomorrow there'll be dancing on the terrace, and the next evening we have one of our regular barbecues."

"Great! We're really going to enjoy ourselves here; I know that. My sister and her husband came to the Moongate last year, and they said it was the best hotel they'd ever stayed at."

"I'm sure you won't be disappointed," Erika said confidently. She had switched the parents from the suite originally reserved for them. The one vacated by the Ephrons had an even better view. Their delighted exclamations at the nighttime scene of moonlight on the water erased some of the sour taste of Walter Ephron's grousing.

After the delay, it was close to midnight before Erika made her way across the fragrant gardens to the villa. When she drew near, she saw that Glen was waiting outside for her, pacing around restlessly on the veranda.

"Look who's finally made it," he greeted her.

"I said I'd come."

"Huh! The way you've been acting lately I wouldn't have been surprised if you'd just stood me up."

Shrugging, Erika walked past him into the villa. Glen followed, and she was glad to note that he didn't draw the curtains.

"Drink?" he queried.

"No, thanks." She sat down, choosing an easy chair, not the sofa where they had made love.

"You're sure? Maybe some coffee?"

She shook her head. "You asked me to come, Glen, so that we could talk. I'm here now, so let's start talking."

"You won't object, I hope, if I pour myself a drink first?"

"Go ahead."

While he was at the bar, Erika glanced around her. There were music sheets spread out all over the piano, and several had slipped to the floor.

"Having problems?" she asked, gesturing.

"Some." Glen sipped his whisky, looking at her over the rim of the glass, his brows drawn together. Then he said, "I think I'm entitled to some explanations, Erika. What have I done to deserve your abrupt turnaround? Why have I suddenly become the object of your hostility?"

She sighed audibly. "Don't you know how to let go, Glen? You should have had enough practice. Or is it because this time it's not your doing?"

"There's no reason *to* let go that I can see."

"Shouldn't that be, you can't see any reason why I would want to?"

"Is this a game of riddles?"

Erika took a deep breath and burst out, "Glen, I heard what you said to Felix Sylvester the night he arrived."

He looked puzzled. "What did I say that was so special?"

"About me, I mean. The way you felt about me. Or rather, the way you didn't feel."

Glen put down his glass and stared at her. "You've left me way behind. When are we talking about? When did I say what to Felix?"

"It was late that night. Think hard—you should be able to remember what you said."

"A conversation that took place *here,* you mean? At the villa?"

"Yes."

Glen frowned. "How come you overheard it?"

"Don't try and put me in the wrong. I wasn't deliberately eavesdropping. I was expecting that you'd invite me over later that evening, for a drink with your friends. When you didn't call, I thought I'd walk over anyway. I heard you and Felix arguing, though, so I decided it wasn't the best moment for a

social visit. I was just about to go back when I heard
you say my name. Joni had apparently told Felix that
there was something going between you and me, but
you denied it, Glen. You denied it very strenu-
ously."

He was silent for several long moments. Finally he
muttered, "You've no cause to get upset about what
I said, Erika. It was just none of Felix's business
about you and me."

"That's not the point."

"So what is the point? He was asking questions he
had no right to ask."

"There was no reason for you to lie about us."

"I simply said what I thought was best."

"He's known about the other women in your life.
You've never made a secret of them. The reverse, in
fact."

"This is different."

"*I'm* different, you mean. I don't have the style
and panache that any woman honored by having her
name linked with the great Glen Hunter has to have.
I'm too ordinary. You want to keep me shut away in
the back room, an off-the-record diversion while
you're stuck here in Bermuda."

"You think that? You honestly think that?"

"Why not? It's the obvious conclusion."

"Oh, Erika . . . you couldn't be more wrong."

"Easy words to say, Glen, but they don't fit with
what I heard. When Felix said there was publicity
value in our relationship, you went right through the
roof."

"To protect *you*," he insisted. "Believe that."

"Try harder. You've never rushed to protect the
reputation of your other women."

"If I had, they wouldn't have thanked me for
doing it. Half the fun for them—more than half—

was all the media attention they received. You wouldn't want that, Erika. I wouldn't want it for you."

He sounded so sincere that Erika was tempted to believe him. She quenched the urge. "Glen, can't we drop this charade? Why go on pretending?"

"I'm not pretending. Why should I be?" He raked long fingers through his hair. "Listen to me. Why would I be saying all this if it weren't true? What would I get out of it—except lost publicity?"

She had no answer to that. Her pulse thudded painfully in the silence of the room. Glen's blue eyes glittered, and she felt pinned by his challenging gaze. Perhaps he could see the beginnings of doubt in her expression.

"If you were really an embarrassment to me, Erika, wouldn't I just ditch you? I want you, darling; I still want you. Isn't that proof of what I'm telling you? I've never been short of beautiful women to choose from. Even here in Bermuda I've had a dozen come-ons I could easily have followed through. I wasn't even tempted."

"That's because you're working on a show. It's been well publicized that you lay off romantic involvements when you're working."

"Right. Only this time I haven't succeeded."

"But you want to keep me hidden in the closet."

Glen released an exasperated sigh. "When I'm working on a show I get left alone by the media people because they know that there's no interesting copy to be squeezed out of me. If something were to leak out about you, the papers would make a big thing of it. Felix knew that, and to his mind it was a chance for some free publicity for *Gossip*. I don't hold that against him; publicity is the breath of life to a producer. But there are limits. I wasn't about to have him blabbing all over New York that Glen

Hunter had found himself a new romance in exotic Bermuda and expose you to all the ruckus that would follow. So I told him that Joni had it all wrong."

Thrown, uncertain, Erika clung to her bitterness as if to a lifeline. "So you repudiated me for *my* sake. How noble of you!"

"Suppose I hadn't? Suppose you'd seen your name and your face plastered all over the gossip columns? Would you have liked that, Erika?"

"That's not the issue. That's irrelevant."

"Then tell me what the issue is," he said. "Explain in words of one syllable, because I'm more than a little confused."

Erika drew a shaky breath. "Whatever you claim, Glen, whatever your excuse, I find it very significant that you could lie about me so smoothly. You flatly denied to Felix that we had any kind of personal relationship. It just goes to show how unimportant I am to you."

"You've got it all wrong," he protested. "Okay, so I lied to Felix about you. But I didn't do it for fun, Erika; I didn't enjoy doing it. That's the truth. It was an instinctive response to what I saw as a threat to you. Maybe it was the wrong decision. Maybe I should have told Felix and Joni how things stood between you and me, and explained to them why I didn't want the story spread around. But it was a risk I didn't feel able to take. Felix would probably have been safe, but I couldn't count on Joni. She and Felix aren't rock-solid, and she knows too many people in the publicity game. She'd have no reason to pass up the chance to earn a favor from a gossip scout."

"Why should I believe you?" Erika flung at him wildly. "If you could lie so convincingly to Felix and Joni, why should I believe a single word you say to me?"

"There's no answer to that," he said slowly. "No answer that I can give you in words. You'll just have to trust me . . . trust yourself, your own feelings." His face was serious, his eyes pleading. "Could we have shared what we have, Erika, if it weren't important to us both? Ask yourself that."

She looked into his eyes, searching for the truth, while her heart pounded in her chest. "Oh, Glen . . ."

He came to stand before her chair, dropping down on his haunches. "Can't you understand, Erika darling? Can't you . . . forgive what you heard?"

She nodded, her throat painfully constricted. Glen reached for her hand, holding it between both of his. But she pulled it away.

"I understand, Glen, and . . . yes, I do forgive you. But that doesn't mean . . ."

"I'm not taking you for granted, darling. I'd never do that."

"I believe you. But what happened . . . well, it's given us a chance to stand back and take a look at our relationship. Where were we heading, Glen? Just on a fast lane to nowhere."

"Don't think of it like that. Think instead what we can give each other now, while we're both here in Bermuda. We're so right together, darling. No one ever gets that many chances of happiness that they can just be thrown away."

"How about your work on *Gossip?*" she persisted. "You're not making a lot of progress, are you? You're worried about it. Felix is worried too. That must be why he came to Bermuda. I can't have it on my conscience that it's *my* fault."

"This isn't the first time I've encountered a block."

"But I'm the cause of it this time, Glen. You'd be better off without me."

"No, I won't have that." In the lamplight his face looked strained, gaunt. "Without you, I'd be in a far worse mess with the show. I realized that in New York. I *need* you, Erika. Waiting for you this evening, thinking you weren't coming despite your promise, I felt frantic. What we have is something very special, darling. We have to cling to it."

Erika closed her eyes. How could she fight Glen when he undermined her at every turn? It was inevitable that they would be lovers again. She accepted that, but for the moment there was no joy in the thought for her. They would be back on the fast lane, hurtling toward the junction where their routes separated.

Glen sensed her capitulation, and a surge of relief washed over him. He'd been so terrified that he'd lost her. But he also sensed that he must tread softly with Erika. Right now she was highly vulnerable, her mood fragile. With a sense of surprise came the realization that his sexual need for her was overlaid by a feeling of tenderness. Being with her, close to her, was the essential thing. Making love together would come later, as a natural consequence, when Erika was ready. If not tonight, then he could wait, secure in the knowledge that he hadn't lost her.

Erika didn't resist this time when he took her in his arms. He held her gently, as something rare or precious, and she let herself melt against him. He put his lips to her brow, her temple, her cheek. Their kiss was a feather-light meeting of mouths.

"Erika, it's so good to have you back."

"Glen . . ." She almost said, I love you.

Their surroundings receded, lost in a mist. The Moongate and her responsibilities were a thousand miles away. As he slid into the chair beside her she was gloriously aware of the touch of his body against hers, the movement of his hands shaping her form, the seeking of his lips. If only this would never cease, continuing until the end of time. The two of them, holding one another.

The stirring of their desire came slowly, as something recognized from far off, steadily approaching. Erika shivered as Glen's tongue tip traced the outline of her mouth, and she parted her lips in invitation. The kiss deepened, and they rocked together. She put up a hand and laid her palm against his cheek, traced a fingertip around the curve of his ear, then moved it upward into the crispness of his hair. She was lost in a feeling of delicious intimacy that only flirted with passion as yet. Even when she unfastened two buttons of his shirt to slip her hand inside, it was to revel in the smooth warmth of his skin and the molded musculature of his chest, not with the intent to arouse him.

"Darling, darling Erika," he whispered against her hair. "Let's go upstairs."

He kissed her again as she rose to her feet. Then, together, they turned through an archway and slowly mounted the curving stairway which on other nights they had hurriedly climbed in eager passion. Glen held her very close every step of the way, as if he couldn't bear a single inch of separation, and her own arms were linked about his waist. In the bedroom, with its king-size bed, he switched on a single shaded lamp. Its light cast their elongated shadows onto the white walls. Glen pulled her down to sit on the blue quilted counterpane and held her to him for a long, drowning kiss.

When at last he drew back, he murmured throatily, "You're very special to me, Erika. Very, very special."

"And you to me, Glen."

He touched his lips to each eyelid in turn. "I've

never known a woman like you before. You're entirely without guile. Just honest and direct."

"That's how I want you to be with me, Glen, honest and direct. It's all I ask of you. Nothing more."

"Erika, I promise you—"

She pressed fingers to his lips. "No, no promises. Promises tie knots that shouldn't be tied. We're both here in Bermuda for a little while longer, and we have a lot to give each other. But we're free agents. . . both of us."

He sighed. "If that's how you really want it . . ."

"You too."

"I guess so. All the same . . ."

Erika cut in quickly, "Them's my terms, buddy. Take 'em or leave 'em."

"Some option. I'll take 'em."

His sigh this time was inaudible. Erika really was a woman in a million. She'd sensed that he was on the brink of a declaration he didn't mean, that he *couldn't* mean. She'd stopped him just in the nick of time. Why wasn't he gladder that she had sense enough for two?

How readily he had accepted her terms, Erika thought. She tried not to let the hurt bite deeper. Glen truly cared for her; she was convinced of that now. Perhaps he cared for her even more deeply than he himself recognized. But that didn't mean he could make a commitment to her, not a commitment that he would keep. She longed to hear him say I love you. If he did, though, the meaning of the words would fall far short of what they meant for her. He would just mean, I love you here and now. I love you for the time being, until I tire of you and want someone new. That wasn't love. Glen wasn't capable of love. Real love.

It was for the best that she had laid down the limits of their relationship. They were both free. To rule out a long-term commitment didn't rule out tenderness and a caring attitude any more than it ruled out passion. She would show him these things just as she hoped Glen would show them to her. She wouldn't need to reveal to him that she loved him with a deep and abiding love.

She lifted her face and put her lips to his. Glen responded instantly, drawing her harder against him and deepening the kiss. When they broke away, Erika pulled back from him a little and completed the unbuttoning of his shirt, then pushed it off his shoulders and tugged it free of the waistband of his slacks. His body glowed with the satiny richness of Bermuda cedarwood. She swallowed hard, marveling. Glen threw off the rest of his clothes, then set about undressing Erika. With her dress, bra, and panties cast aside, he pressed her down onto the bed and adored her with his lips, murmuring soft endearments as he traced trails of tingling sensation across her face, across the smooth flesh of her throat and down to her breasts, always moving, his hands following where his lips had explored.

"You're so beautiful, Erika."

Smiling, she laid her hands on his powerful shoulders, kneading the firm flesh. "You too. You have such a marvelous body."

"I was half out of my mind when I thought that I'd lost you."

Did it really matter that much to Glen, when their affair was destined to end quite soon? A few more weeks with her . . . could they be so important to him? Even as Erika asked herself these questions, she knew how precious this brief time together was to her. So why not to Glen also?

"Forget about all that now," she said. "We're together again."

"Yes, thank heaven. Tell me you want me, darling."

She was without guile, Glen had said, honest and straightforward. Erika looked up at him and smiled. "I want you, Glen."

"You're the most wonderful woman I've ever known," he said. "You're perfect in every way."

Since he'd known so many women, wasn't it a great compliment? Yet Erika felt a sting of jealousy. She tried to subdue it by making a flippant remark. "I do have one or two minute flaws, believe it or not."

"Such as?"

"Let's see. I'm just short of twenty-twenty vision. I have a mole under my left armpit. . . ."

"That mole I was supposed to search for. How did I forget?"

"I'm a duffer at languages, which is not a good thing in a hotel manager. I only have a smattering of French, German, and Spanish."

"Terrible. I had no idea you were such an ignoramus."

"My biggest flaw, I guess, is this weakness I have for handsome men who write musical shows."

Glen's tongue curled out and he slowly and carefully licked her chin. "With such poor ingredients, how come you still manage to taste so delicious?"

"I'm the flavor of the month," she said gaily. Then her face flamed. What had possessed her to say such a stupid thing?

Glen saw her distress and understood it. She wants more than I'm offering, he thought. Not just to be this month's flavor, but next month's, next year's, and for always. He thrust away the pleasing, cosy, stifling concept. It couldn't be. He'd be a miserable failure like his father, and he'd drag her down with him. There could be no future for them together.

A shadow had fallen across their mood. Erika knew that she had to be the one to dispel it, to erase Glen's feeling that he was failing her. She had to be bold, provocative. For the moment teasing was out; their way back to togetherness lay through passion.

Firmly, insistently, she rolled him onto his back till she was above him. She felt Glen's muscles tauten, but he lay still. His eyes held hers, waiting for her next move. Erika laid her hands flat on his shoulders and slowly drew them downward, riding the contours of his chest, down to the hard plane of his abdomen, and still downward. Glen's body jerked convulsively, and his quick intake of breath hissed in his throat. He uttered her name hoarsely as he pulled her hard against him.

Their need now was for speedy gratification, for release from the unbearable tension that had gripped them both. Their lovemaking was frantic, ungentle, fiercely demanding. Together they surged toward the summit, together they reached the breaking point of ecstasy. Glen's cry of triumph mingled with hers, seeming to shiver in the quiet of the room. Then they lay still with legs entwined, their bodies still united, shuddering with echoes of the joy they had shared. It was a while before either of them spoke.

"Erika," Glen murmured huskily against her throat, "when you're not here with me, I think I can remember how good it can be between us. Then when I hold you in my arms again, you astonish me afresh each time. My memory never does you justice."

He kissed her softly, just brushing his lips against

hers. Erika glowed with happiness, swept by a flood of tenderness for him.

"Oh, Glen," she whispered, and again she only just held back from adding, I love you.

Glen kissed her eyes, the tip of her nose, the soft lobes of her ears. Pushing aside her fanned-out hair, he kissed the warm flesh of her shoulder. "How about a dip?"

"A dip?"

"A swim."

"Sounds great. But . . ."

"Come on." He rose from the bed and pulled her up after him. Erika reached for her clothes, but he stopped her. "You won't need those."

"No clothes? But where are you taking me?"

"Down to the villa's private beach."

"Just like this?" They were already halfway down the stairs.

"You can give the fishes a treat. I often skinny-dip after dark."

Outside, a flagged pathway curved downward to a flight of zigzag steps. Pale moonlight guided them as they descended, with rocks high on either side. They emerged onto a small, perfect crescent of sandy beach which Erika hadn't seen before. Wavelets lapped in soft murmurs, and from behind them in the shrubs that clung to the rocks came the chattering chorus of tiny tree frogs. The water was calm after the previous night's storm, and the lights of Hamilton shimmered across the way.

"Oh, this is lovely!" she exclaimed. "I didn't even realize this beach was here."

"I told you that you should spend more time exploring the territory. Come on, let's test the water."

Erika gave an instinctive shiver as the water swirled around her ankles before she realized that it was not cold at all, but deliciously cool. Glen released her hand and struck out in a lazy crawl, leaving a phosphorescent glow in his wake. Erika followed, finding the sea surprisingly buoyant. It was the first time she had ever gone swimming naked, and it felt wonderfully exhilarating as the water caressed her skin silkily. After a minute or so she turned onto her back and gazed up at the glittering display of stars, keeping afloat by paddling slowly with her hands.

Other hands reached up from beneath her. She felt herself tugged down into Glen's arms, pulled hard against his nude body. His palms closed over her breasts, and his teeth gently nipped her shoulder. Then they surfaced, gasping for air and laughing. Erika pushed away from him and struck out, tempting Glen to follow. He caught her in a few yards, and this time when his arms encircled her she was facing him. Her hair streamed around their faces as they clung together in a kiss of parted lips and curling tongues. Glen's muscular legs encompassed her, closing like a vise. The strength of his desire, hard and insistent, made a promise that brought her body to a state of tingling expectation.

Locked together, they again sank slowly into the world of pale luminescence, down and down until they touched smooth polished stones. Then, with a powerful thrust of his legs, Glen sent them soaring to the surface again. Breaking through, they gasped air into their lungs, laughing and exchanging tiny breathless kisses, and all around them the ruffled water glittered in the moonlight like a million diamonds.

They swam shoreward together until there was sand beneath their feet, then waded. At the water's edge they fell into one another's arms again. The sand on the tiny beach was soft and yielding. Shallow

water still lapped around their legs, its ripples caressing Erika's calves while Glen's hands caressed her
thighs. Propping himself on one elbow, he leaned
forward and trailed the tip of his tongue across her
abdomen, pausing to lap up the drops of seawater
trapped in her navel.

Time stood still as they made love. The night was
theirs . . . the land and sea and sky, the quarter
moon which rode serenely against the dark velvet
canopy. It was all theirs, existing just for the two of
them. Lying on the soft sand, Erika began to float
again, borne along on a mounting, rolling wave of
bliss that soon . . . soon would break with a torrent
of incredible delight. It was rapture just half a step
from being beyond bearing. When Glen covered her
with his body and entered her at last, the ultimate
moment was very near. Ecstasy beckoned as she
moved with him, receded, and returned, always
closer . . . but slowly, slowly. She felt Glen tremble
from his need, but still he held back, pacing himself
to her, on and on. Until . . . it was here, it was now,
it was a glorious certainty. A rushing, roaring sound
filled her ears as her body jerked in delirious spasms
and the whole universe seemed to explode into a
cascade of golden stars.

They remained entwined, their passion spent,
tenderness taking its place. With a fingertip Glen
pulled a strand of her hair away from her face; then
he put his mouth to hers. Erika felt a shiver ripple
through him, and it brought a flooding response
deep within her being . . . the sweet contentment of
fulfilled desire. They kissed again, clung together,
murmuring half-coherent endearments. The moon
rode serenely on its ordained path, and the shadow
of their joined bodies widened on the silver sand.

Chapter Ten

Erika sat in the prow of the sleek little dinghy as it skimmed the turquoise waters of Mangrove Bay. She was idly watching the graceful, silken flight of the longtails—Bermuda's national bird—in the sky above her. She wore a bikini, two yellow and black wisps, and the sun was deliciously hot on her back. Behind her, in dark blue swim briefs almost as diminutive as her own, Glen sat at the tiller.

Again she twisted her head to look back at him, unable to resist doing so for very long at a stretch. His finely planed face was serious, his brilliant blue gaze resting on her. But when their eyes met he smiled quickly and, as always, his smile filled her with tenderness and longing.

"Hi, sexy," he said.

"Hi to you."

"There ought to be a law against women like you, Erika."

"What have I done now?"

Glen was making love to her with his eyes, and little shivers of excitement pulsed through her bloodstream. "It's what you're putting into my head," he said. "Lascivious thoughts."

"Lascivious. That's a long word."

"There're shorter ones."

"Let's stick with lascivious. I like it."

They were approaching a small island, about a mile offshore. Glen ran the dinghy onto a shelving beach, jumped out, and hauled it farther up the soft sand. Erika stepped ashore and reached back for the cooler containing their picnic lunch. Leaning past her, brushing against her as he did so, Glen picked up the insulated water flask and an armful of snorkeling gear that he'd rented with the boat back at Somerset Village.

"How's this for a picnic spot, darling?" he asked.

"Perfect." Erika glanced around in appreciation. The land sloped up gently from the beach, covered by scrubby grass and low bushes, with a few stumpy trees marking the island's highest point. She had gauged, as they approached, that it wouldn't be more than thirty yards across. They had the little island, and the water all around it, entirely to themselves.

Glen dumped the snorkeling gear beside the picnic box, and came to stand behind her. He closed his arms about her slim body and drew her back against him. Erika felt his lips burrowing into her hair.

"It's really lovely here," she said in a husky voice. "How did you know about it, Glen?"

"I didn't . . . except that I knew there were dozens of islets like this. It was just a matter of selecting a good one."

"Which you did. Clever you. When do we go snorkeling?"

"Don't rush me. You're forgetting those thoughts I had on the boat."

"The lascivious ones?"

"None other."

She leaned back against him as his hands traced patterns on her skin, riding up over her breasts to linger at the sensitive pulse points of her throat. With a little whimper of need that she couldn't stifle Erika turned in his arms and tugged his head down to bring their lips together. Glen responded by deepening the kiss and holding her pinned against the thrust of his hips. It was several minutes before he drew back and muttered with a shaky laugh, "Snorkeling, you said."

"Did I?"

"Don't look at me like that, Erika."

"Like what?"

"Like you're holding out an apple. Let's go get into our gear."

Erika felt rather grotesque in the black mask and flippers, but she became a snorkel devotee the instant she dipped her masked face into the water. She let herself float, staring down in delighted astonishment at the fascinating marine life that swarmed in the crystal-clear sea around Bermuda. Fishes of every rainbow hue darted or gracefully glided against a carpeting of fine pink sand. Glen floated beside her, and every now and again they dived for a closer inspection of some exotic shell or writhing fern-shaped frond of seaweed that caught their interest.

When they finally swam back to shore, Erika felt as excited as a child. "I'm going to buy a book and identify all those marvelous fish," she said breathlessly as she peeled off her mask. "They're so beautiful."

She threw herself down on the sand and lay back

luxuriously to gaze up at Glen standing above her. He looked magnificent, so magnificent it caught at her throat . . . his legs long and powerful, his stomach hard and flat, his taut waist broadening to his deep, muscled chest.

"You'll be sticky with salt if you let the sun dry you," he pointed out.

"Who cares?"

"It might be a good idea to rinse it off." He bent to pick up the large insulated flask that he'd carried from the boat. Before Erika guessed what he was up to, he'd unscrewed the cap and was pouring a silver jet of water straight onto her stomach. Erika yelped, scrambled to her feet, and darted out of range.

"You pig. It was ice-cold."

"That's modern technology for you."

"Okay, if you think it's so funny, give me the flask and stand still while I pour some over you."

"We mustn't be wantonly extravagant with water," he said virtuously, putting the flask aside.

"Coward."

She dived past him to get the flask but Glen grabbed her, and in the struggle her bikini top came adrift. He kissed her with parted lips, and while her defenses were down he seized a further advantage, cupping the soft weight of her breasts in his palms and kneading them sensuously. He drew back from the kiss enough to murmur, "Am I still a pig?"

"Yes. Pig, pig, pig."

He resumed the kiss, his tongue spearing in to glide over the smooth ivory of her teeth. His hands slithered down her back, pushing under her bikini briefs until his fingers could clench the soft flesh of her buttocks. Again he drew back.

"Still?"

"A very nice pig," she conceded. And then, in a rush of love for him, "Oh, Glen, this is so wonderful. Just the two of us here together, away from everyone. I wish it could go on forever and ever."

She'd made a mistake; Erika sensed that instantly. Glen still held her close, but now he seemed withdrawn, without that wonderful sense of oneness between them. She took a quick, covert glance at his face and saw that he was frowning.

"I guess we'd better eat now." His tone was flat, neutral.

She wanted to take back her foolish, impetuous remark and put things right between them. But she sensed that the wisest course was to let it go now and just watch her words in the future. She had to reassure Glen, in everything she did and said, that she wasn't trying to stake some sort of claim on him.

These past ten days she had established a pattern for their relationship. Given his choice, Glen would have seen her every day and made love to her every night. But Erika had resisted that—though at a cost to herself. Instinctively she knew that it would be a mistake to allow their affair to run at such fever heat. If she couldn't get through a day without him now, how would she fare when they'd parted for good? Also, though Glen was spending long hours at the piano, she avoided asking him how things were going. Such a question would always touch off a dark mood in him. It worried Erika that she was reducing his ability to turn out good work. But she had to believe—on the evidence of his sudden return from New York, if nothing else—that he'd be even worse off without her. Here and now she filled a need in him.

"Good idea. Let's eat," she said gaily, breaking away from Glen and putting on her bikini top again. "I'm starving. Let's see what Denver has packed for us." Kneeling, she shook out the yellow linen cloth and spread it on the sand. From the cooler she first took out a bottle of wine, which instantly misted over in the warm air. "Hey, Chardonnay '79."

"He's done us proud." Glen took the bottle and corkscrew she handed to him. He drew the cork and filled the two glasses, giving one to Erika. Then he stretched out beside her, propping himself up on one elbow. "Here's to . . ." He paused, and finally said, ". . . all that's good."

"I'll drink to that." She sipped, then set her glass down on the small metal tray that had been thoughtfully provided. "Chilled vichyssoise . . . yummy! Seafood salad, cheeses, banana bread, apricot mousse. What a spread."

Watching Erika as he sipped his wine, watching her fluidly graceful movements, the smooth-slim lines of her scantily clad body and the exciting swing of her breasts as she leaned over the outspread picnic cloth, Glen felt the familiar flood of heat in his loins. If only it were just that, he thought despairingly, how simple his problem would be.

He moved his legs restlessly, oddly ashamed of his desire. He felt a kind of resentment against Erika. Why couldn't she see things the way he did? Why didn't she understand that these few weeks in Bermuda could be a time of sheer pleasure for them both? No strings. No heavy emotional entanglement. They could spend time together, enjoying one another's company and making love. And at the end of it, they could smile and part as friends.

Why couldn't she see that?

Erika passed him a bowl of the chilled soup, smiling at him tentatively, nervously. Glen had to stop himself from leaning forward to kiss the slender fingers that held the bowl. He wanted to tell her not to be unhappy; he wanted to tell her that he loved her. . . .

His breath caught in his throat at this treachery of

his subconscious mind. His hand shook so much as he took the soup from Erika that he almost spilled it. Why did his imagination refuse to remain in the here and now, content with the prospect of an afternoon of making love on this secluded island? These days, whenever some picture of the future flickered in his thoughts, it was always a picture that included Erika. Her presence was unexplained; she was just there at his side, as if his brain refused to imagine life without her. But that was crazy. No way could he allow that to come about.

They said very little as they tackled their lunch. Neither of them had much appetite anymore, and most of the delectable food had to be packed away again.

"That was good," said Glen. "Tell Denver I said so."

"Will do."

There was another tension-filled silence between them. Close by, waves unceasingly broke against the sandy beach, making a tiny swishing sound. From far across the water, the sound of a cruise boat heading for the coral reef was just audible.

Glen said abruptly, surprising himself as much as her, "My father was a bitterly unhappy man in the last years of his life."

"Really? But why, Glen?"

"Because nothing was going right for him. When he died, the London *Times* gave him just eight lines. 'A man who failed to sustain his early promise.' That was the gist of it. I was only nine years old then. But later, when my mother was also dead, I looked up what had been said about him."

Erika sensed that this conversation was somehow important to Glen. She had a feeling that now he'd started, he should be encouraged to talk about his father.

"What went wrong?" she asked. "Why did he fade out the way he did?"

Glen didn't answer that directly. His blue eyes took on a faraway look. "I'd like to think that I'll be what *he* could have been, if only . . ."

"You will be, Glen," she said. "You are already."

"No. I'm just about where my father was when everything fell apart for him."

"Are you scared that history will repeat itself?"

His eyes became hard as he refuted the possibility. "I won't let that happen, Erika."

She hesitated, anxious not to say the wrong thing. "I told you, didn't I, that I once saw a revival of a Thorley Hunter show? *Summer Magic.* I thought it was terrific."

"That was his last success. And it was an outstanding one. My father wrote the liveliest, most innovative musicals of his time. There were no loose ends in his shows. Everything came together with a marvelous feeling of unity . . . story, musical score, lyrics."

"How did he get started writing musicals?" she asked.

Glen wrapped his arms about one knee and stared moodily toward where the water lapped the beach. "He had a musical background of sorts. His father was a pianist at a movie theater in the days of silent films. To his credit, my grandfather saw his son's potential, and he sent him to the Royal College of Music, though he couldn't really afford the fees. Dad had his early struggles, like most people in the music game. He composed incidental music for radio dramas at first; then he had one or two hit tunes. Some friends persuaded him to try his hand at the score for a show based on the life of Benjamin Disraeli. When the lyricist walked out halfway through, my father discovered that he had a talent with words, too, and he completed the show by himself. That was *Dizzy*, of course. The London audiences loved it, and it moved to Broadway. Soon he was riding high with a string of successes."

"And then?"

Glen gave a twisted smile. "And then his life changed overnight. I know the story in detail. As a child I often heard it from Dad, when he was in a maudlin state."

"He drank?"

"By that time he was drinking heavily," Glen said. "Anyway, it goes like this. One fine spring evening he was walking down a street in Chelsea, on his way to meet some friends for dinner, when he heard the hit number of his latest show floating out through an open window just ahead of him. Someone was playing it on a piano. Tickled, he stopped when he came to the window and stuck his head in. He saw that it was a young woman playing, a very beautiful young woman. She was startled and nervous until my father introduced himself; then she asked him in for some coffee. I guess she must have felt flattered to be entertaining the famous Thorley Hunter. She was a student, she told him, and she really ought to have been practicing arpeggios, but she adored his music. My father was enchanted. He forgot about his dinner arrangements and stayed the evening with her. Within three or four months they were married.

"This was your mother?"

"Right." *Why did I ever get into this?* Glen wondered wretchedly. *Erika would never understand, not in a million years, what he was trying to tell her.*

"So they married," she prompted. "And then?"

"From then on," Glen said, "it was downhill all the way."

"Why was that?"

He shrugged. "They were just wrong for each other—in age, in temperament, you name it. Any woman would have been wrong for my father. He completely lost his touch, and nothing he wrote after that was any good. When the royalties from his past shows dried up, there was nothing more coming in. The debts piled up, and he and my mother were always fighting. They were both very bitter, each blaming the other. When I was nine my father killed himself. He took a whole bottle of sleeping pills, washed down with whisky."

"Oh, Glen, how terrible it must have been for you."

"My mother found it very hard to forgive him. She tried to, but she couldn't help feeling that he'd taken the easy way out and left her with the problems—not least of which was to raise me. She'd already started giving piano lessons at home, just to make ends meet, and she kept that up. But it was hard work. Before marrying, she'd dreamed of being a concert pianist, but it was too late for that by then."

"Were you and your mother close, Glen?"

"In a way—but there was a reserve about her. She always told me that I looked a lot like my father, and I think she resented that. She didn't want me to take up music, but she didn't stand in my way."

"Was she able to send you to the Royal College of Music like your father?"

Glen shook his head. "My mother was dead by the time I was sixteen, so I had to fight my own way up. I took a job at a music publishers to start with. It gave me a breathing space, and then I won a scholarship to the College."

"You've done brilliantly, Glen."

"Not badly." He met her eyes with a steady, determined look. "That's how I intend to go on, Erika."

"And you will, no doubt about that."

Erika felt a deep compassion for the young Glen who had suffered through his parents' misalliance. It seemed to draw her even closer to him, since she had suffered in a similar way. Yet it also put her at a distance from him. She knew only too well why he had chosen to tell her the story today. He was warning her gently not to expect too much from him. But she didn't need Glen's warning. She'd already settled for the few brief weeks of happiness that he was offering her. That, and nothing more . . . except in her dreams.

She sensed, though, that Glen had been warning himself as much as her. She truly believed that he felt differently about her than he had about any of the previous women in his life. Perhaps he was close to loving her. But bred into his makeup was a conviction that love and marriage spelled disaster for a creative artist. Suppose . . . suppose she were to declare her love for him. No, it wouldn't be any use. He would reject her—as kindly as he knew how—and softly close the door on even their limited relationship. Glen Hunter was a man with only one route to go . . . the route he'd laid out for himself.

They were still looking at one another, and the silence stretched—a heavy, loud silence, filled with tangled emotions and things unvoiced. Erika kept very still, almost holding her breath. She felt a kind of panic lest she say or do the wrong thing. It had to be Glen who made the next move.

As if idly, he scooped up a handful of the fine, pink-gold sand and let the grains trickle over her bare feet. Erika gave a quick laugh, letting go of her tension, and wriggled her toes as the sand ran between them.

"Hey, that tickles."

"Does it?" Glen lifted her foot in his hand and blew away what sand still clung. His breath was like silk on her skin. "Want to go into the water again?"

"Not really. I'm comfortable here."

His hand still clasped her foot. Erika could feel the light pressure of each fingertip, the warmth of his palm. She imagined his hand running up her calf, her thigh.

"You can't be cold," Glen said, noticing her shiver.

"No, I'm fine."

For seconds that stretched to eternity they talked with their eyes of their need for each other. Erika was hardly aware that Glen had actually spoken when his tense, husky voice broke through the silence. "Erika, I'm hungry with longing for you. I want you."

"Yes," she responded. "Yes, yes."

Her affirmation was in reality a surrender to his terms. I'm yours for as long as you want me; that was what her yes conveyed. I'm yours against reason and common sense, against my best interest and perhaps against yours too. I'm yours because I can't summon up the willpower to resist you.

Glen moved slowly, as in a dream, and folded his arms around her. Erika's trembling increased. Against her hair, he murmured, "Why do you have to be so perfect? So perfect in every way?"

She laid a hand on his thigh and smoothed the sun-warm skin . . . down to his knee, then up again. She heard Glen's quick catch of breath; then his mouth was locked to hers in a kiss of fast-kindling passion. Desire blazed between them like a spark on dry tinder.

Erika was hardly aware of his pulling away the two bikini scraps, nor of his removing his own swim trunks. They lay together naked, and it seemed so right, so wonderfully right and beautiful. There was an urgency gripping them both, a kind of panic that they might not find again the wild magic that their lovemaking had always brought them before. Glen entered her swiftly, and they moved together in a frantic climb to the high peaks until they were both rocketed into the golden glory of fulfillment.

Afterward, when his breathing had slowed, Glen gazed into her eyes and saw that they had filled with tears. -

"Erika, darling . . . please don't cry."

She knew that she had to play it cool. If she let emotion take over, she would find herself clinging to him and uttering all the words of love and eternal fidelity that she must not say.

"Hey, mister, you don't know what you do to a woman."

"Nor you, sweetheart, to a man."

Her heart rebelled against these flippancies. We're not talking about men and women, she wanted to burst out. We're talking about you and me. You and me, darling.

Instead, she blinked back the tears and smiled at him, forcing a laugh as her fingers riffled through his tousled hair. Behind her smiles and laughter she was weeping from the joy of his lovemaking, but that was only part of it. She was weeping too for that time in the future, only a few weeks away, when they would part forever.

Chapter Eleven

*T*he call came on the direct line to the manager's desk, so it was someone who knew the number. Erika picked up the phone and announced herself.

"Hello, Miss Talbot. This is Bruce Oldfield, calling from Boston."

"Why, hi, Mr. Oldfield. How are things with you?"

"The doctors reckon that I'm fine, and I must say I'm feeling pretty well. I would have called you before, but I didn't want you to get the feeling that I was on your back. How are things at the Moongate?"

"No major problems. You have a really smooth operation going here, and there hasn't been a lot for me to do."

He chuckled. "Nice of you to say so. But you don't fool me for one minute. There isn't a hotel in this world which wouldn't go to pieces in two days

189

without a firm hand at the helm. I was mighty relieved when I heard that the owners had engaged someone with your qualifications to stand in for me."

"I was glad to have the chance to come. Bermuda is just beautiful." Then Erika asked the question that had jumped into her mind the instant the caller had said his name. "Does this mean that you're ready to return to the Moongate, Mr. Oldfield?"

"Not quite yet. The doctors say they want me to stick around here where they can keep their eyes on me for another week. I thought I'd return to Bermuda next Wednesday, and perhaps we could run in tandem for a couple of days while I get back into stride. How does that sound to you?"

"Oh, great!" It was like a reprieve. She'd been scared that Bruce Oldfield would say that he was coming back immediately.

"Of course," he went on, "there'll be no need for you to leave before the agreed time. You could treat the rest of your contract as a paid vacation. I'm sure you deserve one."

She was sorely tempted. To be at the Moongate with no duties to pin her down would mean that she could spend all her time with Glen, every hour that he wanted her. According to the original agreement she'd be leaving Bermuda just two days after Glen was due in New York. Assuming that his plans stayed the same, it would give them five uninterrupted days together. But at the end of those five days, their parting would still have to be faced—and would probably be even more agonizing.

With a curious feeling that she was betraying her heart, she said, "I don't think I'll take you up on that offer, Mr. Oldfield. I'd better get back to England and see about my next post. Thanks all the same."

"Whatever you think best."

After she'd put the phone down it was hard to concentrate on her job. She was thinking ahead to the evening, when she'd have to break the news to Glen. She decided to keep quiet about Bruce Old-field's suggestion that she should stay on at the Moongate for a few days as a guest. If Glen knew that, he would press her to accept, and she doubted her ability to resist him. It had been hard enough to make him accept her ruling that they didn't see each other every night.

When she made her way across the dark gardens to the villa, her footsteps lagged with apprehension. Glen sensed that something was wrong the moment he took her into his arms. He drew her inside and closed the curtains.

"What is it, darling?"

She couldn't dissemble and make it sound like good news. "I had a call from Bruce Oldfield this afternoon. He's returning to his job a week from today."

"A week from today?" Glen looked stunned. "But your contract has another . . . another ten days to run after that."

"I know. But I won't be staying that long. I'll work with him for a couple of days; then I'll leave."

Glen pulled her to him harshly. "You can't do that, Erika."

"I must."

"Why? If there won't be any room in the hotel for you, you could come here. In fact," he went on eagerly, "that would be wonderful. Think about it, Erika . . . just imagine being together all the time. Not having to say good night."

She closed her eyes against the lovely thought. It was unfair of Glen to conjure up pictures she had already conjured up in her own mind—and thrust out as impossible.

"No, Glen. Forget it. I'm returning to England a week earlier than I planned."

"How can you be so damned cool about it?" The look in his blue eyes was harsh and accusing. "Don't you care, Erika?"

She shrugged. "With Bruce Oldfield coming back, I won't be needed here. I have a life to get on with."

"You've got it all worked out, haven't you? Where do I come in, Erika? Don't I have any say?"

"In your heart," she said, "you know it's the best thing for us both. For me to stay on a few days more wouldn't make it any easier for us to say good-bye. Besides . . . I know you don't like my mentioning it, but you do have a deadline to meet."

Glen cupped her face between his hands and kissed her with rough tenderness. "Darling, stop being the voice of reason and logic."

"One of us has to be."

"There are times when reason and logic should go out the window. Those few extra days together would be so wonderful."

"And where would that leave us? The weeks here *have* been wonderful, Glen, and we still have a little time left. But if at the end we were to change the tempo and become . . . more intense, it could ruin everything."

"I don't see how," he said stubbornly.

She wished that she dared to throw the truth at him. She wished she dared to say straight out that they obviously loved one another and that it was crazy to be talking of parting—ever. This summer in Bermuda should be just the beginning of their relationship, not its sum total.

But it was impossible to say any such thing. Once voiced, it couldn't be retracted. Glen's twisted ideas about love and marriage, based upon his parents' disastrous life together, would make him reject her.

Or even supposing that the unlikely should happen and Glen let himself be persuaded by her, the time would inevitably come when he'd blame her for ruining his life. If the realization that he loved her didn't come freely to Glen himself, it couldn't be implanted in his mind.

"Hey, mister, snap out of it." She forced herself to speak lightly, hating such false brightness. "I didn't come here to pick a fight."

Glen regarded her in thoughtful silence. Then, as if he too were making an effort to cast off gloom, he said with a faint smile, "Maybe, if I work at it, I can get you to change your mind."

"No chance." Then she added on a giggle, "But I won't mind your trying."

Glen laughed and drew her back against him, swamping Erika with feelings of love for him. "Like this?" he said, sending his hands on an erotic exploration of her back. "Like this?" he said again, and brought his lips onto hers in a kiss that drowned out all but the present moment. Instantly they were embarked on a familiar journey that had only one destination. But tonight there was a new fever to their lovemaking. Each of them wrestled with fumbling fingers to remove the other's clothes, impatient for the intimacy of naked contact. Erika felt the burning heat of Glen's skin against hers and could almost hear the wild pounding of his heartbeat as he pushed her down onto the couch—the couch where they had made love that very first time. With parted lips and searching tongue he roamed her body, bringing her to a searing need for fulfillment. Her fingers, digging into the hard flesh of his shoulders, were a frantic entreaty.

"Glen, oh Glen . . . please!"

He gave in to her pleading, or perhaps he could no longer control his own need. Together they soared.

Erika cried out his name, holding him, clawing him to her. But there was desolation behind the ecstasy. They were on a countdown to the end. They had so little time left.

"Erika! What a nice surprise. What are you doing in Bermuda?"

The new arrival was a tall, powerfully built man in his early forties. His squarish face, with frank pale-blue eyes, was beaming with pleasure.

"Why, it's Tony Sutton!" Erika exclaimed in delight. "I never thought, when I saw that a Mr. A. Sutton of London was arriving today, that it would turn out to be you."

"I've come up in the world since we last met." He grinned modestly. "I'm finance director of the company now, based in London."

"That's wonderful for you, Tony."

"How about you, Erika? How long have you been running this place?"

"Less than two months. I'm only here as temporary manager. I leave at the end of next week."

"Then back to England?"

She nodded. "I guess so."

Tony Sutton looked gratified. "I came at just the right time, then."

After he'd registered, when Erika was escorting him to his suite, she asked, "Are you here on vacation, Tony, or business?"

"A little of both. The firm's thinking of headquartering one of its subsidiaries in Bermuda. Tax reasons. I've come to sound out the possibilities, but I won't be working round the clock."

"Bermuda is a marvelous place to relax," she said, leading him along one of the covered walkways. "Sun and sea, plenty of entertainment."

"A bit dull on one's own, though. It would be

great if we could get together a bit while we're both here."

About to say that she'd have no free time, Erika amended that to, "We'll have to see what I can arrange, Tony." A thought was forming in her mind: that Tony Sutton's presence in Bermuda—the presence of a friend—might help her to keep sane when the time came to part with Glen.

Tony admired the suite he'd been allotted, and the magnificent view. "My chairman stayed here once a few years ago, and he recommended the Moongate highly. I can see he wasn't wrong. If the food is as impressive as the accommodations . . ."

"Even more so. Unless you exercise iron self-control, Tony, you'll put on pounds."

"Middle-age spread?"

"You middle-aged?" she said scoffingly. "You have years to go before that."

He looked pleased. "About this wonderful food, Erika . . . will you have dinner with me this evening?"

She hesitated. "I don't normally sit down with the guests."

"Break a habit for an old friend," he urged. "I'll be fascinated to hear what's been happening to you lately. The first time we met you were at that hotel in Bristol. I can remember thinking to myself, That lady is really going places. It looks as if I've been proved right."

She smiled at him. "Put it like this . . . I'm on my way."

"I like to see ambition in a woman."

"Glad to hear it. Not all men do, even in the nineteen-eighties."

"You're the sort of woman to strike terror in the hearts of chauvinists, Erika. Not only are you supremely confident and competent, you still remain delightfully feminine. It's quite a combination, my dear. Formidable. A man has to be pretty sure of himself not to turn tail and run."

"Well, that's fine by me. I'd never be interested in a man who wasn't."

"Can I surmise from that remark that you *will* have dinner with me this evening?"

"That's a heck of a big leap you took there, Tony. Still, why not? I'd enjoy it."

He smiled with pleasure. "We can continue this very interesting conversation. Cocktails first?"

"Sure. I'll see you in the lounge at seven. Or outside on the terrace, whichever you prefer."

Returning to her office, Erika reflected on Tony's unexpected arrival. She'd first met him when she was the banquet manager of the hotel in Bristol. Tony's firm had thrown a farewell party for two of their top men who were retiring. She and Tony had formed an instant liking for one another, sensing in each other the sort of drive and ability they both respected.

A year later, when she was working at a five-star hotel in Birmingham, Tony had booked a room for two nights while he visited the firm's local factory. It felt to Erika like picking up an old, well-established friendship. Tony, she discovered then, was a corporate accountant, and a widower, his wife having died eight months previously. On his second evening, on a trip to see Hamlet at Stratford-upon-Avon, he had made it clear, without being pushy, that he found her very attractive. In response, Erika had made it clear that she wasn't looking for either a husband or a lover. She liked Tony and enjoyed his company, but that was all. They'd parted with mutual hopes that their paths might cross again sometime. And Erika had sincerely meant that. She thought of Tony Sutton as a friend.

And now Tony had turned up again; at just the

right moment. It would help her pretend to Glen that she wasn't disconsolate about parting from him. That she didn't want permanency in their relationship any more than he did. To that end, she dressed for dinner with Tony with all the care she normally took for Glen.

When she entered the cocktail lounge and smiled around at her guests, Tony rose at once from a table by an open window.

"You look terrific, Erika," he said as she joined him. "Whatever happened to all those other attractive women who were here a minute ago? I can't see any now."

"That's a good line, Tony. Enough to make me purr."

"Like a lovely sleek kitten."

"Huh! Sleek cat, you mean. My kitten days are over."

As they sipped their drinks they fell into an easy, amiable conversation, filling each other in on what had happened since they last met.

"It's great news about your promotion, Tony," she said. "I'm really happy for you."

"The trouble is, success doesn't mean so much when you're on your own."

Erika had a sudden flash of foresight to the day when she'd be managing one of Britain's most prestigious hotels, at the top of her chosen profession. Once it had been her sole aim and ambition, but it no longer seemed to beckon so enticingly. The traditional female role of wife and mother still had a lot going for it.

"Okay, I'll give you that, Tony," she said, forcing a laugh. "But don't expect me to believe you don't find success good for your ego."

She was aware that Glen was entering the cocktail lounge. Though her back was to the door, she felt a prickling of the hairs at her nape. She laughed louder, talking with bright animation.

"It must be great to be able to switch vast sums of money around the world."

She didn't hear Tony's reply. Glen was coming over; it was as if she could hear his footsteps on the soft pile carpet. A shadow seemed to fall across their table.

"Hello, Erika." His voice made her breathless. She looked up and saw Glen standing above her. He wasn't smiling.

"Oh, hello, Glen. This is Tony Sutton. Tony's an old friend of mine from England, so I'm breaking my rule and having dinner with him tonight. Tony, meet Glen Hunter."

Tony stood up and extended a hand, which Glen took with patent lack of enthusiasm. "Glen Hunter! I thought your face was familiar. I'm a great fan of yours."

"Thank you."

There was a pause, tinged with uneasiness. Then Tony said, "Won't you join us, Glen?"

"Thank you," said Glen again. He avoided Erika's eyes as he sat down. "So you two are old friends?" he asked Tony.

"Our paths have crossed from time to time."

Bless Tony, she thought. That reply could mean anything.

Amos came over and took Glen's order. Erika could sense Glen's gaze moving between herself and Tony. He was trying to size up the situation, trying to gauge the extent of their past relationship.

"We don't see all that much of Glen in the hotel," she explained to Tony. "He's occupying a separate villa in the grounds. The idea is to give him space and quiet, because he's at work on a new show."

"Is that so? I'll look forward to seeing it when the time comes. What's it called?"

"Gossip."

"Intriguing! You must be having fun with a theme like that."

"Sure, it's what makes the world go around."

"I thought it was love that was supposed to do that," said Tony dryly.

"Love more often jams up the machinery."

Tony laughed. "Listening to you is like being at one of your shows. Is he always such a cynic, Erika?"

"Unfailingly."

She wished Glen would go away, because she couldn't bear the look of reproach in his eyes. She wished now that she hadn't started this. But since she had, she might as well go through with it.

"Tony is one of our captains of industry, Glen."

"Really? What line are you in?"

"Electrical goods. But I'm not quite a captain. More a lieutenant."

"He's the finance director of his firm," she said.

Glen gave her another long, stony look, then switched his gaze back to Tony. "The man who controls the money! Could be useful. I'm always on the lookout for new backers."

"Oh . . ." Tony's alarm showed. "I'm sorry, but I'm afraid that my company already has a program of arts sponsorship."

Glen drained his drink and rose to his feet. "Don't worry. Fortunately, my producer has no problem raising money for my shows. See you around, no doubt."

"He did that deliberately." Tony was staring with resentment at Glen's retreating figure. "Why did he want to put me down?"

Erika shrugged, still crushed by the looks Glen had given her. "Well, he didn't succeed, Tony. Shall we go through to dinner?"

Somehow the evening wasn't as easy as she'd expected. There was a tenseness in their conversation now that hadn't been there before Glen's arrival. It was her own fault, Erika knew, because she couldn't keep her thoughts off Glen. As the meal proceeded she realized that he wasn't going to use the dinner reservation he'd made for that evening.

As she and Tony rose from the table, Erika excused herself on the plea that she had work to attend to. "I'll see you around tomorrow, Tony."

"Sure. I can arrange to have the afternoon free. Could we go somewhere together?"

"Well, I'm not sure . . ."

"Leave it open," he said. "I'll check with you at lunchtime."

"Okay." She smiled. "Was I right about the Moongate's food?"

"It was a fantastic dinner. But I'd hardly have noticed if it wasn't." His eyes lingered on her warmly. "You make a man forget things like food, Erika."

"My word, what a compliment," she said lightly. "I won't let it go to my head."

Oh damn, she thought as she headed for her office, she should have foreseen this possibility. Tony's interest in her had been rekindled and, unwittingly, she'd given him a certain amount of encouragement while she'd busily concentrated on forming a cosy little tableau for Glen to see. Now she'd have to make it clear to Tony once more that she was only offering friendship.

It was one of those evenings when, at her insistence, she and Glen weren't seeing each other later on. She wasn't surprised, though, to get a call from him after she'd gone upstairs to her room.

"Are you alone?" he demanded.

"Of course I'm alone."

"I thought you might be prolonging the fond reunion with your old friend."

"There was never anything like that between Tony and me," she protested.

"No?"

"No, Glen. But even if there had been, it's no concern of yours. Right?"

"What's your game, Erika?"

"I don't know what you mean."

She heard his impatient intake of breath. "Since you're free now, come over."

"No, not tonight. We've already argued about that."

"I want to see you, Erika. I *need* to see you."

"Too bad! I'm not at your beck and call, Glen. You'd better remember that."

"How could I forget? You've made it brutally clear. Can I take it that we still have a date for tomorrow night?"

"Of course. That's what we agreed."

"Good. I couldn't be sure. You might have decided that the time would be better spent with a captain of industry. You could be onto a good thing there."

Anger shook her, chilling her voice. "If you say a single word more like that, Glen, there's something you *can* be sure of: that you won't see me tomorrow night."

"Okay, I apologize. I shouldn't have come on so hard. But I really hated that guy's guts tonight, having your company. It was all I could do to stop myself from hitting him."

"You should hear yourself," Erika retorted. "You sound just like a jealous husband. If we're going to keep seeing each other, you'll have to promise me something."

"What?"

"That you won't overstep your limit again. You don't own me, Glen, any more than I own you. You're free to take or leave what I offer you."

"You think so?"

"Nobody's forcing you."

"Except myself."

"I don't follow."

His sigh was audible. "Why should you, Erika, when I don't understand myself?"

She felt a compelling urge to drop the phone and hurry across the gardens to him right now. The anguish in Glen's voice was tearing her apart, and she longed to hold him, to comfort him. But to do that would be to throw away what she had achieved this evening. They would be back in the fast lane, hurtling at destructive speed toward that terrible moment when their lives divided. Somehow they had to slow down. That was as important for Glen's sake, she truly believed, as it was for her own. The final parting had to be made bearable.

"You haven't given me that promise yet," she reminded him.

"Okay," he said sullenly. "I'll watch what I say in future."

"Very well. Good night, Glen." She hung up before he could say anything more.

At the villa, Glen glared at the dead phone in his hand. "Just where did that get you, chum?" he asked himself aloud. He'd been a fool to obey the impulse to call Erika. Now he'd made her angry, and some of the precious time that was left to them would have to be wasted in reestablishing their closeness.

He slammed the phone back onto its cradle and poured himself a stiff drink. Then he crossed to the piano, sat down, and thundered out a series of chords until he had simmered down.

Glen worked long into the night. It was as if his desperation had inspired him at last. Melodies poured through his brain; lines of lyrics seemed to leap at him from nowhere. He was unaware of the passage of time, unaware of anything except the excitement of creation. Finally, emotionally and physically exhausted, he climbed the stairs, flung off his clothes, and rolled into bed.

He awoke early and stared around him in a daze. Remembering, he stumbled downstairs, where stave sheets made a sea of white around the piano. He gathered some together, read them through, collected more and scanned them. The cold hand of fear gripped him. With a muttered cry he gathered all the sheets together in a careless bundle and tossed the lot into the wastebasket.

Chapter Twelve

On Tony Sutton's last afternoon before he flew back to London, Erika agreed to go out with him. She felt she owed him that. They decided on the Crystal Caves, and wandered awestruck around the great cool limestone caverns, which were so spectacularly floodlit.

"Which are the stalactites and which are the stalacmites?" Tony asked her. "I can never remember."

"It's stuck in my head from school days. Stalactites hang on tight; stalacmites stand mighty. Easy."

Over coffee in a nearby restaurant, Tony grew wistful. "Are we going to meet up again, Erika? I hope so."

"Me too," she said lightly. "I've got your address. I'll let you know if I'm ever near enough for us to get together."

"But I'd better not count on it?" He gave a wry

smile. "When I arrived at the Moongate and found you there . . . well, I guess I thought it was fate at work."

"I'm sorry, Tony," she said. She didn't pretend not to get his drift.

"A career isn't the sum total of life," he said. "I ought to know. After Gillian died I tried to kid myself that I could make my job enough for me, but there's . . . an emptiness." His glance was serious. "Even if you're not interested right now, Erika, don't close your mind to the idea of marriage."

She toyed with her salad, her thoughts floating in forbidden directions. "It takes two to make a marriage."

"I'm one," he said. "And you'd make two."

"Oh, Tony, I really am sorry," she said again.

"It's okay." He laughed ruefully. "Well, it's not okay, but you know what I mean."

"You're a nice man, Tony Sutton."

"I'd better not say what I think of you, or you'll accuse me of being pushy."

"I can't imagine you being pushy."

"That's because you've never seen me in action in the boardroom." He reached across the table and ran the back of a finger down her cheek. "Come on, send me away with a smile."

"Sure." Her smile was genuine. "I wish the very best for you, Tony."

"That I won't get. Second best, maybe."

Back at the Moongate, Erika went straight to her office. A bunch of sweet peas lay on her desk, and she knew who'd put it there. This was the third time Frankie had made such an offering since he'd returned to work. Touched, she inhaled the delicate fragrance as she glanced down at her message pad.

A Mr. Richard Mackenzie wanted her to call him back urgently . . . it seemed to be a British number. A prospective guest, no doubt. Some people insisted on dealing with no one but the top executive.

She dialed the number, and the answering voice said, "Glenbrae Castle Hotel. May I help you?"

"I believe you have a Mr. Mackenzie registered with you. A Mr. Richard Mackenzie."

"Mr. Mackenzie is the proprietor, madam. Do you wish to speak with him?"

"Apparently he wants to speak with me. My name is Erika Talbot, and I'm calling from Bermuda."

"Oh yes, of course, Miss Talbot. He's expecting your call."

While waiting, Erika pondered. The Glenbrae Castle Hotel was a small and super-select golfing hotel near the famous St. Andrews course. She knew it by reputation, but she'd never had any direct contact before.

The man's voice was friendly, but seemed overlaid with anxiety. "Good of you to call back, Miss Talbot. I was sorry to have to ask you to, but this is a wee bit urgent."

"How can I help you, Mr. Mackenzie?"

"I'll come straight to the point. I have to find someone to take over here on a temporary basis. My wife and I run this place together, and we just heard today that our daughter in New Zealand has been involved in a car crash. She's quite badly injured."

"Oh, I'm sorry."

"Yes, well . . . my wife is leaving right away, and I shall follow her as soon as I can make arrangements for someone to stand in for us here."

"I see. May I ask what made you contact me, Mr. Mackenzie?"

"It was through our friends Douglas and Catrina

Montrose. They said what a wonderful job you were doing running the Moongate, and they thought you'd be finished there around about now. I realize you may have another post already fixed."

"Not yet. There are two or three I'm still considering. I finish here in three days' time. But—forgive me, Mr. Mackenzie—you would hardly put the management of a prestigious hotel like yours in the hands of someone unknown to you, merely on the recommendation of friends who are not in the trade."

"You're right, of course. I'd better be frank with you. This had to be settled quickly, and it would have taken too long to go through the usual process of calling for references. The Montroses happened to remember that your last post before Bermuda was at Bramley Court in Leeds. I know one of the directors there, so I checked with him. He gave me a glowing report on you. He also said that the references you'd given them were equally good. I knew I didn't need to look any further. So . . . will you accept, Miss Talbot? It would be a load off my mind, I can tell you."

Erika thought rapidly. She'd planned to take a few days off before starting another job, to shop for clothes and so on. But this was a request that was difficult to refuse.

"How long do you expect you'll need me?" she asked, wondering what she'd be committing herself to.

"I can't really say. It depends on how my daughter's recovery goes. But I'd be happy to give you a minimum period. How would six weeks be?"

"I think that's fair."

They discussed terms, including her salary. It was all very satisfactory. "I'll let you know when to expect me after I've checked the flights," she promised. "I hope you'll soon have good news about your daughter."

Bruce Oldfield was due that day, and he arrived just before dinner. He was a brisk man in his mid-forties, prematurely gray, with sharp features and a small mustache. They had dinner together in a quiet corner of the dining room while Erika filled him in on events at the Moongate during his absence. Bruce listened attentively, asking a question now and then. He was clearly very much on the ball, as she'd expected.

"The food and service are well up to scratch," he said approvingly. "I'm sure everything else is, too. Have you decided to stay that extra week, Miss Talbot?"

"Erika," she corrected. "And no, thanks all the same. I've accepted a post in Scotland, starting Saturday."

"May I ask where?"

"The Glenbrae Castle Hotel. Have you heard of it?"

"Who hasn't? An establishment of considerable distinction, Erika."

"Like the Moongate."

He inclined his head. "Nice of you to say so. I can see that you're heading for the big time."

Erika laughed. "I hope to get there one day."

"You will. You have the right kind of determination."

Did she still? Tony's words came back to sting her again. A career isn't the sum total of life. She'd thought, once, that she could make her career the only thing that counted. That was before Glen. She knew now that, at best, her career would only be a partial compensation for what she couldn't have.

"You're looking very thoughtful," Bruce Oldfield observed.

"Am I?" She dredged up a smile. "I was just wondering whether there was anything I'd forgotten to tell you."

"We'll have plenty of time to get down to details in the next couple of days," he said easily.

"There is one thing I ought to mention right away," Erika said, suddenly remembering. "I agreed to let Lalla Bishop have an advance on her salary."

"Really? Lalla's not the sort of person to get herself into money difficulties, so what . . . ?"

"It was Frankie." She had to tell Bruce the story, but not quite all of it. "Out of bravado he rode another boy's motorbike without permission and smashed it up. Frankie's underage, of course, and to avoid trouble with the police Lalla had to pay for the damage. I agreed to advance her the money, and arranged for her to repay it over a period of twelve months."

He nodded. "Yes, that was a good idea. Lalla will be conscientious about the repayments."

"Maybe you could see your way to giving her a raise soon," Erika suggested. "As I told you, she's been very helpful to me during your absence."

Bruce Oldfield's eyes twinkled. "That's a subtle order, if I ever heard one. I'll think about it. Poor Lalla, she has a lot to contend with."

"It's a shame; she's such a nice woman."

"It would appear," he remarked, "that she also has the ability to win friends."

"Friends are fine as far as they go," Erika said, "but what Lalla really needs is a man in her life."

Bruce chuckled. "Is that your panacea for women with problems?"

If she'd been asked that same question a few weeks ago, Erika would have answered with a brisk "No way!" Now, she gave an evasive shrug. "Lalla is competent, very competent, but she's not the sort of person to shoulder burdens alone. There's her mother, too, as well as Frankie. It's a lot of responsibility for her."

Bruce nodded thoughtfully. "It's a great pity about Frankie. He's a likable lad."

"I think there's more to Frankie than shows on the surface," Erika said. "He's got a lot going for him, but he's very vulnerable, very sensitive." She went on to tell Bruce about the incident with Walter Ephron and its near-tragic aftermath. "It seems to me that Frankie is being condemned to spend his life as an unskilled laborer when the potential is there for something much better."

"Such as?"

She gestured helplessly. "I don't know enough about Bermuda and what possibilities there are for a young man like him. But there must be something he could be trained for."

Bruce nodded again. "I think you're right. When I suggested to Lalla that Frankie come to work in the gardens here after leaving school, it didn't strike me that I might not be doing him a favor."

"Oh, I wasn't criticizing."

"I know you weren't, Erika. You've just pointed out something that needed pointing out."

After dinner they spent an hour in the manager's office, going through the books and generally talking business. They fixed their schedule for the next day; then Erika was free. Only ten o'clock. She took her time over a shower, and more time in deciding what to wear. Delaying tactics, she realized as she finally chose a cool-blue jersey-silk dress with a deep V neckline and thin shoulder straps. Then she quickly brushed out her hair, arranging it in loose waves haloing her face. She longed to be with Glen; it was a longing that was always with her. Yet tonight, somehow, she dreaded going over to the villa.

On her way across the gardens, an impulse made her detour to the moongate. In the starlight the stone arch showed up as a pale silhouette as she approached. Erika stood there within its circle, wondering what to wish for. That she could part from Glen without breaking down? That she could survive the following days without too much pain? That she would soon manage to get over him? These were the sensible thoughts she allowed her conscious mind. But thrusting up from deep within her came the wish that had always been there since she'd first known Glen. The wish that was only a beautiful, impossible dream . . .

"Making a wish?" It was Glen's voice, right behind her. Erika's heart thudded as she spun around to face him.

"Glen! What are you doing here?"

He came and wrapped his arms around her. On this sultry evening he was wearing a thin white cotton shirt and slacks, so his body felt almost naked against hers.

"But, Glen, how did you know it was me, in the dark?"

"Because I have ESP where you're concerned. I can scent you, taste you, breathe you. I feel a tingling on my skin if you're anywhere within a hundred yards."

"What were you doing out here?"

"I was restless, waiting for you. I felt caged. I came out for air, knowing that I'd hear you if you came along the path. And then . . . I just knew you were at the moongate, so I came across."

He bent his head to kiss her, and Erika clung to

him. They were within the enchanted circle of the
moongate, where so many honeymooners had stood
and made their wishes, and she had a curious
sensation that this was a uniquely magical moment.
Glen didn't believe in romance, but just for this
instant she could pretend that the two of them had a
shared future. When he ended the kiss and turned
toward the villa with his arm still about her waist,
she felt reluctant to leave the spot. Yet her senses
were already tingling with the anticipation of their
lovemaking.

"Did Bruce Oldfield arrive on schedule?" Glen
asked prosaically.

"Yes, we had dinner together, and I was with him
until just a short time ago."

"Has he changed your mind about leaving before
your contract ends?"

They had reached the steps, and they went inside
before she answered. "About that, Glen . . . I've
made a reservation to fly home on Friday evening.
My next job starts immediately."

"When did you fix this?" he asked coldly.

Erika explained the situation. He listened in grim
silence; then he gave a short, harsh laugh. "So it's
due to our friends the Montroses that you're leaving
so soon."

"You can't blame Catrina and Douglas; they were
doing me a favor. Besides, I was going by the end of
the week anyway. I told you that."

"You'd have changed your mind when it came to
the crunch."

"No, Glen. I'm not saying that I wouldn't have
been tempted, but I'd have stuck to my decision."

His mouth tautened. "I don't understand you,
Erika."

"Perhaps you don't understand yourself," she
responded sadly.

"What's that supposed to mean?"

"Nothing. Forget I said it."

Glen regarded her thoughtfully, his eyes serious. But he veered off onto another subject. "Will you be seeing Tony Sutton again?"

"Maybe, one day. Who knows?"

"Is that the truth? You haven't made any plans to see him?"

She wanted to tell Glen that Tony Sutton meant nothing to her. She wanted to tell Glen that he faced no competition for her love. *Love?* She had to stifle the word, even stifle the thought.

"What is this, Glen? An inquisition? I warned you before about that."

His eyes flashed with anger. "So how much more *am* I going to see of you?"

"You're seeing me now."

"And tomorrow?"

She killed temptation before it flared. Too many last-chance emotional encounters would be more than she could take. "No, not tomorrow."

"Why not? Bruce Oldfield's here to run things now, so you can't say you'll be too busy."

"There are other things I need to do. Shopping, for one. And I have letters from several friends of mine that need an answer."

"That's not going to take you all day."

"I said no, Glen. Forget it."

Glen poured himself a drink as if he needed one. Then, almost as an afterthought, he asked, "Do you want anything?"

"No, thanks."

Where he was standing, the lamplight fell slant-wise across his face, casting dark shadows. His hair was rumpled, and there was a gauntness about his features, a look of tiredness. Erika felt anxious for him. Was he working too hard? She wanted to ask about his progress with *Gossip,* but she knew how touchy he could be about that.

"We'll do something special on your last day," he said.

"Great!" she said, injecting brightness into her voice. "But just remember that I have to catch the night plane."

"Am I likely to forget? I know, let's go back to our island in Mangrove Bay."

Our island! The place where Glen had spelled out to her his pessimistic philosophy of life by telling her the story of his father's failure. And in doing so, he'd revealed his deeply embedded fear of following that same downhill route. Did she want to return there? Would the little island be marred with the taint of hopelessness? But their lovemaking had been wonderful.

"That's a good idea, Glen. I'll ask Denver to have a picnic put up for us again."

"Fine." But he sounded remote, almost uninterested.

Glen was watching her face, trying to read the direction of her thoughts from her uncertain smile. A smile that didn't reach her eyes. Had he been wrong to suggest the island? He wanted perfection for their very last time together, somewhere they could be safely alone. He wanted to recapture the glorious feeling he'd had that the whole universe existed just for the two of them . . . the land and the sea and the sun-filled sky. But the island also held less-than-perfect memories.

"We could go somewhere else, if you'd prefer," he said.

"Would *you* rather we didn't go there, Glen?"

"It's not that. I thought that perhaps you . . ."

"The island will be fine by me."

"We'll go there, then."

Suddenly they seemed to have distanced themselves from one another. They were talking stiltedly, almost like polite strangers. In an effort to break through to Erika, Glen sat on the sofa and held out his hand to her.

"Come on," he said with a smile. "Tell me about this Scottish hotel you're going to."

Erika sat down beside him, and Glen held her hand. While she talked, he caressed each finger in turn. The contact was so tenderly erotic that she found it difficult to concentrate.

"It's called the Glenbrae Castle, and—"

"Hey, you didn't mention the name before. I've stayed there."

That came as a jolt. The Glenbrae Castle wouldn't be the total escape from Glen that she'd envisaged. If he had stayed there, some subtle aura of his presence would inhabit the place.

"When was this?" she asked.

"About eighteen months ago. I was taking part in a pro celebrity tournament at the Royal and Ancient Golf Club, and I wanted a small hotel that would offer me privacy. I got that all right. The Glenbrae Castle is a sort of super-Moongate. The ultimate in discreet luxury. Should be right up your street, Erika."

"Meaning?"

"It'll be another rung up the ladder of your famous five-year plan. A step nearer the Ritz."

Her five-year plan seemed suddenly to have become irrelevant, as if it were on another plane of existence. At this moment she was intensely aware of Glen, and she wanted him to put his arms around her, to kiss her. She wanted to run her hands over the molded tautness of his body.

"That's right," she said, and there was a note of defiance in her voice. "Another rung up the ladder."

"You'll need a good head for heights where you're going."

"It's lucky I have one."

Time hung suspended; there was a breathless, calm-before-the-storm tension. Then they were reaching for each other, unable to wait another second, greedy for the closeness they both needed. Glen's body seemed burning hot, and when she pushed aside his shirt, his chest was moist with sweat.

With his lips pressed against the softness of her hair, Glen whispered hoarsely, "I've wanted you all day, darling. It got to be unbearable, the longing I had for you."

She clung closer, harder, lifting her face for his kiss. It enveloped her with sensations, the smell, the taste, the feel of him, and she let the rest of herself forget the imminent future. Together, temporarily united, they cast adrift from reality and floated into their own private, secret world. . . .

A long time later, when Erika awoke in the bedroom upstairs, she lay in a state of dreamy contentment. The room glowed with soft amber light, and a faint night breeze stirred the drapes. She was lying within the circle of Glen's arms, pressed against his strong, warm body. With one finger she traced a pattern of circles on the smooth skin of his shoulder. Glen grunted pleasurably, but he didn't waken.

With her lips she formed the words *I love you*, words she would never be able to say aloud to him. It must be late, she thought, and she reached down to shift his arm a fraction so that she could read the face of his wristwatch. The movement roused Glen.

"Hi, gorgeous female," he said sleepily.

"Hi, handsome male."

"Sexy female."

"Oh, come on," she said, laughing. "That's fishing."

He laughed too, and kissed the tip of her nose. "Them that don't ask, don't get."

"You've had quite enough compliments from me," she quipped. "It's late, Glen. I'll have to get going."

"Not yet," he pleaded, holding her tighter.

"Well . . . soon."

"Soon," he agreed, and began tracing the long groove of her spine, moving slowly downward until his fingertip was moving sensuously over her buttocks. "But not too soon."

The sky to the east was flushed with pearly pink light when Erika finally made her way back across the gardens. The early-morning air was fresh and delicious. Bruce Oldfield had courteously insisted that she should remain in the manager's room until she left, taking other accommodations for himself. After climbing the steps to her balcony, she stood at the rail, staring out across the rippling waters of the wide harbor. Dawn today didn't seem like a new beginning, but the poignant end of something beautiful and precious and irreplaceable.

By eleven o'clock on Friday morning, Erika was all packed except for the change of clothes she would need for traveling. For her outing with Glen she was wearing a pale blue striped skirt with a cotton-knit top and a navy linen blazer. She had stuffed a swimsuit and towel into her waterproof duffel bag.

Bruce had readily agreed to let her use his car. When she went downstairs she found that the car had already been brought around for her and was parked just outside the front entrance. Denver himself carried out the picnic basket and stowed it for her.

"Thanks, Denver. I feel pleasantly pampered, like a V.I.P."

"We shall miss you, Erika."

"And I'll miss you . . . all of you."

"Some more than others, I hope?"

"Men!" she exclaimed. "You're always fishing for compliments." She held out her hand to him. "You'll be up to your ears in work when I leave for the airport tonight, so I'll say good-bye now. It's been nice working with you, Denver. Maybe we'll cross paths again one day."

"I'll drink to that."

Erika walked back into the hotel to say her good-byes to other staffers who'd be off-duty or busy when she returned from her day out with Glen. Afterward, she sought out Frankie and found him hosing down the steps to the jetty.

"I've come to say good-bye," she said. "I'm off this evening."

He looked at her, his brown eyes soft and gentle. "I wish you weren't going away, Miss Talbot."

"So do I, in a way. But there it is." She smiled and held out her hand. "Take care, Frankie, and try not to give your mother any more nasty scares. You mean so much to her, you know."

She drove around to the villa, where she found Glen all ready. He was sitting on the veranda steps, waiting for her.

"You're late," he accused.

She checked with her watch. "Four minutes, to be exact."

"Late is late," he said as he climbed in. He leaned across to kiss her, and his hand lingered on her arm, his warmth and essence flowing through to her.

"Well," she said briskly, "if I'm so dreadfully late, we'd better get started."

How could it possibly work, this last day with the man she loved? How could it possibly be happy? Yet Erika vowed to try to make it so. Somehow she would retain the flippancy that marked their relationship . . . that, and passion. To be serious with Glen except in passion was dangerous.

On the drive to Somerset Village they tossed remarks back and forth between them, laughing at things they spotted, like a beaten-up old truck painted all over with slogans, and a monstrously fat man clad in Bermuda shorts, looking grotesque. They admired the fabulous views of land and sea, pointing things out, relating odds and ends of local information that one or the other of them had picked up. Anything to avoid what loomed largest in their minds.

The first flaw in the day came when the boatyard at Somerset could only provide a rather battered dinghy that smelled of fish.

"I should have called ahead and booked the one we had before," Glen said gloomily. "It never occurred to me that there'd be any problem."

"Don't worry about it," Erika told him. It was only a minor disappointment, after all.

They had both changed into swimwear. Glen wore black briefs, and Erika was wearing a new one-piece suit she'd bought in Hamilton the previous day. They pushed off and clambered aboard, having dumped in the picnic box and snorkeling gear. With the outboard humming noisily, they headed across the blue water. Away to the west clouds were coming up, but here the sun still shone brightly, and the air was deliciously warm.

This time Erika sat facing Glen. She felt an ache in her throat as she watched his smooth, economical movements at the tiller, watched the ripple of muscle under his bronzed skin.

"Damn!" he said suddenly.

"What is it?"

"The island. There's a bunch of teenagers there."

Erika twisted on her seat and stared ahead, dismayed. Among the little knot of stunted trees on the hump of the island, she saw some teenagers rushing around chasing each other.

"Curse it," said Glen. "This would have to happen."

"Where now?" she asked as he tugged the tiller and they changed course abruptly.

"We'll find some other island that isn't crawling with people," Glen said irritably. "There are plenty to choose from."

For Erika a shadow had suddenly fallen across the day. Their beautiful last outing had turned into something faintly sordid—a search for somewhere secluded enough for lovemaking.

Despite her downbeat mood, she said nothing as Glen headed for another islet a quarter of a mile away. But when they reached it, there was a lot of litter strewn around. Glen veered away and chose another possibility. This time they spotted a dinghy similar to theirs pulled up on the beach, though there was no sign of life. Another couple with the same intent as theirs? Her sense of depression deepened.

Again Glen pulled the tiller around and headed across the open water. The clouds that had seemed so distant earlier had crept nearer by now. The sun was suddenly blotted out, and a chill had descended. A wind sprang up from nowhere, and the water was marked with white caps.

The sun appeared again, but fitfully. On a sudden impulse, Erika said, "Glen, let's go back."

"Go back? Where?"

"I don't know. Let's return this dinghy to the boatyard, and . . . and find a pleasant spot somewhere for our picnic. There are some nice beaches."

He frowned at her. "Where are we going to find anywhere that's this private? An island is our best bet."

Best for sex! Why not say it straight out? she thought bitterly. Was there nothing else on Glen's mind? Couldn't he see that just being together was what counted? Two people in love could be as alone on the crowded streets of Hamilton as on a deserted island.

"No," she said, shaking her head. "I want to go back. I can't explain, Glen. It's just how I feel."

In silence, Glen yanked the tiller across. The dinghy rocked wildly until it settled on its new course. She'd made things even worse, Erika realized, by upsetting him. The lovely day they'd planned together was ruined. The hours ahead offered nothing but growing unhappiness. She wished that the day was over, wished that the parting was over, and that she was on the plane heading out from Bermuda.

They ended up at Warwick Long Bay. In the lee of a rocky outcrop they found shelter from the persistent breeze. The sun was chasing shadows of clouds across the sea, making a beautiful sight, but the gloom which had settled on both of them was too deep to be shaken off. Their conversation was forced, unnatural. They just picked over the delectable food that Denver had provided for them, and tossed what they couldn't eat to the gulls. For long minutes Glen lay propped up on one elbow, gazing in the direction of a family playing with a beach ball.

"How about going back to the villa?" he suggested.

"No . . . I don't think so."

His dark look switched to her, hard with challenge. "Don't you want us to make love this one last time?"

Erika drew patterns on the sand with her forefinger. It was useless to pretend; she had to come straight out with what was in her mind.

"Today was a mistake, Glen. I guess we both expected too much from it. Perhaps it never stood a chance. Let's just cut our losses and go back to the Moongate. I'll drop you off at the villa, and that will be good-bye."

"But there're hours yet before you have to leave," he protested. "And anyway, I'm taking you to the airport."

"No," she said. "I'd rather you didn't." She wanted to weep. Did the parting have to be like this? Couldn't she somehow by an effort of will make everything different? The ending of their affair should be poignant and beautiful, not edgy and bitter and accusing. But it was no use. "No, Glen. We'll go back to the Moongate now and say good-bye. Bruce Oldfield offered to drive me to the airport."

"You've already fixed it with him?"

"No. He just said to let him know if I wanted to take him up on it."

Glen picked up a pebble and flung it angrily across the sand. "Doesn't being with me mean a thing to you, Erika?"

"You know it does." She felt shocked by the unfairness behind his words.

"Then how can you—"

"Glen," she broke in, "we're not going to get anywhere, talking like this. Please . . . let's go."

They walked in heavy silence to where they'd left the car. A ten-minute drive brought them to the

Moongate. Erika swung into the driveway and stopped outside the villa.

Glen turned in his seat to look at her. He spoke in a cold, clipped voice. "So this is how you want it to be—good-bye and good luck. Right?"

"Glen, please don't be like this," she begged.

"It's your choice, Erika, not mine. Change your mind and come in for a while."

"No, I won't do that."

Glen felt a sudden sense of panic, his whole being flooded through with desperation. Desolation. Until this moment he hadn't fully realized that he wasn't ever going to see her again. He'd planned this last day together as a beautiful good-bye, tender and wistful and sweet. He'd envisioned them reaching sublime heights in their lovemaking beyond anything they'd attained before, and parting with warm and lovely memories of each other that would linger for always. Now the final moment was here, and the parting was ugly.

"Erika," he found himself saying in a cracked tone, "this doesn't have to be the end for us."

A surge of hope made her catch her breath. But she schooled her voice to remain steady as she asked, "What are you suggesting, Glen?"

"I have to go to New York when I leave here, you know that, but I won't need to be there for long. Then I can return to England." His imagination began to catch fire at the idea. It made sense; it made wonderfully good sense. "My plans are still fluid, but I'm likely to be in London for a while. You and I can keep in touch, and get together whenever possible. Maybe we could take a vacation together somewhere. Greece, or Spain. How about that?"

Erika closed her eyes, fighting down the pain of disillusionment. "No," she said quietly, "that wouldn't be a good idea."

"You don't *want* to see me anymore?"

"Glen, you don't understand. I'm not like you. To me, a love affair can't be something casual, switched on and off according to whim . . . not the way it is to you."

He leaped on that, his voice harsh with protest. "You think this has been something casual for me? Oh, Erika, you couldn't be more wrong. You're very special to me . . . far more special than anyone I've ever known before. That's why I can't bear saying a final good-bye to you."

"It wouldn't work," she said miserably. "I couldn't handle it . . . starting up again, seeing you sometimes, then not. A clean break—this is the only way."

Glen sat hunched in the passenger seat. His eyes met hers, and his expression was resentful. "Suppose I were to say that you can make all the rules?"

"No, Glen."

"My God, you're hard."

"Not hard," she said. "I'm trying to be sensible . . . for both of us."

"Sensible, you call it." He reached for the door handle. "Okay, Erika, you win."

For a dreadful moment she thought that he was about to get out of the car and walk away, just like that. She said quickly, "Glen . . . kiss me one last time."

He hesitated, then leaned across and put his lips against hers. She wanted to cling to him, but she held back. Glen's arms came up as if to enfold her, then hovered and fell away. He reached for the door handle again.

"Good-bye, then, Erika." He laughed hollowly. "You know something? Words are supposed to be my specialty, but I've no words for this moment. There are all kinds of things I wanted to say to you, but . . . Look after yourself, darling. Have a good life."

"And you." She gulped back a sob. "Good-bye, Glen."

As Erika drove off, half blinded by tears, she knew that Glen was watching her. She couldn't know that his eyes, too, were misty with emotion.

.

Chapter Thirteen

This was the first time that Erika had visited the Montroses since she'd arrived in Scotland four weeks previously. They had driven over to see her at the hotel a few times, just for a drink, or for dinner.

There was a distinct chill in the evening air as she drove alongside a small loch, then through a pretty village of stone-built cottages. She found the Old Manse without difficulty, an impressive building of gracious proportions.

Catrina must have been on the lookout for her. She came hurrying down the front steps as Erika swung the hotel station wagon in between the granite gate pillars. Douglas appeared a moment later, looking slightly breathless.

"Hi!" she greeted them as she climbed out. "I hope I'm not too early."

"No, it's me," said Douglas cheerily. "I'm behind today." When the two women kissed, he complained, "Don't I get one too, Erika?"

"I should think so." She put her lips to his cheek, and he squeezed her arm in a fond gesture.

They did a short tour of the garden while it was still light. There were flowerbeds brilliant with dahlias and early chrysanthemums, plus a few remaining roses. The lawns were smooth and green.

"Which of you is the gardener?" Erika asked.

"Milady," Douglas said. "I just cut the grass."

"Well, you do a beautiful job between the two of you."

"She's the soul of tact, isn't she, Catrina darling?" Douglas walked between them, his arms linked through theirs. "I imagine it comes from her training in hotel management."

"Or could it be just my nice nature?" said Erika.

Laughing, they entered the house. It was spacious and comfortable, with tall ceilings and paneled walls. The living room had a fine white marble fireplace where a small log fire burned, offering cheer more than warmth. Douglas inquired about drinks, then went to fix them at a carved oak buffet.

"I had a letter from Lalla Bishop this morning," Erika told them after they'd discussed how things were going at the Glenbrae Castle.

"Oh, really?" Catrina's eyes sparked with interest. "What's her news? How's Frankie?"

"He's fine, and Lalla's very cheerful. Apparently Bruce Oldfield—he's the regular manager I was replacing—has pulled a few strings on Frankie's behalf. He talked to a man he knows who runs a flower nursery, and as a result Frankie's been offered an apprenticeship. The job at the Moongate was rather a dead end for him."

"I'm glad," said Douglas. "Frankie will give good value to anyone who employs him. He'll never be brilliant, of course, but a little encouragement should work wonders with him."

Actually, there'd been more news in Lalla's letter than Erika had revealed . . . more, perhaps, than Lalla had intended to reveal to her. She'd written:

I already owe you so much, Miss Talbot, and now this. Mr. Oldfield told me that it was you who put the idea in his head. I just don't know how to thank you. He made an appointment for me to take Frankie to see Mr. Outerbridge who owns the nursery. He's such a nice man, you wouldn't believe, and he was very kind to Frankie. He said that he'd think things over, and two days later he called to say he'd like me to have lunch with him to discuss the details. He's someone I can really respect. After lunch he took me around the Botanical Gardens, and he told me lots of things that I never knew before about Bermudian plant life. He's going to come and have supper with us on Sunday. I'm so happy for Frankie, I just can't tell you.

And pretty happy for yourself, too, Erika reflected. With good reason. Bruce Oldfield was an even wilier bird than she'd taken him for. In one deft move, he seemed to have lined up a job with prospects for Frankie, a sympathetic sponsor for the boy, and a possible husband for his mother.

Dinner was eaten in the Montroses' pine-paneled dining room. After Scotch broth, there was a roast of venison, served with baked potatoes and a dish of mixed vegetables. When Erika made complimentary remarks, Catrina gave a doubtful laugh.

"I feel terribly nervous about cooking for someone like you, considering that you're accustomed to the very best gourmet food."

"You needn't be," Erika assured her. "This is really delicious. Believe me, Catrina, however good restaurant food may be, it can never quite equal good home cooking."

"I'll second that," said Douglas, helping himself to another slice of venison.

"You'll get a paunch," Catrina warned, but fondly.

The phone rang, and Douglas went off to answer it. He looked gloomy when he returned. "I'll have to love you and leave you," he said. "An emergency appendectomy at the cottage hospital. Sorry and all that." Still standing, he forked up another mouthful of the roast meat. "Scrumptious! Who said something about my getting a paunch?"

After he'd hurried off, the two women sat in silence for a moment. Erika realized it was the first time since Bermuda that they'd been alone together, and presumably the same thing was in Catrina's mind.

"Well?" They spoke together, then both laughed. "You first," Erika said.

"You already knew the most important part, Erika—that Douglas and I are back together again. Oh, I'm not saying that everything is suddenly wonderful between us. It takes longer than a few weeks to rebuild bridges. The point is that we're *both* trying now, not just Douglas."

"I'm so glad, Catrina."

"It frightens me, looking back, to realize what risks I took with Douglas's love. You always hurt the one you love; that's what the song says, isn't it? And it's absolutely true. I feel so awful about the way I piled all the blame onto Douglas for Alistair's death —and for losing the other baby, too. It was dreadfully unfair of me, but . . . I just couldn't see things in perspective anymore."

"We all make mistakes," Erika murmured sympathetically.

Catrina nodded slowly. "I guess so. But mine was a king-size blunder—quite unforgivable. It took Bermuda to make me see sense . . . the things you said, Erika, and then that night Douglas and Glen went off in the storm to look for Frankie . . . what Glen said afterward about Douglas saving him." She shook her head disbelievingly, and there were tears in her eyes. "How I could ever have thought that Douglas was uncaring, I just don't know."

Before Erika could say anything, Catrina sprang up from the table and hurried out of the room with a tray of dishes. When she came back a few moments later she was in control again, and smiling. She carried a crystal bowl of fresh raspberries.

"Our second crop," she announced, placing it on the table in front of her. "I thought raspberries would be safer than trying to compete with the sort of gooey gateaux that you're used to."

"I hardly ever touch desserts. If I do, this is the sort of thing I always go for."

"That's a relief." Catrina doled out generous helpings, then passed Erika a dish of thick cream. "Now, tell me about yourself . . . about you and Glen."

"There's not really anything to tell."

"Oh, come on. How were things left between you two when you came back from Bermuda?"

"They were left, period."

"So it's really all over?" Catrina looked distressed. "I must admit that I'd been hoping . . ."

"You knew the score, Catrina. In fact, you told me that I'd be crazy to expect anything more lasting from Glen."

"I know I did. All the same, I couldn't stop myself from thinking that Glen had a very special relationship going with you. I thought so even more after that episode with Frankie. When Glen and Douglas got back, I noticed the way Glen looked at you."

"And how was that?"

"Sort of . . . hungry."

"Well, he'd missed dinner."

Catrina showed her scorn in a look. "I'm sure that Glen was in love with you, Erika, in his way."

"What way was that?" Erika felt that if she didn't keep this light she might burst into tears.

"He's a creative artist, Erika . . . a genius. Any woman he married would have to accept that a lot of his emotional energy would always be given to his music, but . . ."

"But nothing. I might as well tell you, Catrina, that Glen let me have it straight between the eyes. It was gift-wrapped in a story about his mother and father, but the message was loud and clear. No commitment! A pleasing interlude in Bermuda, then the big finish."

Catrina smiled sadly. "So I was mistaken."

Erika hesitated, tempted to say more. She knew, though, that to confide in Catrina about the love she was certain Glen *did* feel for her, the love he couldn't even acknowledge to himself, would be sheer indulgence. That was something she had to keep forever locked within her heart.

"Let's change the subject," she said gaily. "As I told you, everything's running as smooth as silk at the Glenbrae Castle. I'm really enjoying the job. I feel very grateful to you and Douglas for recommending me for it."

"Forget that. The Mackenzies were frantic to find someone reliable to take over, so they were the ones we handed a favor. Not you. I wonder how Sally, their daughter, is."

"Doing very well, it seems. He called me yesterday from New Zealand and said that they hope to be leaving for home in about ten days' time.''

"Well, I'm glad for them. But Douglas and I shall miss you, Erika. We will keep in touch, won't we?''

"Yes, we certainly must.''

As Erika was leaving, she said, "Give Douglas my love, won't you? I hope the appendectomy went okay.''

"I'm sure it did. Douglas is very capable, and very conscientious.''

"He's the right sort of doctor to have.''

"He's the right sort of husband to have.'' Catrina gave a shy smile, then suddenly burst out, "I just have to tell you, Erika. I wasn't going to because it's really much too early, but . . .''

"You're pregnant?''

"Well, I think so . . . I'm sure so. Douglas says that I'd better have a test, and then we can really celebrate.''

"Catrina, that's wonderful.'' Erika hugged her. "I'm so happy for you.''

It was a twenty-minute drive back to the hotel along almost deserted roads. The Scottish landscape was serenely beautiful, washed by silver moonlight. She swung the car between the hotel gates and followed the curving driveway through immaculate parkland where statuary gleamed whitely among the trees. Glenbrae Castle was a solid Victorian structure boasting a French-chateau-type facade. Inside, there was an air of hushed refinement. The guests were chiefly VIPs. who came to play golf. Accustomed to the media limelight, what they paid for at the Glenbrae Castle was an interval of privacy, an unaccustomed luxury for them.

Erika crossed the spacious lobby to let the girl on duty at the desk know that she'd returned.

"Oh, Miss Talbot, I have a message for you. A

Mrs. Phyllis Talbot wants you to call her back as soon as possible." She ripped a page off her pad. "Here's the number. Shall I get it for you?"

Phyllis! Her father's second wife. It could only mean that something had happened to her father. She felt stunned, engulfed by confusion.

"What time did Mrs. Talbot call, Joan?"

"Only a few minutes ago. I tried to reach you at Dr. Montrose's, but you'd just left. Is it your mother?"

"My stepmother. Yes, Joan, get her for me, will you? I'll be in my office."

The call came through a minute later. Erika's stomach was jumping with nerves as she picked up the phone. "Phyllis, this is Erika. What's wrong?"

"It's Alec." There was a fraying edge to the voice, as if Phyllis were finding it hard not to break down. "He's in the hospital, Erika . . . a massive coronary. He's had this heart condition for some time, and I'm always warning him to take things easy. But you know your father."

Do I? Erika wondered with a shaft of pain. The man I thought I knew and loved as a child turned out to be a hollow sham.

"When did it happen?" she asked.

"Earlier this evening. He collapsed in the garden and I called the doctor. He had Alec rushed straight to the hospital. He's asking for you, Erika. He very much wants to see you."

"Which hospital is he in?"

"Oh, St. Mary's. Can you come at once? I've had such a job tracing you. In the end one of the hotels I tried gave me the name of the agency you use, and they were able to tell me where you were. Fortunately, they were late at the office or I'd have had to wait until—"

"How serious is it?" Erika asked, cutting across her stepmother's babble. "What's the outlook?"

"It's not good, I'm afraid. In fact . . . oh dear . . ."

"You mean he's not expected to pull through?"

"No . . . they don't think he will."

Erika thought quickly. At that moment she felt numb, unable to analyze her feelings. She had virtually written her father out of her life all these years, and now, suddenly, he was asking for her. She experienced something she thought she had lost . . . the tug of kinship.

She had to go to her father; she knew that. The Yorkshire city where he had moved a few years ago was about a hundred and fifty miles away . . . a four-hour drive.

"If I started right away I'd arrive in the early hours," she pointed out to Phyllis. "It might be better to wait until the morning."

"They'll let you see Alec whatever time you get here, Erika. I'm at the hospital now, and I won't be leaving till . . . till . . ."

"Okay, then, I'll come at once. I'll be with you as soon as I can."

Erika put down the phone and walked out to the reception desk. "Joan, my father is critically ill . . . he's not expected to live. I have to go at once."

"Oh, Miss Talbot, I'm so sorry."

"You have the hospital number, in case you need me urgently. See that it's given to Derek first thing in the morning. He'll be in bed by now, so I won't wake him." Derek Sims was the young trainee under-manager. "I don't think anything's likely to come up, but tell Derek to call me if he has any problems. I can't say when I'll be back, but I'll keep in touch."

It took Erika no more than twenty minutes to

change her clothes and pack a few items. Then she was heading south. Fortunately the night stayed clear, and she made good time. It was a little after four A.M. when, having asked for directions from a police patrol car, she reached St. Mary's hospital. The forbidding Victorian exterior changed inside to quiet efficiency and concern. The night sister in the intensive care unit explained to Erika that Mrs. Talbot had been persuaded to take a sedative and get some rest in a side room.

"I'm glad you're here, Miss Talbot," the sister said. She was fiftyish, gray strands glinting in the auburn hair that showed beneath her white cap. "It may be just my fancy, but it's as if your father is hanging on to life until he can talk to you."

Erika nodded, swallowing hard. "We've had our differences."

"I guessed that. I expect he wants to try to put things right between you before he goes."

"Perhaps." Erika felt tears pricking her eyelids. "There's no chance that he'll make it?"

"None—not really. He's very weak."

"I'd better go to him, then," she said, bracing herself.

It was a shock to see the gaunt figure on the bed in the small, clinically-white room. All around were various life-support systems and monitoring devices. Her father was awake, just, and Erika wondered if he were afraid that to fall asleep would mean the end. His longing to talk to her before he passed away showed in the brightening of his tired eyes as she stepped into his range of vision.

"Erika . . . my dear. Thank you for coming."

"Dad, I . . ." She drew up a chair and sat where he could see her. Feebly, he lifted a hand as a sign for her to hold it. His skin felt cold and dry in her fingers.

"I want to tell you . . . to ask you . . ." he whispered in a thin, breathy voice.

"Don't exhaust yourself, Dad."

"But I must . . . say this. I want you to understand . . . perhaps forgive."

"There's no need."

"There is! I treated your mother very badly . . . yes, I know it. But it wasn't *all* my fault, Erika."

"I guess nothing ever is completely one-sided," she murmured.

"Poor Jeanette was such a possessive woman . . . always so jealous when there was nothing to be jealous of. Until one day, there *was*. It's no excuse, I know, but . . ."

"Jealous? Mother?" It came as a complete surprise to Erika. "I didn't see that side of her, Dad. I just saw that she was broken up when you left."

"I know she was. I was desperately torn, not knowing what to do for the best. Phyllis was pregnant, you see, and besides . . . I loved her, Erika; I truly loved her. I still do. She's been a good wife to me."

Erika nodded, trying to see things from her father's point of view. She wanted to tell him that she understood, but the words wouldn't come.

"Phyllis wasn't to blame," he went on. "She's a good woman, Erika . . . a fine woman. But she doesn't possess the inner strength to carry on alone when I'm gone. So will you . . ."

"What are you asking, Dad?"

"Just that you show her understanding . . . friendship, if you can. She's always felt so guilty about being the cause of the rift between you and me. It would help her so much now, dearest, if you'd show that you don't hold her to blame."

Her heart full, Erika made the promise that her dying father was pleading for. A promise that she vowed to keep. "I'll try to make things up with Phyllis. Truly I will."

A faint smile of relief touched his ashen face. But she could see what the effort of talking to her had cost him. Swallowing a sob, she leaned over and kissed his cheek. For several moments they gazed at one another in silence, and she knew that a feeling of peace and calm was stealing over him.

His second daughter, Deborah—Erika's half-sister—arrived soon after nine, having caught an early train up from London. Both daughters and his wife were sitting at Alec Talbot's bedside when he peacefully slipped away in his sleep three hours and ten minutes later.

"I'm glad you came to see him before the end," Phyllis said to Erika as they were leaving the room. "It will have comforted him. It was always such a sadness to Alec that you weren't part of his life."

"Yes, to me too."

Deborah glanced at Erika diffidently. "Will you be going back now?"

"I shall have to, soon. I'm temporarily managing a hotel in Scotland, and the owners are depending on me."

"But you'll come again?" Phyllis asked anxiously. "I mean, for the funeral."

"Yes, of course." How was it possible, she thought unhappily, to break through the barrier of hostility that had been there for so many years? Yet she'd made a promise to her father, and somehow it had to be kept.

"Will you . . . come home with us for a little while?" Phyllis invited. "You'll need something to eat before you drive back to Scotland."

"I suppose I will. Yes, all right, I'll come."

Phyllis and Deborah both seemed relieved. Erika drove them to the suburb where they lived in a small modern house. They were all too wrapped up in thoughts of the man they had lost to exchange more than the occasional word. At the house, Erika went upstairs to wash. Her head felt prickly from having her hair pinned up for so long. She pulled out the pins, gave her hair a good brushing, then fastened it back with a tortoiseshell barrette.

When she went downstairs again, Phyllis was in the kitchen, and Deborah was setting the table in the living room. Again she gave Erika a diffident glance, as if she wanted to say more than her actual words.

"Mum's going to be lonely, Erika."

She was a pretty girl, with Phyllis's coloring and dark curly hair. Only the clear blue eyes made her unmistakably Alec Talbot's daughter, whereas Erika had inherited her golden-gray eyes from her mother. She's not at all like me to look at, Erika thought. Yet emotionally, she's so like I was at eighteen— insecure, anxious about what the future will hold, and protective toward her mother. She felt a wave of sympathy for the girl, and in the same instant, for the very first time in her life, a stab of sisterly love. Deborah wants my friendship, she decided; she wants to think of me as an older sister. Well, it wasn't all one-sided. A sister would add a new dimension to her own life.

Phyllis came in with a tray. "I just did scrambled eggs with toast and coffee. Is that okay, Erika?"

"Yes, fine." They sat down. The coffee was reviving. Erika said into the growing silence, "At least he didn't suffer too much."

"No, that's a blessing."

How to break through from these formally stilted exchanges? "Phyllis, shall we keep in touch?"

Her stepmother's unhappy face lit up. "Oh yes . . . I'd like that, Erika."

"Dad explained a few things I didn't know

. . . about my mother. I've not been altogether fair . . . to either him or you, Phyllis. I realize that now."

Deborah looked from one to the other of them, obviously not fully understanding this conversation.

"Alec faced one of those situations where nothing he did would be wholly right," Phyllis said sorrowfully. "I don't mean to put any blame on you, Erika. But it did seem cruel, the way things worked out, that as a result of marrying me, he lost his firstborn daughter. I know he always felt badly about that, and I felt badly about it too. I mean, having been the cause of it all."

"That's in the past," Erika said. "There were wrongs done on all sides, I can see that now, and every one of us has suffered as a result. Let's try to put what can't be changed behind us, Phyllis. It's what Dad wanted. He begged me . . . he made me promise to try and make friends with you."

"Oh yes. Now that Alec's gone, it's what I want more than anything. You'll always find a welcome here, Erika. Won't she, Debbie?"

"Sure thing."

The door chimes pealed. Phyllis immediately looked anxious. "Oh dear, it will be one of the neighbors to inquire after Alec. They mean well, but just at the moment . . ."

"I'll go," said Erika. "You both stay here."

She crossed the hall, fumbled with the unfamiliar latch, and opened the front door. Then she gasped in astonishment. The man who stood on the doorstep was Glen Hunter.

Chapter Fourteen

"Tell me if I'm intruding, Erika, but I just thought there might be something I could do to help. I know about your father's death, and the hospital gave me this address."

"But . . . but Glen . . ." she stammered, and then no more words would come.

"I'll go away if you want me to. I just thought . . . well, this is a bad time for you, and I wanted to be with you."

"I don't understand." Her heart was thudding painfully, and her knees felt shaky. Right after the night's trauma, she was too thrown by Glen's sudden appearance to register anything except bewilderment. "How did you hear about my father . . . being ill, I mean? Who told you?"

"They told me at the hotel—the Glenbrae Castle. I arrived at London Airport from New York early this morning, and took the shuttle up to Edinburgh."

"But why did you go to the Glenbrae Castle?"

The look in his eyes told her everything. There was tenderness, and longing, and a kind of suffering. He said, very simply, "I went there to see you, Erika. What else?"

Behind her, Phyllis called from the living room, "Who is it, Erika?"

"Oh . . . it's a friend of mine, Phyllis." She realized that Glen was still standing on the doorstep. She stood aside and motioned him in.

"This is Glen Hunter, Phyllis. I met him when I was working in Bermuda recently. Glen . . . my stepmother." Another face appeared around the living room door, and she added, "And my half-sister, Deborah . . . Debbie."

Glen shook hands with the two women. "I was just explaining to Erika that I don't want to intrude. I just thought, when I heard the news, that I might be of some use."

"How kind of you, Mr. Hunter. We were just finishing a meal. Will you have something?"

"Thanks, but no."

"A cup of coffee, at least." Phyllis led the way back to the living room and they all sat down around the table. "We're rather at sixes and sevens, I'm afraid. It's a bit difficult to get ourselves together."

"That's only natural," Glen said sympathetically. "It must have come as a great shock."

"Yesterday morning Alec was his usual self . . . even when he got home from the office. And then . . ." Phyllis gulped down a sob. "I'm sorry, I . . ."

"Please don't apologize, Mrs. Talbot," Glen said. "I do understand. And you have my deepest sympathy . . . all of you."

"Thank you, Mr. Hunter."

Erika guessed that the name Glen Hunter had

registered with Phyllis and Deborah, but they probably felt inhibited from saying so in the present
circumstances. "In case you're wondering," she
said, "Glen is *the* Glen Hunter."

"I thought you must be," said Phyllis. "Your face
looked familiar. . . . I've seen your picture somewhere."

Glen smiled, dismissing his fame with a gesture.
"I'm just here as a friend of Erika's anxious to help
in any way I can."

They sat talking for a while, largely about the
funeral arrangements. Erika said finally, "I don't
think there's anything more I can do at the moment,
Phyllis, so I'd better get back. I don't like leaving the
hotel for long. I'll call you this evening. You'll be all
right, won't you?"

"Yes, I have Debbie. She's not going back to her
vacation job for a few days." Phyllis smiled tremu-
lously. "Having you here has been such a help,
Erika. I can't thank you enough for coming. I'm so
glad that poor Alec had the comfort of seeing you
again before the end."

Erika kissed Phyllis and Debbie good-bye, then
left with Glen. He had come in a rented car that was
parked just behind hers.

"I'll return this to the firm's local office, Erika,
and then drive back with you. How's that?"

"You're coming to the Glenbrae Castle?"

"Of course I am," he said firmly. "Look, I'll drive
off first and you follow me till we get rid of my car.
Okay?"

It didn't take long to dispose of the rented car;
then Glen joined Erika in the station wagon. As she
drove he questioned her about her father and what
had happened. It was a relief to talk, and she
surprised herself by telling Glen more than she'd
intended, spilling out some of the anguish in her

heart. She could feel the depth of his sympathy, and was touched.

"I can see now," she said, "that my mother was overly possessive with my father, and inclined to be jealous. I didn't realize it at the time, but she was like that with me, too, all through my childhood. She would put on a hurt face when I wanted to go out with my friends instead of staying home with her, and afterward she would always question me minutely about what we'd done . . . where we'd been. It used to irritate me a lot, and I can understand now how it must have been for my father. It's strange, though; I only saw the situation from my mother's point of view. And it was really for *her* sake that I stopped seeing my father, because she always got so upset each time I did." Erika sighed deeply. "It was so easy, as a child, for me to see things the wrong way around."

"You and me both. I've carried a load of emotional luggage from my childhood that's given me a completely distorted picture of reality." Glen pointed ahead. "There's a turnoff coming up. Let's find a quiet place where we can talk. I have things to say to you."

Her heartbeat quickening, Erika nodded wordlessly. She took the turnoff and found they were on a narrow country lane. A little way along a small bridge crossed a stream, and beside it there was a space to stop the car under the spreading branches of an oak tree. When she cut the engine, the only sound was the gurgling of water from the stream.

For a brief moment Glen sat beside her in silence, his fingers twisting restlessly together. He had come to seek her out . . . what did that mean? No more, perhaps, than that he hoped to continue what they had begun in Bermuda, despite all she'd said. Or had he faced his true feelings about her and come to terms with them? She waited in an agony of expectation.

"I love you, Erika."

The directness of his words jolted her. "You . . . you mean . . ."

"Just that. I love you. I want you; I need you. I want to marry you."

Her heart skipped a beat, and she closed her eyes. "Glen . . . this goes against everything you've ever believed. Everything you've ever said."

"I know. It hasn't been easy for me to get to this, Erika . . . but then again, it was the easiest thing in the world once I let myself. Don't you see, it's *because* the way I feel about you is different from anything I've ever felt before. No woman I've ever known has come within miles of having the effect on me that you do. You've taken me to heights I never dreamed existed."

"You're talking about sex, Glen."

"Yes . . ."

"But you can't equate sex and love," she protested, doubts swirling in her head. She wished suddenly that he hadn't reappeared in her life to disturb her afresh just when she was beginning to forget him . . . or rather, when her memories of him were beginning to feel less painfully raw. But she immediately snatched back the foolish wish. It was wonderful to have Glen here—on whatever terms.

"I agree, love is altogether another dimension from sex," Glen said somberly. "Genuine, lasting love is a concept I've always denied before. When I met you that first evening, I desired you. I wanted to carry you upstairs right away and make love to you. But even that first evening, although I didn't understand my feelings and tried to dismiss them from my mind, I knew there was something more than just desire in the way I felt about you. Something mysterious, something very wonderful." He gave a soft, wry laugh. "I've always regarded myself as an expert at sex, but when it comes to loving, I'm just a novice."

"I guess I am too."

"Then how about our learning together?" he said eagerly. "Let's teach each other the wonder and the magic of being in love. You mentioned sex . . . I know now why it was always so different with you. Not just *better,* not just a matter of degree. Love-making with you brought a totally new understanding of the word to me."

"Oh, Glen!" she whispered.

He took her hand where it lay on her lap, enclosing her fingers within his. It was a restrained, unpassionate contact, yet it brought them beautifully close.

"You've always thought that falling in love would mean the end of your career," she said huskily.

"It would be a small price to pay, if that were true. But I was wrong."

"How can you be so sure, Glen?"

"Remember the evening you had dinner with Tony Sutton, and I called you afterward in your room and we had a fight on the phone?"

"I remember."

"I was as jealous as hell," Glen said, "even though I knew it was irrational of me. I needed the reassurance of having you in my arms, darling. I desperately wanted you to come to me that night, and you refused. I tried to kid myself it was just that I was hungry for sex, but even at the time I knew differently in my heart. I had to do something to stop myself from charging over to the hotel and finding you, so I turned to the piano. The mood got hold of me, and I seemed inspired . . . ideas just churned out so quickly that it was hard to get them down on paper fast enough. I know now that it was the passionate outpouring of love for you that I couldn't express in any other way. I worked half through the night until I was exhausted. Then in the morning I looked at what I'd written, and it all seemed to be the tritest, most sentimental slush ever written. In despair I bundled it up and threw it away."

"But, Glen, that was criminal."

His slow smile was half ashamed, half prideful. "I wasn't such a total imbecile as that sounds. Later I rescued the bundle and shoved it away in a suitcase . . . out of sight, out of mind, I thought. After you left the Moongate I produced nothing. Nothing at all. I went to New York, and Felix fixed me up with a studio. But it was still no use. Felix was on my back all the time, but I gave up trying. I didn't really care anymore. The idea grew in my brain that I had to go after you . . . see you and tell you that I loved you. I fought against it until I couldn't fight anymore. I fixed a flight to London, and at the last minute—just to keep Felix quiet—I sent him the bundle of stuff I'd written that night in Bermuda and thrown out."

Erika felt prickles of excitement. "And . . . and he likes it, Glen?"

"He's crazy about it. There was a message for me when I reached London Airport early this morning to call him immediately. My first reaction was to ignore it. . . . I expected him to ask me what the hell I was playing at, sending him a load of rubbish. I didn't want any delay in getting to you, and anyhow it would be the middle of the night in New York. But then it struck me that Felix would have *known* that. Yet he still wanted me to call at once . . . his home number."

"So you called him?"

"He'd obviously been waiting up, and he was bursting with excitement. He said that the new stuff

I'd given him for *Gossip* was the best I'd ever written. What really got to him was the marvelous romantic feeling. . . . The new Glen Hunter, he called it."

"Oh, Glen, that's wonderful."

Glen chuckled. "Felix is nobody's fool. He said the only explanation for the sudden change in my style had to be that I'd fallen in love. Joni must have been right all along, he insisted. Was it Erika Talbot? When I told him yes, he said that if I had any sense in my head I'd ask you to marry me right away. I told him what the hell did he think I'd come to Britain for, except that?"

"I'm so happy for you, Glen. But how you feel about me . . . will it last?" The words of the song came back to mock her: How long will it last, their frantic affair? "For how long, Glen?"

His eyes burned with intensity as he looked at her. "You love me, Erika darling, don't you?"

"Yes, Glen. I have from . . . almost from the first moment."

"You could be honest enough with yourself to admit it. I clung doggedly to my stupid belief that falling in love spelled creative ruin."

"Because of what happened to your father."

"Right. I was driven by an obsession to succeed where he had failed. As if *my* getting to the top would in some weird way balance out the wreckage of *his* career. Crazy. My father was a gifted man, who for some reason couldn't follow through. Some of his gift passed down to me. I'm grateful for that, and proud. But I'm my own man, Erika. I don't have to live in my father's shadow."

"So all those years . . ."

"Like you said just a while back, it's so easy to see things the wrong way around as a child. And I've had a distorted view of things ever since. All these

years, I've never once been in love. . . . I've never
let myself begin to fall in love." His voice took on a
note of tenderness. "Then I met you, and love finally
succeeded in breaking down all the stupid barriers
I'd erected. You want to know for how long I'll love
you, darling, and the answer is simple. Forever. That
song you helped me with will stay in the show, sung
by one character or another each time a new love
affair is starting. 'How Long Will It Last?' But in the
final scene, the way I visualize it now, there'll be
another song that's sung as a duet by Adam and
Vanessa, the man and the woman who are the two
main characters. It will counterpoint 'How Long?'
growing in volume and finally taking over. 'Forever
. . . forever, my darling, forever.'" He turned to
Erika. "And that's the way I love you—*forever*.
There are no doubts or fears or reservations in my
mind. Just this wonderful certainty that I'll love you
for as long as I live."

"Oh, Glen . . ."

He gave her a tentative little smile, as if coaxing
an answering smile from her. "I'd make it longer if it
were possible, darling, but as it is . . . those are my
best terms."

"You've got yourself a deal," she said, laughing
through a mist of tears. "Do we shake hands on the
bargain?"

"I'd rather kiss on it."

Their kiss was one of sweetness and thankfulness,
of gentle wonder that fate could truly be so kind. For
long minutes they sat hugging one another, clinging
together. But at length Erika said with a wistful sigh,
"I'm a working woman, Glen. I have a hotel to
run."

"How about my taking over the driving now?" he
suggested. "You've been up all night."

"I wouldn't mind," she admitted.

As they were moving off, Glen said, "I used to resent your work bitterly. It always seemed to come between us."

"Not now?"

He shook his head. "Your work is part of you, and I love you just the way you are." He grinned. "Anyhow, there'll always be free accommodations for the manager's husband—right?"

"What, at the Ritz? You have to be joking."

"It'll be worth paying for the ritziest suite they have, to spend the night with you."

"I have no intention," she stated, "of spending more than the barest minimum number of nights away from my husband and our home. My career will take second place from now on."

"Likewise."

Erika turned her head to look at him. "You don't mean you've lost the urge to write brilliant musicals, I hope?"

"Let's say that I've managed to get my priorities right at last. You first, and my career . . . important, but definitely second."

She sighed her deep pleasure. "Oh, Glen . . . we're going to be so happy together."

"It won't be my fault if we aren't. That's a promise."

A purple-blue dusk was deepening over the hills when they arrived at the Glenbrae Castle. Erika had called the hotel from the hospital to explain about her father's death and say that she'd be back later that day. Now, Derek Sims had a few minor queries for her, but luckily no problems. She registered Glen as a guest; then they both went upstairs to bathe and change for dinner. Erika made the promised call to Phyllis from her room.

She and Glen ate together in a secluded corner of

the sumptuous dining room, with its oak paneling
and gilt-framed oil paintings of the Scottish moor-
lands.

"You're so beautiful," he whispered to her. "I just
can't believe my luck."

"Nor me." Erika felt a curious detachment from
reality, as if everything that had happened since her
return from the Montroses' last night had been a
dream. Sadness and happiness were swirling through
her brain in confused waves. She felt very, very
tired, and it was a relief that Glen didn't try to talk
much.

They had reached the coffee stage when he said,
"If I promise to be very discreet, will it be okay for
me to come to the manager's room tonight?"

Erika felt a tiny frisson of disappointment. After
the traumas of the day, the tragedy and the joy, this
seemed too soon. But could she find a way to explain
that to Glen?

There was no need, though. Glen could read what
was in her mind. He shook his head and smiled at
her tenderly. "I just want to be with you, darling,
that's all. To hold you. I think it's important . . . for
both of us."

Erika understood then what he had already seen
. . . that the night would be lonely if they weren't
together. She smiled back at him, and reached
across the table to touch her fingertip to the tiny scar
on his upper lip. "You don't need to be so terribly
discreet."

Rising from the table, they separated while Erika
made a few last routine checks. Then she went up
early to her room, and presently Glen joined her
there.

In bed, between the cool, lavender-scented
sheets, they lay together, holding one another gently, chastely. Passion had no place tonight. That

would come later, and Erika knew that it would be wonderfully good. Always. Forever.

As she felt herself drifting off to sleep in the comforting circle of Glen's arms, she realized that at last she was free to speak the lovely phrase she had always before forbidden herself to say out loud. But she was so burned out that she could hardly make her throat squeeze out the words.

"I love you, Glen," she mumbled sleepily against the curve of his neck. "For . . . forever."

Silhouette Special Edition. Romances
for the woman who expects a little
more out of love.

If you enjoyed this book, and you're ready for more great romance

…*get 4 romance novels FREE when you become a Silhouette Special Edition home subscriber.*

Act now and we'll send you four exciting Silhouette Special Edition romance novels. They're our gift to introduce you to our convenient home subscription service. Every month, we'll send you six new passion-filled Special Edition books. Look them over for 15 days. If you keep them, pay just $11.70 for all six. Or return them at no charge.

We'll mail your books to you two full months *before they are available anywhere else.* Plus, with every shipment, you'll receive the Silhouette Books Newsletter absolutely free. *And with Silhouette Special Edition there are never any shipping or handling charges.*

Mail the coupon today to get your four free books—and more romance than you ever bargained for.

Silhouette Special Edition is a service mark and a registered trademark.

An epic novel of exotic rituals
and the lure of the Upper Amazon

THE TAKERS RIVER OF GOLD

JERRY AND S.A. AHERN

THE TAKERS are the intrepid Josh Culhane and the seductive Mary Mulrooney. These two adventurers launch an incredible journey into the Brazilian rain forest. Far upriver, the jungle yields its deepest secret—the lost city of the Amazon warrior women!

THE TAKERS series is making publishing history. Awarded *The Romantic Times* first prize for High Adventure in 1984, the opening book in the series was hailed by *The Romantic Times* as "the next trend in romance writing and reading. Highly recommended!"

Jerry and S.A. Ahern have never been better!

READERS' COMMENTS ON SILHOUETTE SPECIAL EDITIONS:

"I just finished reading the first six Silhouette Special Edition Books and I had to take the opportunity to write you and tell you how much I enjoyed them. I enjoyed all the authors in this series. Best wishes on your Silhouette Special Editions line and many thanks."

—B.H.*, Jackson, OH

"The Special Editions are really special and I enjoyed them very much! I am looking forward to next month's books."

—R.M.W.*, Melbourne, FL

"I've just finished reading four of your first six Special Editions and I enjoyed them very much. I like the more sensual detail and longer stories. I will look forward each month to your new Special Editions."

—L.S.*, Visalia, CA

"Silhouette Special Editions are — 1.) Superb! 2.) Great! 3.) Delicious! 4.) Fantastic! . . . Did I leave anything out? These are books that an adult woman can read . . . I love them!"

—H.C.*, Monterey Park, CA

*names available on request